I0630383

The Queen's Return

Copyright © 2024 Alexandra Louise

All rights reserved

Cover design by: Alexandra Louise

Go ahead, buy this book and the other one (or seven) you're thinking about.

You can say it was my fault.

Author's Note:

The feelings Leon possesses toward a certain couple on a certain T.V. show, in no way reflect my own opinions on the matter. He was just really pissed.

The Queen's Return

Prologue

Talvia. Five hundred years ago.

He walked through the aftermath of the battle. His boots crunched over the blood-soaked snow beneath his feet and the bodies of the brave lying across the fields. The Blue Queen was gone, her reign of terror was over and the people of Talvia would soon be able to regain what was once theirs.

He clutched the small diamond in his hands and watched as her spirit swirled angrily within.

"What shall we do with it?" Lord Evian asked, looking at the diamond.

"It must be hidden far away. So hidden that it will never see the light of day," he replied.

"No, we should keep it," the King of Talvia interjected. "It is a trophy; a symbol of our defeat over the Blue Queen."

"We should destroy it. It would ensure it will never be found," pushed Lord Evian.

"You know as well as I do, that is easier said than done. There's nothing that can shatter this," added the king. "It will be perfectly safe in my hands, and the hands of my bloodline."

Lord Evian hesitated, "No, I will ensure its safekeeping. It will be hidden where none will ever find it. Not even the sun's rays or the moon's beams will ever touch light upon its surface."

He handed over the diamond to Lord Evian.

"Come on, Evian. You are too uptight. She can't be released and she can't hurt anyone now," pushed the king.

"Where will you go now?" Lord Evian asked, turning back to the man.

"I'm not sure. I think it is time for me to live a solitary life. One where I won't be bothered with such things," he nodded to Lord Evian's pocket where the diamond lay.

"Well, then, my old friend," Lord Evian patted a hand on his shoulder, "it was an honour fighting with you, and I hope you find the solitude and comfort you're looking for. I hope we never have to meet under such circumstances again," he smiled.

The man gave a sideways smile with an undertone of dread, and looked at the ground, "I hope so too." But it was almost as if he knew hoping for such things was pointless. He turned and walked away, heading for the mountains. He didn't quite know where he was going yet, but as Lord Evian watched the retreating man's figure get smaller and smaller in the distance, he heard the familiar cry of an owl overhead.

1

It began with a snowflake, as it once had before. The cold occasionally got to Eira, but she revelled in those winter days that were warm enough to venture outside in light layers. It had been a year since she was dragged back to Talvia, and she couldn't be happier with her life currently. Her friends that had become her family were making the transition to this world easier than she had expected and everyone seemed to be embracing the other-world flair she brought with her. She thought that when she finally did move to Talvia, there would be a significant adaption period, but she blended in to life there seamlessly, as if she had always lived a life of a Talvian—like she had always belonged there.

Her people welcomed their new queen with open arms and were overjoyed to begin this new period in Talvia's history. It was difficult for her to do anything without the people fawning over her. Anytime she ventured into the town of Trillium Nivale for shopping or lunch or dinner dates with Leon, or anyone who would join her, she was always stopped by the people and given free merchandise, regardless of how much she insisted on paying for it. She didn't mind, though. It showed her how happy her people were to have her back and only solidified in her heart and her head that she had made the right decision to embrace being queen. She was truly in her element and nothing could take this feeling away from her.

****

"What is that?" asked Gideon, perking up his ears to the beats travelling through the halls. Leon raised his eyebrows and tilted his head in the same direction the music was coming from.

"I'll be right back," he said. The music only grew louder and more distinguishable as he walked down the halls of Trillium Nivale castle. His boots clicking on the stone floor were barely noticeable as he got closer to the source of the noise. He opened the door and was greeted with the sight of Eira and Killian snuggled up on the sofa with a bowl of popcorn and two boys bouncing around the room as a cartoon played on the white screen Eira had set up. He frowned, moving to Eira's laptop and paused the movie.

"Hey!" yelled one of the boys and they all turned to see Leon standing there.

"Yeah, dude. What'd you do that for?" complained Killian, turning in his seat.

Leon walked up to the sofa, behind where Eira was sitting. "You know we can hear this down the hall."

"Sorry," she turned to him and smiled. "It's almost over, though."

"What in the world are you watching anyway? What's that?"

"That's Goofy," she smiled.

"What's a Goofy?"

"No," she shook her head, "that's his name. His name is Goofy. I think he's a dog? Or maybe a cow? He dates a cow."

"Okay, well, Gwen will be here soon to pick up the boys."

"Come on, Uncle Leon, watch the rest with us," one of the boys pleaded.

"Sorry, buddy. I have a lot of work to do—unlike some people," he grinned at Eira.

"Yeah, come on, Uncle Leon—it's fun," teased Killian.

Leon simply rolled his eyes, "I'll have fun tomorrow for Solstice and Eira's birthday." He leaned down and kissed Eira on the cheek. Then turned the movie back on and headed back to where Gideon was waiting for him.

When Eira awoke the next morning, the sun was flooding the white stone floors of her bedroom with a warm glow. The world outside was sparkling in the sun's beams, and every inch of it was covered with fresh snow. It was a beautiful Solstice morning. She could smell the crisp mountain air and the subtle note of the pine trees wafting through the crack in the window. She lay there for a moment, in the warmth of the furred blankets. Turning to her side, Eira noticed that Leon wasn't there. It wasn't like him to leave the bed before her. They usually woke together and just enjoyed each other's company in the privacy of their room for a while.

Her curiosity about where Leon had gone didn't last long though, as he soon walked through the doors of their bedroom carrying a tray of breakfast. He placed it on the coffee table in the sitting area.

"There you are," she smiled. "Where did you go this morning?"

"I just had something to do."

"This early?" she asked as she got out of bed and walked over to the settee to start on her breakfast.

"Well, it's not actually that early," he chuckled. "I let you sleep in. Figured you'd need it after the night you had." Eira thought back to the night before and the copious amounts of alcohol she had consumed while preparing for her birthday/ Solstice party tonight. "Although, I'm not sure the staff fully appreciate you...and Killian, trying to help with the set-up. You know, I already have one Killian to deal with; I didn't think I was going to end up with two."

"Yeah, I hope they didn't have to redo too much," she replied through a mouthful of strawberry waffles, completely ignoring his latter comment.

"I wouldn't worry about it," he smiled.

"Well, anyway," she reached a hand out for him, "we could go back to bed."

He sat down beside her. "As tempting as that is, I have a surprise for you."

"A surprise? For me?" Eira questioned with a hand placed over her chest. "It's not a ring, is it? I will not be proposed to in my pyjamas," she added.

"You're so difficult," he joked. "But it's not a proposal, don't worry. Get dressed and meet me downstairs." She stared at him for a moment, unimpressed by the fact that he was urging her to hurry.

"I'm not finished eating, and you know how I get when I'm hungry."

He smiled back at her, "Yeah, I know. I have an entire cross-country journey to prove it." She didn't respond, just smirked through a full mouth. "Okay, fine. I guess you don't have to get dressed right this minute." He leaned in and stopped her from saying anything else by placing a small kiss on her lips.

"So, what sort of surprise is it?" she pushed again.

"Half the fun is not knowing—that's why it's called a surprise. Just finish your breakfast and then I'll show you," he smiled, reaching for a strawberry and popping it into his mouth.

"Fine, but it better be good. I have important things to do today."

"Not today, you don't."

"What are you talking about?" she asked, squinting at him.

"I cleared your schedule—for the whole day. You have nothing better to do than to hang out with your boyfriend."

"Oh, really?" She sat back on the ornate sofa and folded her arms across her chest. "Since when do you have the power to just clear my schedule? I figured even on my birthday, a queen still has to work."

"Hey, as future king, I have that power."

"Future king? You do realize for that to happen, that would actually require us getting married?"

He shrugged his shoulders, "That's just a formality, really."

"Um, kind of an important one."

"Well, also, as one of your advisors, I have the power to clear your schedule."

"Yeah, I've been meaning to talk to you about that. I appreciated your help at the beginning, when I didn't really know what I was doing, but I'm not sure if I like the idea of you telling me what to do now."

"Advising, not telling."

"Oh, so now you know the difference?" she retorted.

"Anyway, hurry up and meet me in the corridor." With that, he left her to finish her breakfast in peace.

She hurried to get ready, pulling on some less-than-regal outfit choices, but they would have to do, seeing as how insistent Leon was. She made her way down the long corridor and down the stairs, where Leon was waiting impatiently. When she met his eye, he gave her a look of frustration, as she most certainly did not get dressed as quickly as he assumed she could.

"Okay, I'm here. What is this surprise?" she asked as she stepped off the last step of the staircase.

"Come with me," was all he said with a smile and he took her by the hand and led her out to the back courtyard. They walked for a few minutes through the castle gardens filled with conifer plants that gave a sharp green contrast to the white world. Even though there was snow all around, a grand garden courtyard could be made with flowers and plants that thrive in the snow. When they turned the corner of the path, Eira could finally see where Leon was leading her. There was a quaint ice rink hidden amongst the evergreen trees. When they got closer, Eira could see a small bench on the side of the rink with two pairs of skates waiting. The only problem was that they both appeared to be girl's skates.

She picked up a pair and looked at Leon, "I don't think these are going to fit you," she said.

"They're not for me," he answered.

"Then who are they for?" At that moment, a pair of hands made their way around Eira's head and covered her eyes. She grabbed the hands, pulled them down to her cheeks, and turned around to see a mess of red hair and a face she missed. Leon had to cover his ears, for the squeals that emerged from the two girls were borderline ultrasonic.

"Nell!" Eira screamed with surprise. She then hugged her friend. "What are you doing here? I thought you couldn't come this weekend?"

"That was part of the surprise. What else would I be doing on my holiday, and your birthday?" Nell had graduated from university recently, a thing Eira would have too if she had not decided to embrace her birthright and come to Talvia. Nell was teaching now and loving it.

Eira smiled at Leon. "Happy birthday," he leaned in and kissed her cheek. "Okay, well, you girls have fun," he said and then turned back down the path from where they came.

"You cut your hair!"

"Yeah, I thought this gave off more girl boss, queen vibes," answered Eira, flipping her now shoulder-length bob haircut.

"It totally does," smiled Nell. "Anyway," Nell grabbed a neatly wrapped package off of the bench, "happy birthday!"

Eira took the package and tore at the paper to reveal a book. "Thanks!" she exclaimed, turning it over to look at the back.

"It's supposed to be really good," began Nell. "It's about like, faeries and shit," she shrugged.

Eira chuckled, "Okay, well, it looks interesting."

"That's the first one," Nell pointed to the book, "but if you like it, apparently the second one is way better."

"Thanks," Eira smiled again and placed the book back on the bench.

Eira and Nell skated for a bit, but soon found themselves not so much skating as sitting in the middle of the rink gabbing about various aspects of their lives and what was happening back in Adelaide. Eira loved Talvia but always wanted to hear what was happening back in the other world.

"Anyway," started Nell after Eira had asked her more about how work was going, "I'm thinking of quitting. I had no idea how much I hated teenage girls until I started working there. I thought an all-girls school would be nice, but boy was I wrong."

"Is it really that bad?" asked Eira.

"Oh, yeah. I once threatened to write the names of the next girls to be kicked off *The Bachelor* on the board if they didn't get off their phones and shut up in the next ten seconds."

"Wow, you went there."

"Hell yeah, I did."

"Oh man, it's times like this that I almost miss Adelaide," smiled Eira. "I'm sure it will get better, though. It's your first year there. It can't be easy right off the bat for everyone."

"Yeah, maybe. If teaching was easy, everyone would do it, right?" she smiled.

"Okay, well, changing the subject..." Eira paused a moment, unsure of how to approach what she was going to say next, "are you going to be okay seeing Killian later?"

"What?" Nell draped a hand over her chest, "Me? Of course I will be. It's him you're going to have to worry about."

"Yeah, I don't know. You two were pretty hot and heavy there for a while."

"Yes, we were. But we both decided it was best to do the whole friends with benefits thing. An actual relationship was never going to work. And then we both decided it was best to end it."

"Why?"

"Seriously, Eira? I can't exactly move here. What would I tell my family? And what, he's going to move to Adelaide?"

"Well, it would make a lot more sense for him to move there. Your parents might not believe you live in a magical other world, but everyone he knows will be fine with him moving," she shrugged.

"Well, still. I don't think he'd acclimate very well. I mean, do they all just speak English, or is there some sort of magic here that lets me understand everyone?"

"I've always chosen to not think about it too much. I mean, I speak Talvian, but still—I think Leon speaks English, though. You understood him when he was in Adelaide," replied Eira.

Nell shook her head, "Look, it's just better this way—we both agreed."

"So...you're not going to fall back into the same routine tonight?"

"Look, I'm not going to sit here and tell you that if he shows up at my bedroom door tonight, I will shut the door in his stupidly handsome face and not let his perfectly chiselled body all over me. But I will tell you, that I will certainly do my best to be extremely quiet about it."

"Oh my gods," Eira just shook her head.

Before the girls knew it, it was afternoon and they had been out on the ice for hours. Although Talvia is constantly immersed in snow, that does not mean it is freezing all the time. The morning was actually a quite pleasant temperature outside and the sun was warming their faces enough to keep their cheeks from becoming redder than they wanted. Suddenly a loud bell rang through the air, and then another ring and another two right after it, signalling to them the time.

"What was that?" asked Nell, turning her head to the sky in the direction the sound was coming from.

"Clock. We should probably start getting ready for the party."

The great hall had been transformed into Eira's vision for her birthday/ Solstice party. The ceiling had been draped with panels of glittering fabric all emerging from the crystal chandelier in the centre. There was a large pine tree that had been decorated with golden lights and all sorts of arctic animal ornaments to represent Talvia. The lighting was dimmed, and the tables had massive cylindrical vases filled with snow and tree branches, all glittering in the lights as centre pieces. Her cake was a masterpiece of culinary delight; it had four tiers and was covered in pale blue fondant with glittering snowflakes cascading down the side. The top was adorned with a large twenty-two made from silver gum paste. She had never been much for birthdays, but this year was different. It was insanely over the top, but she couldn't help but love it. She had people who could not wait to celebrate with her, and she was starting to realize that nothing would ever be simple again; living in Talvia. The party was not like any party the people of Talvia had ever been to before, but everyone who knew Eira first hand, or lived in the castle, were starting to realize that things were never going to be the same as they were. The people were used to elegant balls with an orchestra playing in the background, nothing like the event Eira was throwing this evening.

Eira was just finishing her make-up when Leon came into the room, not at all ready for the party. "How are you not ready yet?" she asked, turning around from her vanity. "You were all on me about hurrying to get ready, and you're nowhere near it."

"I had last-minute things to do. Plus, I know how long it takes you to get ready for things," he said, sticking his tongue out at her and wandering into the expansive walk-in closet to change while Eira finished her make-up.

He was sitting on the bed buttoning up his cuffs when she stood up from her vanity to reveal the dress she was wearing. It was a high neck, sleeveless cropped top made entirely of gilded and beaded lace in a dusty purple.

The skirt was a full length a-line made from the same dusty purple coloured tulle overlaying a pale pink satin. The waist was the same gilded beading that was on the top.

"Wow," said Leon, running his eyes up and down the woman standing before him. "You know, we don't have to go to the party right away," he said, reaching out for her waist and pulling her close.

Eira laughed, "Not a chance, buddy," she smiled. "It took way too long to do this hair."

He reached behind him and pulled out a small gift-wrapped box, "No, I meant we have just enough time for this." He handed it over. "Happy birthday," he smiled.

Eira took the box and smiled, then undid the bow and opened the lid. Inside was a bracelet with a charm in the middle, holding the two strings of diamonds together. The charm looked like a snowflake encased in resin surrounded by the same tiny diamonds that made up the chain. Eira took it out and held it up to the light to see the snowflake better.

"That's a snowflake from the first snowfall Talvia saw after the dragon was defeated."

"What?" exclaimed Eira. "That's a real snowflake?"

Leon nodded and took the bracelet from her and put it on her wrist. "It's perfectly preserved. It'll never melt, to remind you why you're here and everything you fought for."

"That's amazing," smiled Eira, admiring it on her wrist. She leaned down and kissed Leon in thanks. "I love it...and you. Thank you."

Leon stood from the bed and headed over to the closet door where his suit jacket was hanging and slipped it on. He looked way too good in his tuxedo. "Well, I guess we should go downstairs," he added, buttoning his jacket closed. He walked over to Eira and held a hand out for her.

They made their way to the great hall and when they entered through the grand archway, Eira was in awe of how it had been transformed. The party had already started with many guests already there, mingling and dancing. When you're the queen, you can arrive at the party whenever you want. The music stopped, however, when she walked in—something Eira was still not used to—and her presence was announced, followed by a boisterous applause from the guests. Leon took her by the hand and led her to the dance floor, where Nell promptly put on one of Eira's favourite songs for them to dance to. Leon pulled her close by the waist and they twirled around the floor amongst the group of other guests dancing.

When the song was over, Eira looked over to Nell who was still by the computer and speakers. She winked at Eira and then put on a different song—one Eira knew all too well. She pointed to Eira and smiled, walking over to her in that half-walk, half-dance way. She took Eira by the hands and the two danced to their song; singing loudly and horribly off-key along with it. They stayed on the dance floor for a few more songs, and soon they were joined by Leon's sisters, Gwen and Amelia—and of course, Killian too.

Eira had not seen Theo and Clea for a couple months now, but she ran over to them and gave each a big hug. Theo's hair was longer and framed his tanned face, but

Clea, with her light olive complexion and dark chocolate hair, looked the same.

"I'm so glad you guys made it," Eira exclaimed.

"Of course we did. We wouldn't have missed this," smiled Clea.

"Yeah, and I have a bet with Leon going that Killian and Nell are going to hook up again," added Theo.

Eira playfully punched him on the arm. "Well, regardless of the reason, I'm glad you're here. Are Oren and Bianca here yet?"

Clea nodded across the room to where her sister and Eira's brother were dancing. Eira smiled and wandered over to them.

"Man, you have to try that game with the cups and the little ball," said Killian, slightly out of breath and tipsy, walking over to where Leon and Eira were talking and drinking champagne later in the evening. He had long forgone his suit jacket and his bow tie was now draped around his neck with his sleeves rolled up to his forearms. His long auburn coloured hair was still neatly tied atop his head, though.

"I think I'll pass, thanks," smiled Leon.

"Oh, come on. It's fun," said Eira.

"This party is awesome," interrupted Nell, coming up to them with a plate filled with various appetizers. "Much better than the ones we had back home."

"Hey, I liked those," responded Eira.

"Yeah, but they were never in a castle," mocked Nell.

The evening was dying down as the number of guests grew smaller and smaller. It was early into the next morning and soon there were only a few people left; mostly Eira's closest friends. They were all sitting around a table looking completely bagged. Eira was leaning against Killian's shoulder when Gideon came up to them.

"Eira, I must show you something," said Gideon, standing beside her chair.

She looked up at him, "Can you show me in the morning? I don't think I can stand."

"Sorry, unfortunately it requires the night."

She rolled her eyes and reached down to remove her heels, then struggled to stand, but when she was finally upright, Gideon helped her to where they were going.

He led her to the astronomy tower, where she had a grand view of the light display cascading across the darkened sky.

"It's beautiful," she gasped at the aurora borealis above; the pinks, greens, and purples dispersing across the horizon.

"It is—but also deceiving." She glanced back at him, changing her expression from one of awe to intrigue. "I have not seen them act like this before, so I consulted every chart I have on the lights. The auroras are restless. It is a bad omen. I fear something is coming."

She could see now what Gideon meant. The lights did not look peaceful as they did in the past. They darted about with ferocity, like they were desperately trying to communicate something. "You know, this isn't exactly the night ender I was hoping for on my birthday."

"I know, but it is serious. As Queen of Talvia, you need to know these things. I will keep an eye on everything and let you know if something comes up."

"Thank you," she smiled.

When she arrived back at the great hall, everyone but Leon had gone to bed.

"What was that about?" he asked, standing up from the table.

"Not much," she responded with a tone of contemplation behind her voice. "He just wanted to show me the lights in the sky," she smiled.

"Sounds nice," he smiled, putting an arm around her shoulders. "Ready for bed?" he asked.

"Yes," she sighed, "I'm exhausted."

"Good. Me too."

Everyone was nursing a collective hangover the next morning. Eira shuffled into the open-air seating area and was greeted by a fire roaring in the fireplace and her friends gathered around. She took a seat beside Nell and Clea.

"How was the rest of your night?" Eira asked Nell.

"Good. Nothing out of the ordinary," Nell gave a quick glance to Killian, who was chatting with Theo across the room.

"Seriously?" groaned Eira.

"What?"

Eira rolled her eyes, "You're really going to have to stop leading him on. He may not admit it, but when you left the first time, I had to watch *The Notebook* with him five times. Five times!"

"Okay, I will talk to him. It won't happen again. I promise."

"Yeah, I've heard that before," she gave a half smile and nudged Nell's side with her shoulder in a playful manner.

"Alright, who's up for sledding?" announced Killian, clapping his hands together.

"I don't think I can do that kind of speed right now," answered Eira.

"Ah, come on, darling. The fresh air will help."

They all begrudgingly went with Killian. When they were all standing atop the hill at the back of the castle grounds, Eira stared at the decline before her. It had never looked so worrying before. She had walked up and down this hill many times; visiting the memorial to her parents. But today, it seemed infinitely daunting.

"Okay, you first," Eira nudged Killian.

He took a deep breath, "Alright, fine." He placed his sled on the ground beside Eira and positioned himself on it. He stared at the hill before him for a moment and proceeded to rock back and forth as if he was trying to psych himself up for it, or gain momentum.

Eira leaned over to Theo standing beside her and whispered, "Oh, Leon owes you ten gold—"

Before Eira could react, Killian reached up and grabbed her, pulling her into his lap and thrusting them down the hill.

She screamed the entire way down.

When the sled slowed to a stop at the bottom of the hill, he let go of her and she rolled off onto the ground. Breathing heavily with her eyes closed she called out, "I hate you right now."

"Yeah, but how's your head?"

Eira cracked an eye open and peered over at him, "Surprisingly okay."

"See, I told you the fresh air would help." Killian stood from the sled and reached a hand down to her to help her up.

The walk back up the hill was also more difficult than it had ever been in the past. At least Olaf and Polar were perfectly content with dragging the sled by the rope up the hill for them.

They spent the good part of the afternoon on the hill, sledding and enjoying the snacks and warm drinks they had packed. It was just as mild as the day before; a perfect winter afternoon for playing outdoors. When they were in the middle of a girls vs. guys snowball fight, a guard from the castle appeared beside the fort that Eira, Clea, and Nell had built in defence of snowballs.

"Your Majesty," he called. "You had better come quickly. There is an urgent matter at the castle." She was distracted by the guard and was smacked in the side of the head with a snowball.

"Sorry," called Theo.

When they arrived back at the castle, Eira and the others were led into a room down the corridor off the great hall—Nell had wandered off to the bathroom. They were met there by Gideon. Leon walked in front of her and Gideon whispered something to him.

"What's going on?" Eira got right to the point. She was no longer an uninformed guest of the castle like she was the first day she had met this group; a girl standing immersed in the grandeur of Trillium Nivale castle wearing jeans and sneakers. She was now a queen, presenting a regal demeanour and leading a kingdom.

"Eira," began Leon, turning back to her. "We just received word from beyond Trillium Nivale. There is a small village in the southern parts of Talvia on the borders, called Durras. They have sent word that there is a man and some of his army on their way here to try to claim the throne over you."

"Is this some kind of weird birthday prank?" she smiled looking into his eyes, but they gave her nothing back but a seriousness she had seen before. He wasn't joking. The two stared blankly at her and she got the hint that it was not a prank. "That can't happen...can it? I'm already queen. He can't just come along and try to steal that from me. Who is this guy?"

"His name is Lord Dundan," began Gideon. "He is the Lord of Durras and he believes he has claim over your throne."

Eira sat down and sipped the cup of tea that had been brought for her as she entered the room they were all currently occupying. She was wearing a cream and grey coloured flowing sweater and when she sat it opened to reveal the shirt that Nell had given her last year; the one that read: *Because I'm the Queen, that's why.* Leon sat down with her.

"You see, my dear," began Gideon as he laid down a large piece of parchment onto the table before them and began to unroll it, revealing a large map of two royal bloodlines and the history of Talvia's monarchy. "Long ago, when the first kings and queens ruled this land, they came from the line of Dundan. They were not kind rulers and believed this land was theirs and theirs alone. They were gods on earth and everyone was inferior to them. The king and queen treated the people and creatures that lived here terribly—to downplay it. One day, the people revolted and drove the king and his family out and sentenced them to exile in the farthest reaches of Talvia. The darkest, coldest reaches. The people chose to continue with the monarchy and they appointed one of their own as king; the man who led the revolt. He was a kind man and knew what was right for this country. That man was your great, great, great, great grandfather. Thus started a new line of royals; the line of Glaciem-Val. The line you come from."

"So, this Lord Dundan wants to take the throne back?" concluded Eira.

"Yes," confirmed Leon. "When the family of Dundan was exiled, they were sent into the tundra of Talvia. They settled in the small villages and over the centuries the villages grew but there they remained, plotting their revenge and every new generation was taught to hate whoever ruled over Talvia. Over the years, they have tried and failed to take back the crown. There have been attempts made on the king's and queen's lives, along with any heirs they had. When the dragon came, we suspect that Lord Dundan knew he could not act until Sirona fell. He was not going to stake his claim over a land ruled by a dragon. He wanted to be king of a prosperous land. He needed you to get the beast out of his way—and you did. Now that Talvia has been restored, he's going to try to take the throne once again."

"But, he still can't just take the throne from me. He has no claim to it," forced Eira.

"Well, he might. If you're out of the picture, there is no one to take the throne. Your brother Oren has abdicated his claim to it and your line ends here. If he gets you out of the way, he could seize it. That's why we need to protect you. He is on his way here and I am worried he might make an attempt on your life."

"How long have you known about this?" she asked.

"A while, but yesterday we got word that he might be a more pressing threat than we thought."

"And you didn't tell me?"

"It was your birthday. We wanted you to enjoy your party. We knew it could wait at least one night." Leon sighed, "Look, we need to get you out of here as soon as possible. There is a carriage ready that will take you to the edge of Lake Isas after the—" Leon was cut off as he reached for Eira's arm in a sign of wanting to protect her, but she forced it out of his reach.

"I am not going anywhere. You can't just hide me away again like you did before. This is my kingdom and I will not abandon it while it is in trouble." Eira stormed out of the room. She was not in the mood to continue the conversation. As she made her way down the corridor back to the great hall, she heard someone calling after her.

"Eira," called Clea. "Wait." Eira paused in her tracks and slowly turned to her friend. "Eira, Leon loves you. He's just trying to protect you."

"I know but, has he forgotten that I'm the one who took down the dragon. I think I can take care of myself," she answered sternly. She did not entirely mean that, however. It was said out of anger, and truth be told, she was glad to have someone in her life that loved her enough to feel the constant need to protect her. Nell came around the corner and joined them in the hallway.

"Eira, what is going on? There are guards everywhere. It looks like the castle is on lockdown," she said.

"Oh, you know, just another day at Talvian court. Someone wanting to kill me and steal my throne—no big deal," answered Eira.

"What?" exclaimed Nell, shocked by the notion. "And I thought this was going to be a nice relaxing weekend in a magical land. I brought *Gilmore Girls*."

In the world which Eira had previously lived, this was somewhat of a foreign concept. While history had its fair share of royal debauchery, it was not something she had experienced first-hand before. "Sorry, Nell, we're going to have to watch it another time," began Eira. "Maybe you shouldn't be here anymore. Leon will take you back. It's not safe if this guy is planning a war against me and my kingdom."

"I'm not leaving you," replied Nell. Then she had an idea, "Come with me," she said. "You can stay at my place until this whole thing blows over. You'll be safe there."

"I can't go with you. My people need me here. Besides, if this Lord Dundan really wants the throne, having me out of the picture isn't going to stop him. Charles would be regent, once again, while I'm away and he'll just try to force the throne from his hands." The three girls stood there while the daylight crept further through the windows until the moment was interrupted.

"Your Majesty," interrupted Ceilidh. Eira had long given up trying to convince Ceilidh to call her by her name, "There you are. Your lunch is ready for you."

"Thank you, Ceilidh, but I'm not very hungry at the moment. I need some time to myself." Ceilidh nodded and headed down the hallway.

Eira then turned back to Clea and Nell, "I've been here a year and my life has already been threatened three times. That evens out to once every four months. That's not normal! I'm getting really sick of it."

"Yeah but, the first two times happened in the same month so...the last few months were good, right?" smiled Clea.

Eira then bid Clea and Nell goodbye and made her way to her room. She spent the rest of the day by herself, refusing to see anyone that came calling. She did not know what to do or when this man would be upon her kingdom, threatening her for the crown. She had just got her throne back, and now she had to fight for it all over again.

Leon found Eira later that evening slumped against the cold stone countertop of the centre island in the grand kitchen. She was laying there with her cheek against the stone, shovelling ice-cream into her mouth. She looked less like a queen, and more like a girl who just found out her crush was dating someone else.

"How's it going?" he asked, leaning down on the counter to meet her eyes.

"Sucky," she responded shoving a large ice-cream-filled spoon into her mouth.

"Look," continued Leon, "I'm sorry for earlier. I shouldn't have insisted that you leave. Having time to think it over, I'm not sure it would be the best decision after all." Eira looked back up from the counter and gave him a look that indicated her agreement with what he had said and that she was right after all. "Anyway, what do you want to do?"

"I don't know. I've never dealt with a throne usurper before."

He chuckled and took the spoon from her hand and scooped some ice-cream for himself. Then he put the spoon in the container and slid it away from her, just out of reach. She shot him a glare. How dare he take her ice-cream at a time like this?

"Look," he smiled as she sat up. He took her hands and looked into her eyes, "We're working really hard to keep this guy away from here. For tonight, you don't have to worry about anything." She faked a smile, and he knew it. He knew her well enough by now to know she couldn't just forget about this for the time being. "Why don't we all watch *Gilmore Girls* for a bit before bed? Killian will be stoked, and honestly, I am kind of curious to know what happens next." She smiled and hopped down from the stool. "You know, life was a lot simpler before you brought television into this world," he joked.

A couple of days later, Eira was sitting on the windowsill bench in her bedroom with Pix curled neatly at her feet, enjoying a pleasant sun nap—as cats often do. She looked at the small tabby sleeping softly and imagined how lovely it must be to be a cat with no worries at all; just wandering from nap spot to nap spot.

A knock came at her door and she called out to allow whomever was on the other side entrance. It was Leon who wandered slowly into the room.

"Whatcha reading?" he asked as he made his way across the sitting room and closer to the window where Eira sat reading a book. She looked up but did not answer. She simply held up the book Nell had given her, in response to his question, then turned her attention back to what she was reading. He took a deep breath, "I have some bad news."

"What now?" Eira asked, finally putting the book down.

"Lord Dundan has been getting closer to Trillium Nivale every day, and we suspect he will be at our doorstep in a day."

"Well, I suppose we should get ready for our guest then," said Eira. Leon sat beside her with a look that suggested he was prying for more and did not really understand what she meant. Eira continued. "He's not going to come here and declare an all-out war and just start tearing through the castle. I'm sure there are some sort of negotiations that can be made that will satisfy everyone. So, we should be gracious hosts for the time being and maybe he will come around."

"I doubt that, but you are right about his intentions. He's not just going to start a war and will most likely want to negotiate things. You really are starting to think like a queen."

"Why do you sound so surprised? Have I ever let you down?" Eira smiled.

"Not yet," he smiled back.

The rest of that day, and the morning of the next, was spent readying the castle for Lord Dundan. A grand banquet would be held in the great hall to welcome their guests and hopefully smooth over the ill will that Lord Dundan was feeling toward Eira and her rule. Just as Leon had predicted, it was when the sun was starting to make its way down from its noonday place in the sky, when Lord Dundan rode across the great bridge that connected the castle to the rest of Trillium Nivale. He came with far fewer men than everyone had thought. Just a few of his companions and a couple of servants.

Eira was poised, standing in front of her throne, dressed as a queen in another one of the elaborately embellished pieces that graced her wardrobe these days. Adorned with another one of her mother's crowns; a golden headpiece forming into tree branches with silver snowflakes hidden within, and a dress that reeked of richness; a beautiful mermaid shaped gown in an ice blue with embroidery that resembled tree branches and roses working their way up her body and across her shoulders. Eira had imagined Lord Dundan to be a small, petty man with size issues, which was probably why he had the desire to be ruler over Talvia. She was waiting, somewhat impatiently, for him to arrive.

"I wish he would hurry up," Eira said, tapping her foot on the floor. "Do you have any idea what he's like?" she asked Clea who was standing beside her. Clea shook her head in response as Eira adjusted her gown. "I bet he's some small pitiful man with a protruding gut and a comb over who just wants to be king to deal with the fact that he'll never find anyone who wants hi—"

The doors opened wide as Lord Dundan's presence was announced to the court. Eira raised her head to see the figure striding through the doors toward her. Her mouth and eyes widened as he made his way closer to where she stood. Even Clea was speechless.

"I told you everyone in this world is ridiculously attractive," whispered Nell in Eira's other ear.

Lord Dundan was not what Eira had expected. No, he was quite the opposite. He was tall and ruggedly handsome, with his shoulder-length brown hair combed back and his facial hair trimmed neatly. His brown eyes were soft and his physique was well kept. There was certainly nothing small about him. He was clearly older than she, ten years at least. Eira found herself staring slightly as every step he took got him closer and closer to her.

She leaned over ever so carefully and whispered to Nell, "I know he's trying to steal my throne, but yum, right?"

"Well, he's certainly not small," Nell replied with a straight face, not moving her gaze from the man nearing them.

"Small of mind, Nell, is what I meant." The two girls gave a small chuckle and kept their eyes on him.

"Still not as cute as Leon though," added Nell, nudging her with her elbow.

"And far more evil," Clea agreed.

"Yeah, well—that too. But still," Eira tilted her head and sighed.

"You know I can hear you guys," whispered Leon.

When Lord Dundan finally approached Eira, she managed to pull herself together long enough to greet him with a smile.

"Lord Dundan," she greeted. He held out his hand for Eira's. She placed her right hand in his and without hesitation he bowed and kissed it. When he did this, she let out a small gasp, which was quickly silenced by Leon coughing beside her. She then noticed a tarnished silver cuff being revealed as his sleeve slipped upward. It looked old, and the gold was starting to wear, but there was a large black diamond in the middle that, for a moment, looked as if the light running through it was moving. Eira was hypnotized by the jewel for a second, but as Lord Dundan let go of her hand and the sleeve covered it again, she was released from its transfixing nature.

"Your Majesty," he addressed her.

She shook off her absentmindedness and addressed him, "As I understand it, you think I should be calling you that," retorted Eira.

"Now, now. There is no need for spite. We can be civil to one another," said Lord Dundan.

"I believe we can." Eira turned her attention to his almond eyes, gazing deeply into them, holding her power over him. "Welcome, Lord Dundan, and your men, to my court."

A dinner was held to welcome the new guests and hopefully create some pleasantries between the two rivals. Lord Dundan was still wearing the jewelled cuff when he took his place at the dining table, which Eira could not stop thinking about. It was not strange for a nobleman to be wearing such a piece of finery but there was just something about this one that had Eira puzzled. Perhaps it was the jewel embedded in it. It looked to be a diamond, but the colouring was unlike any diamond Eira had ever seen. There appeared to be swirled shades of blues and greens dancing around inside of it. She thought it must be a trick of the light because there was no way there was something actually moving inside. Despite her rational thinking, she could not rein in the uneasy feeling brewing inside her that it appeared as though something was trapped and trying to get out.

She turned to Leon sitting next to her and asked, "Have you noticed that cuff Lord Dundan is wearing?"

"What about it?" he asked taking a sip of wine.

"There's just something about it that doesn't seem right. He seems to constantly be pulling his sleeve down to cover it. It's as if he does not want anyone to see it, yet he wants to keep it on his person at all times."

"Maybe he stole it," joked Leon.

"No, there was something about it when I saw it when we first met. The jewel is very different. There's something unusual about it."

"Why don't you just ask him about it?" whispered Leon with a slight annoyance in his tone. It was understandable that Leon was not comfortable with the situation. He didn't like having a man in the castle who was trying to hurt Eira.

"Maybe I will," replied Eira in a way that said, *I'll do what I want because I'm the queen.*

Dinner was served and then dessert. The evening's entertainment was still playing their various selections of music, and the party was just beginning. Various members of court were starting to take their places on the dance floor and Eira thought it an excellent opportunity to get to know

Lord Dundan on a different level—without provoking him. Everyone would be watching the two and it would keep the conversation from rising. Eira got up from her seat at the head of the table and made her way over to Lord Dundan who was rather preoccupied by the beautiful countess sitting next to him.

"Lord Dundan," she interrupted, "might I request a dance?"

"How can I refuse an invitation from the queen?" he responded in a playfully flirtatious tone.

"You can't—lucky for me," she bantered back with a coy smile. Lord Dundan stood and offered his hand to her. The two walked onto the dance floor and he took her by the waist. She was surprised at how well he danced and how much delight she was getting from it. He was obnoxiously charming in his ways, and Eira was not the first to get caught up in it. Then she remembered why she had asked him to dance in the first place. The ruffled hem of her gold sheer and silk gown swirled around her with every turn and he pulled her closer with the timing of the music and she looked him in the eyes. "I was wondering what the story was behind the cuff you have on your wrist? It is an interesting jewel, isn't it? What is it?"

"It's just an old family heirloom, worthless really," he answered and tried to pull her closer so they were no longer face to face and she could not pester him with any unwanted questions.

"You want me to step in?" asked Killian from the sidelines, leaning into a clenched jaw Leon who was getting increasingly angrier watching Eira and Lord Dundan move around the dance floor.

"No," Leon grumbled. "She can handle him."

"And why do you cover it up?" Eira asked Lord Dundan, pulling herself away from him to look him face to face once more.

"No reason. Just one of the last mementos I have from when my family ruled the land. Perhaps, I think, some people would not want to see me wearing it."

"I have a hard time believing you are the kind of man who sympathizes with the people and would not want to cause an uprising amongst them."

"Despite what you think, Your Majesty, I am simply here to get what my family deserves," Lord Dundan responded calmly.

"Your family deserves nothing," snapped Eira. "Your people have established a new life in the South and frankly, my forefathers were far too generous with their sentencing."

"Oh really? And what would you have done?"

"Let me just ask you one thing?" Her tone changed snarky, "Do you just sit in your big mansion in front of your roaring fire drinking your hot nonsense, planning ways to exact your revenge? Don't you have anything better to do with your time?"

Leon and Killian were still watching the whole interaction, and Leon couldn't contain his growing distress about the fact that Lord Dundan had his hands on Eira. Then Leon could see in both of their eyes that if he did not intervene, there would soon be an all-out war in the middle of the ballroom.

Leon stepped over to Lord Dundan and Eira. "If you don't mind," he began in a patronising tone, "I'd like my fiancée back." And without hesitation, he and Killian separated Eira and Lord Dundan, Leon taking her one hand in his and placing his other on her waist, the same way Lord Dundan's hands had just been, and moved them away from the man he despised. Killian, too, took Lord Dundan's hands and spun him around the dance floor until Lord Dundan pushed himself away from Killian and made his way back to his seat at the table.

"Well, that looked like a pleasant conversation," Leon started as he led Eira slowly in a dance.

"It was," she sneered. "You seem like you're having a good time though," she said with a sarcastic undertone.

"Hardly," he responded.

"You were the one who told me to ask him about the cuff. But it was useless anyway. I got no information about it. He said it was just a family heirloom, but there's something about it—I just know."

"I can look into it tomorrow if that will pacify you for now?" Leon snapped. Eira looked at him and realized she was getting more flustered.

"Wow, tone much," she responded.

He tilted his head at her with an uneven look on his face, "Sorry, I just don't like him."

"I get it, I don't either." Eira placed a hand on Leon's face, which seemed to calm him.

"Perhaps Gideon knows something about it," he added.

The next day, Leon went to the library to ask Gideon if he knew anything about the mysterious cuff Lord Dundan had. Gideon was puzzled at first, but then he pulled out a dusty old book and riffled through the pages for a bit until he came to the one he seemed to be looking for.

"Is this the cuff?" he asked Leon as he pointed to a hand-drawn sketch that mirrored the cuff exactly.

"Yes, that's it!" exclaimed Leon, and he turned the book to get a better look.

"That's what I was afraid of," said Gideon. Leon looked up at him, intrigued by the tale Gideon was about to tell. The words written around it were piled together like a train wreck, making it hard enough to decipher without the added bonus of it being written in some ancient language Leon could not interpret.

"It is the Diamond of Azul Sorceress, better known as the Blue Queen's Diamond." Leon listened as Gideon told him the legend of the Blue Queen. "Long ago, there was a terrible sorceress called the Blue Queen that terrorized the land. She had powers beyond any imaginable. She was finally defeated and entrapped inside a diamond. That diamond was then fashioned into a cuff to be worn by the great kings of Talvia as a trophy of their triumph over her. Eventually it was decided that the power contained inside the diamond was too powerful for any man to hold and the bracelet was taken from Talvia and hidden in an unknown location, never to be seen again. It was hidden for fear that one day the Blue Queen might be released. Before she was trapped, she swore an oath to whomever would release her from her prison."

"Can she be released?" asked Leon when Gideon was finished with his tale.

"She can, but only if he knows how. It says here that she can only be released when the fullest moon of winter pierces the diamond."

"What does that mean?"

"It means that to release her, the light from the first full moon of winter needs to shine through the jewel." Gideon then pulled out a moon chart and unrolled it in front of Leon. He studied it for a moment.

"That's only in a couple of weeks. If he intends to release her, we need to act now," urged Leon.

"Yes, but, you should make sure this is in fact the Diamond of Azul Sorceress. It could be a fake, to sway Eira in his direction—to get what he wants. The real jewel was hidden centuries ago. There is no way of knowing where it was hidden. The men who hid it were instructed to go out and never tell anyone where they were going or write anything down. And—sad to say—it was a suicide mission. To ensure none would ever find it."

"And what if it is the real thing? What if someone did find it?"

"Then you had better pray Lord Dundan does not know how to release this wrath into the world."

Leon ran to find Eira and tell her everything Gideon had told him. When she found out her suspicions about Lord Dundan were right, she wanted to confront him right away.

"Wait," urged Leon. "You can't confront him right now. What if Gideon is right and the jewel is a fake? You may anger him and squander any chance we had at making peace. You cannot accuse him of things you are not one hundred percent sure of."

"Fine. So, how do we find out for sure that is the real diamond?" Just then, Ceilidh walked into the room with a tray of essential oils and other items she was using to ready Eira's bath for the evening.

"Ceilidh!" she exclaimed. "I didn't even know you were here."

"Sorry, Your Majesty. Quiet feet, I guess." Eira looked at Leon and she knew he had the same thought she had. They both looked back at Ceilidh who was still standing sheepishly by the door.

Ceilidh was informed of the plan and what she was listening for. Any mention of the diamond or the Blue Queen, she was to come straight to Eira.

For the next couple of days, Ceilidh took on her new role with great ambition. She quietly attended to Lord Dundan, bringing him his meals and anything else he needed. All the while, negotiations went on between Lord Dundan and Eira. She was trying to please him without having to give up her throne. Finally, one night, Ceilidh heard what she and Eira were waiting for. She was about to bring in Lord Dundan's tea one evening when she overheard him talking to one of his men.

"We are almost there," he began. "The first full moon of winter will be here in a week's time, and then she can be free. We just need to manage to stay here a bit longer and keep the negotiations going." A loud clang rang through the hall and it stopped the men talking inside, as Ceilidh had dropped the tray she was holding. She ran to tell Eira what she had heard, leaving the tray and spilled tea behind.

Eira and Leon were right. Lord Dundan had the jewel and intended to release the Blue Queen. They now had to get to him before it was too late. He could not release the Blue Queen without the moon, so they were safe for the time being, but Eira knew that would not stop him. He had been relentless in his pursuing of aspects of her kingdom during negotiations and Eira had a feeling a little moonlight was not going to get in his way.

3

The sun was setting on this informative day at Trillium Nivale. Eira and Leon knew they needed to confront Lord Dundan right away about the diamond. They could not wait until the next morning now that they knew it was the real Diamond of Azul and he knew how to release the Blue Queen. Lord Dundan was in the great hall, sizing up Eira's throne with his men around him.

"It's quite comfortable, really," he said as he was perched atop the throne.

Eira marched into the great hall feeling about as red as the shade her flowing gown was coloured in. "What do you think you are doing?" she asked.

"Well," Lord Dundan began as he stood from the throne, "when you started asking those pesky questions about my bracelet, I knew it would not be long before you discovered its true power. I decided it was now or never to claim my position over you. Let's face it, there were going to be no negotiations between us anyway."

"How dare you come here and challenge my throne," Eira commanded as she stepped closer to Lord Dundan.

"Your throne?" snapped Lord Dundan as he fled from his position and came face to face with her. "You are an outsider that took advantage of the first available position at court."

"This is my home, whether I have lived here for one or one hundred years," replied Eira. "It doesn't matter now, anyway. We know you have the Diamond of Azul and you intend on releasing the Blue Queen. Did you really think we were going to let you get away with this now? Your threats are useless. You and I both know you can't release her until the first full moon of winter. You'll have to wait and we won't give you that time."

"That's what you think, my dear. You see, I thought about that little predicament myself, and then I realized there had to be another way. And, there is." Eira looked at Leon who had the same bewildered expression on his face. Gideon had not mentioned another way, and Eira did not think Lord Dundan was smart enough to find one on his own. "You see, I don't need the actual moon to release her, just the light from it." He pulled a small vial from his jacket pocket and its contents shimmered like liquid pearls.

"Bottled moonlight," gasped Leon.

"What? That's a thing?" whispered Eira to Leon.

"Where did you get that?" Leon ignored Eira's ignorance.

"That's none of your concern now, is it? The point is, I can release the Blue Queen whenever I want."

Eira turned to her guards and ordered them to seize Lord Dundan and his men and remove the cuff from his wrist. But when she did this, they simply stood there. She looked at them again as if they did not hear her the first time, but they remained still.

"Seize them," Lord Dundan ordered her guards. Then the guards moved in, taking hold of Eira and Leon.

"What are you doing?" Eira called to her guards as she tried to free herself from their clutches.

"You see, my dear," began Lord Dundan as he walked slowly toward Eira. "I knew a queen would come back one day—it had to turn out that way, and I had to be ready for the day you did."

"You've been planning this all along. You had your men infiltrate my castle and pretend to be my guards until you got here."

"You are a smart one, aren't you?" he caressed Eira's chin with his hand.

"How long have you been planning this?" she shook herself free of him.

"Years. Ready and waiting for this exact day."

"You won't get away with this," said Leon, who had his arms behind his back, being held beside Eira. "You can't hold us captive forever."

"I can and I will—until I get what I want, that is." He turned to Eira, "The way I see it, I have a few options: I can kill you and take the throne, I can release the Blue Queen and she can force you to give it up, or…" He paused for a moment and glanced back to Leon with a look of sheer sadistic pleasure in his eyes, then back to Eira. "I can marry you and become king. The choice is yours, really."

Eira was shocked at the audacity of Lord Dundan's statement. His true nature was showing and Eira knew that he had her momentarily beat. "I will never marry you," she said through clenched teeth.

"I thought you would say that. So, I will give you some time to think over your options. Meanwhile, my guards are taking over the castle. I own this place now. No one does anything or goes anywhere without me knowing about it."

With that, the guards led Eira and Leon away. It seemed that the number of Eira's friends in the castle were rapidly diminishing and becoming increasingly outnumbered by foes. Lord Dundan had successfully taken siege of Trillium Nivale and his guards were working around the clock to protect him, the diamond, and the vial of moonlight.

Eira stormed into her room with Leon following behind. The doors were closed behind them and a couple of Lord Dundan's guards stood on the other side.

"'Oh, if I just wasn't a lady, what wouldn't I tell that varmint'," she said, mustering up her best Scarlett O'Hara impression, feeling that particular sentiment suited the situation quite nicely.

"What?" asked Leon.

"Never mind," she sighed.

"So, what do you think we should do?"

"What should *we* do? I have no idea what *we* should do. My only options are to die, forfeit the crown, or marry that spiteful man."

"Look Eira, I wish I could tell you I had some plan to get you out of this but, I can't. He has the castle and there is nothing you can do. I'm certain he is monitoring any messages coming in or being sent out. We can't send for help."

"What are you saying?" she questioned him when she saw the torture in his eyes that what he was about to say would bring him.

"Eira, there is no other option. You have to do it."

"What? Marry him or give him my crown? Which would you rather me do?" Eira argued. Her tone of voice was increasing rapidly with the anger Leon's words were bringing to her heart.

"At least if you marry him, you will remain queen," Leon responded, his demeanour shifting.

"I cannot believe you just said that! I would rather die than marry that despicable man."

"If you die, then he becomes king, and I'll lose everything that ever mattered to me. There's no winning here, Eira. Can't you see that?"

"No, I'll just give him the throne. Then we can go live in some estate somewhere and be perfectly happy."

"Really? You'll be happy giving up your throne and watching as he turns Talvia into a place of corruption and the people's free will is stripped from them? You know he's not going to rule peacefully over this land. He's going to be a dictator, the likes of which Talvia hasn't seen since his ancestors ruled."

"Maybe not. He just wants to be king. What benefit would it be to him to be a vengeful king? He would want the people on his side."

"Trust me, sweetheart. A guy like that doesn't care how he wins the favour of his people. They won't take too kindly to him stealing the throne from you, so he'll likely threaten them into worshiping him," he sighed and took a step closer to her, taking her hands in his. "At least if you're still queen, you can prevent that from happening. You and I both know you wouldn't abandon your people like that."

Tears were now forming in Eira's eyes as she breathed through the waving in her voice. "We can make sure that doesn't happen. I can make sure that the only way I will give up the throne will be if he keeps everything the way it is."

Leon shook his head, "You can try, but we know it won't work. He might agree to it now, but once you sign over your throne, you have no say in what he does. Believe me, you have no idea the terror he can release on this land.

If the Blue Queen is free—you don't want to see Talvia under her rule. We were all taught it in school as kids. Think of the worst possible event in the history of your world. The worst possible leader your world has ever known—and trust me, she is a hundred times worse."

"There is a way—we just haven't thought of it yet. I will not marry anyone but you." She looked into his longing eyes. She could see the look; that he was searching for another option too, but there was no other.

He loved her too much to let her give up her kingdom or sacrifice herself and when he finally responded, his words hurt her, crushing her soul to the very core, but they didn't hurt her nearly half as much as they hurt him to say, "Then I refuse to marry you." Those were his last words. He turned from her bewildered gaze and headed for the door, resisting the urge to look back. For he knew one look into her eyes, he would not be able to continue walking out of her life.

"You are sentencing me to a deathless death! Can't you see that?" she ran after him and pounded on the doors after the guards had already shut them behind Leon. She called after him through tear-filled eyes, "Leon. Leon." She fell to the floor of her chamber and wrapped her arms around her waist in an effort to comfort herself. She was trapped in her chambers; a prisoner in her own castle.

Everyone in the castle was ushered into the great hall where Lord Dundan sat on Eira's throne.

"Attention all," he called out. "From this moment forward, this castle is under my control. You will all listen to me until the time your queen has made a decision regarding my propositions."

"What the hell?" whispered Killian to Theo. "We were gone two minutes and suddenly he's taken over?"

"I don't know what's going on here, but it can't be good," whispered Clea.

"Where are Eira and Leon?" asked Nell, who was now trapped in the castle. She was not allowed to leave, and she for sure was not going to be able to sneak home through the Almaluna door in the library.

"I don't know," answered Killian. "I haven't seen them all day."

"Well, he didn't release the Blue Queen," noted Theo, nodding to the cuff still on Lord Dundan's wrist. "At least we have that."

They turned their attention back to Lord Dundan's voice, bellowing through the great hall. "No one enters or leaves this castle without my approval. Is that clear?"

The crowd's silence was response enough and Lord Dundan waved for the people in the castle to be dismissed.

That night, Eira wept herself to sleep for the first time, in she did not know how long. The last time was probably when she had found out that Leon had done everything in his power to prevent her from having to face the dragon. The night they were still in the Valley of the Ethereal, celebrating Myrrvintrel. As she was falling asleep, she tried to devise some sort of plan that would get her out of this, but came up with nothing. Finally, the strain from her emotional day lulled her into a welcomed sleep. Sometimes, a good night's rest and a new day are all that is needed to find a solution.

"What are you doing?" Killian asked as he stumbled upon him. Killian watched Leon pack up Harwin in the dead of night. "You can't leave the castle," he whispered, moving closer and looking around for Lord Dundan's guards.

"I have to," responded Leon. "I ended any relationship I ever had with Eira and I can't stay and watch her marry someone else."

"You did what? Have you lost your mind? Is everyone in this palace just losing it?"

"No, but he's going to kill her to get what he wants, and I can't let that happen."

"You don't know that—have a little faith in her. And since when would that have stopped you? You are a man who stays and fights, not abandons the people he loves," Killian argued back.

"I do have faith in her," Leon shot back. "I have faith that she will do what is right for this country, and I'm not it. If we decide to fight, there's a good chance we'll all die. Haven't you seen how many guards Dundan has? We're greatly outnumbered in this castle, and I'm sure he has an entire army just waiting on our doorsteps. Without greater numbers, we can't defeat him."

"So you're just going to leave and turn your back on her?"

"I love her too much to see her give up everything and her life for me. She can't marry me and you know that."

"No, I don't. What I know is that you're letting what you feel for her get in the way of rational thinking."

"Rational thinking? I seem to be the only one who *is* thinking rationally around here. Would you rather Lord Dundan release a terror on this land and kill the people most important to us?"

"If you just stay, we can find a way."

"She is a queen. She has her country to think of. I'm insignificant compared to that. I knew it from the beginning that love isn't always a luxury people like her can afford. She needs to do what is best for her people and she knows that."

"You are giving up everything you—both of you—fought for. She will never forgive you, you know that?" declared Killian.

"She knows why I did what I did and if I see her again someday, I know she will."

Leon shook off his friend and readied himself atop Harwin. Killian grabbed the reins and held him back. "You need to learn a thing or two about love."

"No, you do. You ever going to tell Nell how you feel?"

"Don't make this about me."

He kicked Harwin and Killian had no choice but to release the reins and watch Leon escape into the night, away from the life that he fought so hard to have.

The pain was increasing in his chest with every stamp of Harwin's hooves, pulling him farther and farther away from Trillium Nivale and Eira. He was uncertain if he truly was doing what was best for Talvia and for Eira, but it was already done. He feared there would be more anguish running through the halls of the castle if he turned around and took back everything he had said. He could not bear to see Eira's throne taken from her and the home she had only just found ripped away as well.

The snow began to fall, just as he was reaching the forest beyond the castle.

Eira awoke the next morning with a clear mind. The first thing she did was visit Gideon to discuss her conversation with Leon. Gideon, unfortunately, could not offer any helpful advice. It pained him to agree with Leon but, where the castle currently stood, she and everyone else were helpless.

"Everything will be alright, my dear," Gideon assured Eira. "Even if this marriage goes through, it is not the end of the world. Things have a funny way of working themselves out in the end. You need to have an awful lot of patience to live in this world. That really is true, and no problem is unsolvable. That is why they call them problems. I find that the defining feature of a problem is that somewhere there is a solution. You simply need to find it. And, nothing is ever lost, just misplaced for the time being."

"I don't think that advice is going to help me here. A marriage is a binding contract. I will be signing away mine and my kingdom's freedom." Gideon gave Eira a clever smile and said a few last words, which let her know that once more, there was more to Gideon than she thought.

"Yes," Gideon smiled, "but he will be signing it, too."

Eira walked solemnly down the corridors back to her room. It seemed the only place she wanted to be after the night she had, was back in the comfort of her bed pretending life was good again.

"I hear your little boyfriend managed to sneak out of the castle," greeted Lord Dundan when he crossed paths with Eira in the corridor.

What? Leon escaped? She thought he had just been avoiding her, but was still in the castle. She did not respond, just looked at him with a blank expression on her face.

"Oh well, one loss won't do much. He can't stop me now. Have you thought any more about my little proposal?"

"Not really," sneered Eira.

"Well, time is ticking, you'd better decide soon," he said, brushing past her and continuing down the corridor, passing Killian on his way.

The tears burst through the moment Lord Dundan was out of sight and Eira raced to her room.

"Eira. Eira," called Killian after her.

When Eira made it back to her room, she just wanted to be somewhere she could let herself go. Let the tears wash over her face. She ran to the bathroom and turned on the shower, sitting under the stream, gown and all.

Killian wandered in soon after and saw Eira sitting there, soaking wet, her dress completely ruined. He wandered over to the shower and turned it off, then sat down beside her and pulled her into him.

She sobbed into his chest, "He's gone, Kil. He just left."

"I know," he sighed, "and I'll kick his ass for it later. But right now, you have to pull yourself together, darling. You can't let Dundan win and see you like this. You have to let him know that he's not getting to you."

She looked up at him and wiped the tears from her face. He stood and pulled her to her feet, then walked across the room, grabbing a towel and wrapping it around her shoulders. She wiped her face dry and smiled up at him. The two walked out of the bathroom, and Killian nodded to something on Eira's pillow. She hadn't noticed it before, but there was an envelope lying neatly on her pillow. She had no idea how it had gotten there, or how Lord Dundan's guards hadn't noticed it. Eira walked over to it and grabbed it off the pillow, opening the sealed seam with her finger and pulling out the hand-written letter inside.

Hey, sweetheart,

I know you're furious with me right now, but you have

to believe I did what I did to protect you.

If I leave now, maybe there is a chance we can win this
thing.

Maybe I can find some people who are still on our side and
willing to fight.

Please believe me that it won't end this way.

She recognized Leon's handwriting instantly. The tears began again—Eira slightly surprised her tear ducts hadn't run dry—and they made little water droplets on the paper, causing some of the letters on the paper to bleed. Once it was read, she handed it to Killian to read. When he was done, she knew she had to destroy it for fear Lord Dundan would discover it. She walked over to the fireplace and threw it in and watched as the sides folded in on themselves and the fire ate it.

"What are you going to do now?" he asked.

"I don't know. But if he believes we can make it through this, then I have to fight for that, right?"

Killian smiled.

Suddenly, the door opened. "Ceilidh," Eira gasped in relief.

"I'm sorry, Your Majesty," she responded, walking in with a tray of tea. Ceilidh placed it on the table and then walked closer to Eira. "Did you get it?" she whispered, tilting her head toward the bed.

"That was you?"

"Leon asked me to get it to you last night."

In that moment, Eira knew what she needed to do. Eira was ready to agree to Lord Dundan's terms with careful consideration. Clea, Theo, Killian, and Nell were there to help her through making a decision. It was a lot of painful deliberation, and sometimes the group offered some less than helpful advice. She had thought over her options for quite some time, but in the end she took Gideon's advice and knew that somehow it would all work out, even if she did not know how yet.

When she was ready to accept her fate, Eira told the guards outside of her bedroom that she needed to talk to Lord Dundan and they led her to the maps room where Lord Dundan was poring over his newly seized lands. When she arrived, he looked rather pleased with himself, for he could sense that Eira was ready to give in.

"Alright, you win," she started. "I will not just hand over my throne and everything that goes with it, but...I will marry you." The moment the words left her lips, she was holding back all the emotion she had within but remained composed and confident as to not let him know what she was really feeling. She did not want him thinking he managed to touch a part of her that she was not sure would ever heal. Swallowing back the tears, Eira stepped forward, "This means that I remain queen, and I still have a say in what goes on in my kingdom."

"Oh, of course," Lord Dundan responded, stepping out from behind the desk and taking a few steps closer to Eira. "I would not want you to lose the trust of your precious people. You see, I am aware that the success of my kingship relies on you still being queen. The people trust you, and in turn, will trust me."

"You—you knew I would give in. All along, this is what you really wanted." He smiled, pleased with himself. "Were all your crayons grey as a child?" He looked slightly puzzled at her remark, then took a few steps closer to Eira still, and softly slid a finger up and down her porcelain cheek.

"It is true what they say about you, Your Majesty," he walked slowly, moving from her front to embracing her from behind and whispering in her ear, all the while slowly pushing her closer to the edge of the desk. "You are beautiful and brilliant in your ways. You might just make a good wife yet. And I'm sure that in time you'll find I will make a good husband." He quickly and forcefully turned her so she was facing him and she was pressed up against the desk in a rather compromising position. There was no room for her to escape. He held her close so she could feel the warmth of his body radiating onto hers. "You might even find my company quite...enjoyable."

Her nose crinkled, *Gross.*

He then moved in and kissed her lips with all the power he had. Eira struggled for a moment, but then was able to push him away. "You are not my husband yet," she said with great force, pushing out all the unwanted impressions brought on by his kiss.

"My lord," came one of the guards from the corridor outside. He turned and left her there, leaning against the edge of the desk with her heart pounding. Eira touched her chest and let out a deep breath. She had to admit he certainly was passionate, but all she really wanted was Leon back and for this to be nothing more than a nightmare she would soon wake from.

Wedding preparations went on over the next couple of days. It did not take long for Lord Dundan to get everything in order. He was not going to draw out a long engagement and risk losing everything he was about to have. The great hall was readied for the wedding to take place. There were no flowers or decorations of any kind that would normally accompany such nuptials. No, Lord Dundan had no time for such things. A hasty ceremony was all that was needed to ensure his hold over the land.

The morning of Eira's wedding was not what she had expected her wedding day would be like. Sure, her friends were there to witness the event. However, it was not the joyous occasion she had imagined it to be, nor did her friends imagine being forced to attend. She had commissioned the royal seamstress to make her a wedding gown for when she would marry Leon but, under the circumstances she could not bring herself to wear that one and instead had the seamstress create something far less elaborate. This was not a happy union and did not deserve the dress she had only dreamed of since she was a little girl playing dress-up. This was a different kind of dress-up she was playing with Clea, Nell, and Ceilidh, who were helping her get ready. She also did not have the desire to look beautiful for Lord Dundan, so instead opted for a simple design with a flowing chiffon skirt and a modest sweetheart neckline with cap sleeves. The bodice was still decorated with crystals and embroidery, but the rest was plain. The colour was not even white. It was more of a champagne, for Eira did not feel this was truly her wedding day and it never would be. She still looked beautiful, though. It was hard for Eira not to, although the sorrow that could be seen behind her sapphire eyes, to all but Lord Dundan, could suggest otherwise.

"I can't believe you're going through with this," sighed Nell as she clasped a necklace around Eira's neck.

"I have to," she quietly responded.

"No, you don't"

"Yes I do, Nell. You don't understand how it works here. It will be much worse if I don't—believe me."

When the doors of the great hall opened, they revealed a dignified and calm Eira ready to make the right sacrifice for her kingdom. She had learned in her short time in Talvia that sometimes being a queen means you have to ignore your heart and listen to your head. As she walked slowly down the aisle, her veil trailed behind her and she was glad for a moment to be wearing it, for a small tear rolled down her cheek, unnoticed by everyone but her. When she finally made it to the altar, she turned to look at the faces of her still loyal subjects that were prisoners in the castle with her. She saw Gideon, Theo, Killian, Clea, Nell and Charles. Leon's absence was all too obvious to her and her heart ached a little more. Even if he were still in the castle, he wouldn't be there. Why would he be? If the situation was reversed, she would not want to watch him marry someone else.

There were other people there that Eira did not recognize, people from the village Lord Dundan was from. His loyal subjects congregated, and were now, under sad circumstances, hers as well. All the faces she knew seemed to share the same expression as Eira. She could only hope that they understood she was doing it all for them.

The ceremony began and before she knew it, the marriage licence was being brought forward for the two to sign. It was placed on a small table in front of Eira and Lord Dundan, who were now kneeling at the altar. The marriage commissioner motioned for Lord Dundan to sign the paper first, so he took the pen and signed his name. Then he looked at Eira next, and she looked back at him for what felt like forever. Glancing back at her friends again, Eira saw Gideon's kind face staring back at her. She turned to Lord Dundan, who was handing her the pen. Eira took the small writing utensil in her fingers and paused again, hovering over the piece of parchment. A smile grew on her face and she looked at the commissioner and laid down the pen where she was supposed to sign her name. She stood and glared down at Lord Dundan, who looked shocked that she would not sign.

"Thank you, Lord Dundan," she began.

"For what?" he stood.

"For giving me back my kingdom. You see, that is not a marriage license. You just signed your name to a confession of attempting to usurp the throne by any means, including regicide."

Lord Dundan pored over the paper he had just signed with utter shock on his face. He stood upright and turned to Eira, grabbing her by the arm. "You can't do this.

Do you think you will get away with this? You're forgetting I control the castle. I will burn this paper."

Eira grabbed his arm as well and leaned in, "You think you have spies in this castle but, you're forgetting one thing." Pausing for a moment to enjoy the look of defeat in his eyes, she then added, "So do I." She pushed Lord Dundan away and called for the guards that were still on her side to take him away.

He moved to grab her again when Killian stepped in, stopping Lord Dundan's arm in the air. "Touch my queen again, and it'll be the last thing you do," growled Killian.

Lord Dundan was thrown into the dungeon, and his bracelet was secured along with the vial of moonlight. Trillium Nivale was reclaimed by Eira and her people, but there was another matter at hand. She rushed to her friends. "We have to go after Leon."

"I told you," started Killian, "he managed to sneak out of the castle the night he called off your engagement. He's headed to Syysia."

"Well, then I'm going to Syysia."

"No, Eira," chimed in Theo, grabbing her arm as she was about to continue running down the aisle. "You can't just leave. You have a kingdom to uphold and a man to prosecute."

"Unless I go after him, he won't know to turn around and come back."

"I'll send for him once he reaches Syysia. He'll receive word to come home," said Killian.

"That will be weeks from now. I can't let him continue on that long thinking I've married someone else. I'm going and you can't stop me. Charles will be steward in my absence. Besides, Lord Dundan is detained in the dungeon. He can't hurt anyone anymore. Let him suffer down there for a while." Turning to Charles, she took his hands in hers, "You did a fine job ruling this kingdom all those years in my father's absence, I think you can manage for a few more days. I trust you."

Eira had to hurry to beat the sun setting over Talvia before she headed out on her journey. Leon had a few days' head start on her and she hoped she would be able to find him. She was rushing out of her room when she ran into her friends in the hall, all with packed bags resting on the floor by their feet.

"What are you guys doing?" she asked.

"You didn't think you were going without us, did you?" Killian said as he reached down and grabbed the bag by his feet.

She smiled at her friends, "You don't need to come."

"We're your family, darling. You can't shake us," smiled Killian, wrapping an arm around her shoulder.

Glad that they were not leaving her to embark on this adventure alone, she didn't need to say her thanks to them—they knew it by the smile. Charles rushed down the hall and ran into all of them. Handing her a small map, he said,

"I've sent word to my cousins in Kevatia that if Leon should stop and rest there, they should tell him to wait for you. It is your best chance at getting to him before you have to embark on the longer journey to Syysia. He always takes the same route back to Syysia. Hopefully, you'll be able to catch him."

"Kevatia?" questioned Eira as she opened the map. "I thought he was headed to Syysia?"

"Well yes," chimed in Killian. "But you have to travel through the Spring Country before you get to the Autumn Country."

"Hasn't anyone ever taught you the order of the seasons? What comes after winter?" patronized Theo, walking up beside her.

"Spring, I know. But, that would mean to get to Syysia you have to go through the Summer Country also?"

"Oh, no," added Killian, "We're going around Kesa."

"Why don't people just travel east and avoid everything, make the journey shorter?"

"We would go that way but, the eastern mountains are treacherous and few people make it through them alive. This is really the only feasible way. Besides, we'll take the train," finished Killian.

"Train?" asked Eira. "How do I not know there's a train?"

"Of course there's a train. Do you really think we travel only on horseback? It goes all around, through all the countries. There is only one train, though, so you have to plan your travels accordingly. Hopefully, if we're lucky, we'll catch it as it is coming into the Talvia station. It is a bit of a journey to get to the station, but once on the train, it'll make our journey easier," said Theo.

"Alright then," Eira sighed, "Kevatia it is." She turned to the group again, "Are you sure you guys are up for this? I hate to ask you to drop everything and come with me. Especially you," she nodded to Nell, looking rather excited to go on a journey through a magical world.

"Haven't you learned by now, darling?" Killian said. "You don't have to ask."

5

The journey through the forest went as expected. A lot of bushes and foliage of the conifer variety to look at. The rest of the trees displayed their grey and white bark being contrasted every so often by some small red berries hanging from their branches. Despite the circumstances, Eira liked the thought of being on a journey again with this company. Although this time around was significantly colder than before, but she was well dressed in her fur-lined hooded cape and mittens. It was not, however, one of those bitterly cold winter afternoons. The kind where you feel perfectly content to sit at home all day not accomplishing anything, in front of a roaring fire and a hot mug of whatever you fancy. No, this was one of those winter days when the sun shone high in the sky, warming the air around you; the kind ready and willing to take you on an adventure.

"How do you do this?" asked Nell, riding up beside Eira. "My butt hurts so much. I don't think I'm meant for horseback riding."

"You get used to it," chuckled Eira. "Hey, are you sure you want to be coming with us?"

"Yes. I missed out on an epic adventure the last time—I'm not missing out again."

"I don't think you really missed out. The last bit of it was kind of intense."

"No, no. That elf place sounded nice. I probably would have just hung out there until you came back."

Eira grinned, "Classic Nell."

"Hey," started Killian in an attempt to break the silence with his unusual sense of humour, "remember the time Eira almost married that evil lord?" he said with all manner of seriousness and reminiscence. The group stared at him, especially Eira, who was hardly amused. "Too soon?"

The group continued to stare and Eira raised her eyebrows to him as if to say, *You think?*

"Right, not ready to joke about it yet, then."

"Remember the time Killian fell asleep in the hot springs?" said Clea. The other two laughed while Killian gave a brilliant re-enactment of his irritated face the first time Clea had pointed out his foolishness. The sun was starting to set when they had almost made it to the edge of the forest.

"Ah, look," stated Killian, changing the subject, "we're almost there. I can taste the hot stew already." In the distance, Eira saw a small wooden cabin with light in its windows and smoke coming from the chimney. It was another traveller's cabin made by the Wintren-elves.

"Oh, good," Eira smiled, her stomach beginning to signal its hunger to her.

When the stew pot was empty, mostly from Killian, and the after-dinner pleasantries had fulfilled the group, they headed out into the now dark world. The days were getting shorter and shorter at this time of year in Talvia. The days were never that long, just as they were in winter where Eira grew up, however at certain times of the year, the days lasted longer. The group didn't have time to stay in the cabin overnight. It was merely a stop for dinner. They then headed out and down the lantern-lit path toward the station and onto the train to take them to Kevatia.

It was as if a path was cut right out of the forest and lined with warm glowing lanterns popping right out of the snowy ground; one right after the other. It all seemed very magical to Eira. Even though she had been in Talvia a year now, its beauty was always surprising her, along with the way people did things. Back in her other world, it would be street lights and probably a paved path. She loved the simplicity of Talvia in some cases, such as these lanterns lighting their way.

A train whistle broke through the air, and they knew they were getting close. Just around the next bend, the massive train and its platform came into view. A large black engine stood at the front and the cars behind went on for what seemed like miles. There were stable cars for the horses, and the passenger cars that were made entirely of glass, with a domed glass roof so you could get a full glimpse of the world outside.

"Alright," started Theo, "five tickets to Kevatia," he said as he passed them around as they got the horses situated in their stables.

Eira's horse seemed a bit unsure about the train. "It's okay, Maeve," said Eira giving her an apple. "It's just a little train ride."

They found their cabins quickly but none seemed tired enough to go to sleep. Well, none except Killian, who was out as soon as he felt the softness of the mattress. They would be travelling all night and half of the next day. Theo, Eira, Clea, and Nell all sat in the bar car, enjoying their drinks. Eira was barely keeping her eyes open as she stared into her mug of hot cider.

"Eira, you need to get some sleep," said Clea. "You've barely slept these past few nights."

"I know, but no matter how tired I seem to be, I never get more than a couple of hours, and then I'm wide awake."

"Hey," started Theo, "everything is going to be fine now. We're going to get Leon and then everything is going to be back to normal."

"I'm not sure it can go back," replied Eira.

"Leon thought he was doing what was best for you and Talvia. Sure, it was stupid, and I probably would not have abandoned the woman I love to marry another man, but he wasn't exactly thinking straight," assured Theo. "Eira, you have no idea how much Dundan was tearing him up inside. He couldn't stand having him in the castle and around you. He thought letting you go temporarily was the only way to ensure he'd never have to let you go again."

Eira didn't know how to respond. She wanted to be ready to forgive Leon, but it was more complicated than that. She just took a sip of her drink and looked out the window at the black world racing by. Every once in a while she could make out the trees when the moonlight broke through the forest, and the falling snow racing past.

"Hey, let's think about something else," said Clea. "I'm excited to see the Spring Country. I've never been there before."

"Yeah, me too," added Theo.

"I think I'm going to go to bed now," said Eira as she stood up. She made her way to her cabin and got ready for bed.

The train cabins were similar to the passenger cars, with domed ceilings made of glass. It was like being inside of a glass igloo built on the train. She couldn't help but let a couple of tears loose as she was trying to fall asleep.

The next morning, Eira awoke to the sun pouring in through the windows. Its warmth on her face gradually pulled her out of her slumber. They were still in Talvia and she could see tiny white flakes falling on the world outside. She spent most of the morning in her cabin, reading and listening to music on her phone—the only thing it was still good for in Talvia—and enjoying the peace and quiet. She was even able to get a nap in, which she was pleasantly surprised about. At one point, she looked out the window to see a couple of bear cubs that looked like pandas playing in the fresh powder outside. Rolling, running and jumping in their white playground. The others were surely enjoying breakfast and having a good time, but she wasn't in the mood for socializing. Close to noon, a knock came at her door.

"Hi," said Nell when Eira slid the door open. "How are you doing?"

"Pretty good. I think I finally got some sleep last night."

"That's good. There isn't much of the journey left. We'll be in Kevatia soon. You should come out and have some lunch."

"That's a good idea," replied Eira as she stepped into the corridor with Nell and slid her door shut behind her.

After lunch, Eira stayed sitting in the dining car, reading her book. The others were off entertaining themselves.

"Look," said Theo as he came up beside Eira and nodded toward the window beside her. "We're crossing the borders of Talvia; where winter meets spring."

Eira turned to look out the window. She could see the snow gradually disappearing and the signs of spring emerging. The trees began to grow bright green leaves and there were flowers blooming and the grass swaying in the breeze. The journey was not long after that. They would be at the Kevatia station in about fifteen minutes.

They got off the train onto the platform and gathered all their belongings. Their horses were brought out to them by one of the stable hands working on the train. Eira could feel the warmth of the spring air as soon as she stepped onto the platform. The smell of the fresh grass and flowers blooming was overwhelming her senses. While she loved Talvia, this was a nice change. It had been a long time since she had experienced the change of seasons.

Eira unzipped her jacket. "Wow, it's so warm here," she said.

"Well, here it is," stated Theo as the train pulled away from the station and they could get a good view of the surrounding countryside. The five stood there in awe, with their horse's reigns in hand. Theo turned back and smiled at Eira, "Welcome to Kevatia, Your Majesty."

Eira pulled the map Charles had given her out of her pocket. It was directions to his cousin's house, and she hoped desperately that Leon had stopped to rest there and received their message so they could return to Talvia and put this whole thing behind them. Knowing Leon, however, she had the slightest suspicion that if he felt even the slightest bit fit for it, he would keep going.

It did not take long for them to find the correct direction to head in, and they were soon making their way through the market roads in the hills toward the first small town in Kevatia. By nightfall, they were on the borders of the town of Kelby. They managed to find an inn for the night and in the morning they asked the innkeeper if she could direct them to the house they were looking for.

"Ah, yes. You are looking for the estate just up the road," said the innkeeper. "It's that road there," she pointed out the window. "It's on a large plantation. You can't miss it."

"Thank you," said Eira as she folded the map up again and tucked it into her pocket. "By any chance have you seen a man pass through here? He would have been riding a white unicorn, hopefully headed to the same place we are."

"I did see that man a couple of days ago. He passed right through town toward the plantation."

"Great. Thank you," said Eira feeling hopeful that perhaps they did not miss Leon after all.

Eira rejoined her crew who were waiting outside the inn, tacking up the horses for the ride. She relayed the information that the innkeeper had given her and then they were off, up the plantation road. About half an hour passed as Eira admired the surrounding beauty of the Spring Country. The road was lined with large flowering trees that shaded the road with their archway of boughs. When they finally reached the right house, she was amazed to see a large yellow and white plantation-style mansion, the likes of which Eira could only imagine. It was the picture of quintessential southern charm, the likes of which she had only ever seen on television on those design shows that make your life seem dull in comparison. When they rode up toward the house, the beauty of it and all its surroundings was only intensified by the lilacs hanging from the porch and the fine craftsmanship of the exterior. They reached the front driveway where a large round fountain was spilling clear water. A man came out of the front doors to greet them. He was Charles's cousin, Lord Edmond, and he welcomed them with open arms. He led them into the foyer and informed them that they had just received the letter from Charles that morning, but sadly, Leon had left only an hour before.

"Great, we missed him," said Eira.

"If he left, how come we didn't pass him on the way up here?" asked Clea.

"He left through the back road. It is a more direct route out of town," answered Lord Edmond. "Since you are all here though, how about some lunch?" Killian's ears perked up at the sound of that.

"That's very kind but, I feel if we leave now we may be able to catch up with him," answered Eira.

"But lunch," whined Killian.

"Maybe, but maybe not. Did he say where he would stop next?" asked Theo.

"Not really. He mentioned he was going to try to make it to the next town by nightfall, so I assume he will stop and rest there. If you stay for lunch, you will still have plenty of time to make it there by night and then hopefully you will be able to find him," reassured Lord Edmond.

The group agreed to stay, and they were presented with a grand feast. Far more elaborate than Eira had expected for lunch. Just as they were sitting down, they heard the front door opening, causing the hanging wind chimes to play their unique tune while someone walked in.

"Uncle," came a voice from the foyer, "I think I forgot my—" and in walked Leon. He stopped in his tracks, looking quite puzzled at the sight of everyone. "Eira? What are you doing here?" At this moment, Eira had a war waging inside her between her feelings. On the one hand, she was excited to see Leon, the great love of her life whom she thought she might not see again for quite some time. On the other hand, she was rather furious with him for abandoning her to marry someone else and then fleeing the country. Before she could move, Nell nudged her to the side and stormed toward Leon.

"Well, well. If it isn't Talvia's favourite roguish abandoner," lectured Nell. "Leon, you have three seconds to get out of here before I make you pay for hurting my best friend," demanded Nell. No one had ever seen that look in Nell's eyes before; the sheer animalistic rage that would only be pacified by killing something. Leon looked stunned as his eyes darted from Nell to Eira. When Nell passed Killian, he grabbed her out of the way and held her in his lap as she squirmed, trying to get to Leon.

"It's okay, Nell. I can handle this," said Eira. Eira rose from her chair and walked calmly over to the man staring at her with eyes she was all too familiar with. The group watched silently, no one wanting to interrupt what was about to happen. Killian casually slid the steak knife on the table out of Eira's reach.

Smack!

"Ow," Leon called, raising a hand to his cheek. "Alright, I probably deserved—" but before he could finish his words, Eira grabbed his collar and pulled him in for a far more passionate kiss than she would have expected from herself. Then, just as quickly, she pulled away and her hand hit his face again.

"What was that for? The first one I get, but that was unnecessary."

"You know what that was for, and I'm still furious with you. And, I actually think the question should be: What are *you* doing here? Why did you leave?"

"What do you mean, why did I leave?" he answered, rubbing his cheek again.

"You know what I mean? You abandoned me to the hand of another man. You couldn't trust me at all to find a way out?"

"There was no way out, Eira. I wasn't exactly going to hang around and watch you marry someone else."

"He makes a good point," chimed in Killian through a mouthful of food, still stuffing more of it in.

"I can't believe you thought I would actually marry that despicable man. Have you no faith in me?"

"That is a good point, too," said Killian again with a sip of his drink.

"Don't say that. I do have faith in you, and I know you. I know that you would have done anything to not marry him and save your people, but that would mean you *dying*, and at the end of it, that wouldn't save your people. I can live my life without you, knowing that you're at least still alive and taken care of, but I can't live with myself knowing that by me staying, I sentenced you to death."

"But you can live with me being miserable for the rest of my life being married to someone else?"

"No. Didn't you get my letter? I said I was leaving to try to find help. Can't you understand that? And besides, we could have had a little forbidden romance thing going on," he joked. She raised her hand to him again and he flinched. "Don't hit me again."

Eira lowered her hand, "You could have let me in on your little plan rather than letting me think you didn't love me anymore."

The argument was getting pretty heated, and the spectators were growing rather uncomfortable. However, there they sat, watching Eira and Leon have it out for each other. It was one of those moments where you cannot look away even when you probably should. Eira got so annoyed at one point that she once again inflicted unnecessary pain on the man she loved by stomping on Leon's foot.

"Ow! Stop hurting me."

"You hurt me first!" She had to hold back the tears that were welling up in her eyes. "You deserved that, and frankly, I can't talk to you right now."

Eira stormed off through the back door into the gardens while Leon stood there holding his foot, bewildered by what had happened. He lowered it and leaned against the sideboard, pressing his fingers against his forehead.

"Women," stated Killian with a shake of his head. Leon gave him a look of un-amusement. "Sandwich?" Killian then offered, and Clea smacked him on the back of the head. "Hey. You know, I'm starting to notice the guys in this group get hit a lot."

"Not me," smirked Theo.

"Yeah, why is that?"

"I don't say or do stupid things."

****

Charles was sitting on the throne when a man made his way into the castle. He strode through with all the arrogance as if he owned the place.

"I'm afraid I am late," he announced, opening his arms at his side.

"For what?" questioned Charles.

"For the wedding. Has it already happened? Where is the happy couple, anyway? On their honeymoon, I suppose."

"The wedding never happened, and Lord Dundan is in the dungeon where he belongs. I don't believe you introduced yourself."

"No, I don't believe I did. He's in the dungeon, you say? Well, that won't do at all." The man ordered the men who were with him to take Charles into custody. Charles called for his guards to come, but none came. They had all been captured and taken into the dungeon with some of the staff and Gideon. Charles was powerless against this unidentified assailant. The man then made his way to where Lord Dundan was being held.

"What took you so long? I was beginning to think you weren't coming," said Lord Dundan as the man unlocked his cell.

"To your wedding, or to break you free from this prison? I have to say, brother, this is an odd way to spend your honeymoon. Where is your beautiful bride, anyway?"

"Alright, enough gloating. We have work to do."

Lord Dundan pried the diamond from the cuff and held it up to the light, "Ah, the Diamond of Azul. It is a thing of beauty. So small, yet so powerful. You can hold all the power in the world between your fingertips."

"Just get on with it, brother."

He placed the diamond on a pedestal and removed the vial of moonlight from his chest pocket. Carefully, as to not spill any of the precious light, he removed the stopper at the top and drop, drop, drop. Three. No more, no less, onto the jewel.

He smiled and stood back as the swirls of colour inside the jewel began to move more quickly, and then, one by one, the streams of light pierced the diamond and flew around the room. The jewel's glow turned from white to a dark blue and then black. The black diamond rested still on the table until a hand picked it up. She held the diamond up to the moonlight and let the light shine through.

"That is beautiful, isn't it?" she smiled. "Now, which one of you released me?"

Lord Dundan stepped forward, "I did, Your Majesty," he bowed.

"And who are you then?" she motioned to Lord Dundan's brother.

"My brother—"

"Ah, it doesn't matter." She raised a hand and with a flick of her wrist, Lord Dundan's brother was dead on the ground. Lord Dundan looked at his brother's lifeless body and then turned back to the Blue Queen. "Ah, that felt good," she sighed. "It is nice to have my powers again. Don't look at me like that. He would have only got in the way, believe me," she said so plainly, as if the worst thing she had ever done was step on a few wildflowers. Lord Dundan continued to look into her eyes—speechless and wondering if it was worth it; what he had done. "If you're serious about taking back the throne, you can't afford to have people like him around to mess things up. Take it from me—people are messy. It's better if you get them out of the way from the start. If you want to be a ruler, you can't let anyone get in your way. Especially family. Now, where's that dreadful child? It's time she learned a thing or two about what it means to be a real queen." She intertwined her fingers and pushed them away from her by outstretching her arms. "Now why is it so cold?" She looked toward the window and saw the vast snowy landscape, "Oh, *Talvia*," the word *Talvia* dripping with disdain. She turned back to Lord Dundan and brushed past him, "Now why would you want to be king of this little snowball?"

****

"Eira," Leon called out to as he ran to where she was sitting in the garden.

"I don't want to talk to you right now. Can you please just leave me alone?"

"No, Eira, you need to come quickly," he said with some urgency. She looked up toward his face with a puzzled expression gracing hers. She could tell by his expression he did not care to talk about what had happened between them, and whatever was going on was a much more urgent matter.

They raced back to the house where she found Lord Edmond, Theo, Killian, Clea, and Nell in the sitting room. Clea had a look of horror plastered on her face and Theo was pacing back and forth in deep thought. When Eira entered the room, Clea ran up to her and placed her hands on Eira's shoulders.

"Eira, it's awful. What are we going to do?" asked Clea, looking deeply into Eira's eyes, searching for some comfort and affirmation that Eira knew what to do.

"What are you talking about? What's going on?"

"You didn't tell her?" asked Edmond, looking at Leon. He then moved toward Eira and presented her with a small piece of paper. When she examined it, it bared the seal of Trillium Nivale. She opened it quickly and read the contents.

"We just received this," began Leon. "I guess Gideon was able to send this out just before the castle was taken under siege."

The letter informed that Lord Dundan had escaped from his imprisonment, released the Blue Queen and had taken command of Talvia's army. Great.

"This can't be—how could your father have let this happen?" Eira looked at Leon. "I entrusted him with the well-being of my country. What have I done?" Eira sank into a chair as she felt faint from learning of the treachery she had brought upon Talvia.

"So, this is all my father's fault?" asked Leon. Eira didn't answer him.

"This was not your doing, Eira," assured Killian, placing his hand on her shoulder for comfort. "Lord Dundan had been planning this for years. You could not have known what he was truly capable of."

"We have to go home—we have to stop him. We're leaving now."

"Eira, we can't just go back. We'll be walking into a trap. The Blue Queen's power is far more than any man can take on."

"Good men are being soured by this witch's spell. Lord Dundan and her, they're on the throne together, ruling over Talvia and you're saying we can't go back?"

"You're right, Eira, but that is exactly why we can't go back yet. Not unless we have a way to defeat her. Lord Dundan is using the Blue Queen to manipulate the people of Talvia to do his bidding, and he will do the same to us if we return. If you love Talvia at all, we can't go back. Not yet," urged Leon.

"Well, what do you suppose we do then? How can we defeat the undefeatable?"

The group stared at each other, hoping someone would present the answer, but none knew what to do.

The Blue Queen's power was the greatest power known to mankind. There was only one power greater, and that was the power of a wizard. A wizard's power is the only thing comparable to that of a witch. The only problem was, there had been no wizards in the land for centuries— or so they thought.

6

It was getting late at the house of Lord Edmond, and the group was no closer to finding a way to defeat the Blue Queen than they were that afternoon. Eira sat there with Gideon's letter in hand, reading it over and over again as if it gave her some comfort or perhaps the solution would eventually present itself. She knew Gideon and his ways. Why would he risk sending a message here if he did not know of a way to help? They tore through every book in Edmond's library and found nothing on the Blue Queen or any way to defeat a witch's power.

"This is hopeless," said Killian as he threw another book on the floor. "We aren't going to find anything of use here. That witch has only ever been defeated once before, and that was centuries ago. And whoever did it then clearly didn't do a very good job, hence, we have to deal with her now."

"That's it," said Leon.

"What is?" asked Eira.

"That's how we defeat her. By finding the person who defeated her the first time."

"She was defeated by a powerful wizard, Leon, a man who does not exist anymore," said Theo.

"We don't know that. Wizards live for hundreds of years—thousands, maybe. He could still be alive."

"Even if he is, we have no idea where he is or how to find him," added Clea.

Eira was only partly listening to the other's conversation. She was still transfixed by the letter that Gideon sent. As it was getting dark out she had to pull herself closer to the light to make out the words on the page and when she did, she glimpsed something small inscribed into the corner of the paper, but she could not make it out. She held the paper up to the lamp again and tried to distinguish the faint ink shapes from the parchment.

"What are you doing?" asked Leon when he finally looked over to see why Eira was being surprisingly quiet during their conversation.

"There's something on this paper."

"It's probably just a smudge. I'm sure he was writing it in a hurry."

"No, there's definitely something here. It's written very small and in ink you can only see under the light." Leon moved closer to see the paper. Eira was right. There was a small collection of words on the corner of the page. *"AsesnoS eTh fo het redOr,"* read Eira when she was finally able to distinguish the words, or rather gibberish, more clearly. She threw her hands in the air out of frustration and let the parchment fall to the floor. "What does that mean?"

None in the group understood the hidden message.

"That's it, Gideon's finally lost it," said Killian.

"Why would he go to the trouble of writing something we can't understand?" asked Eira.

"I don't know. Maybe he used a piece of paper from something else. Perhaps he didn't even know the message was there," added Clea.

"No, I don't think so," replied Eira. "Do you think it could be another language?"

"Could be but, it doesn't sound like anything I've ever heard," said Theo. "If he was going to send us a hidden message in another language, you would think he would write in something one of us would recognize."

"Maybe it's a cipher. There are capital letters mixed in, indicating they might be the beginning of words." Eira sat back down with a pencil and the parchment trying to work out what the scrambled letters could be. She placed the capital *'T'*, *'O'*, and *'S'* at the beginning of the words they were mixed in with and ended up with: *Sasesno The fo het Odrre*. From there, it was quite simple to find the right word and in no time, she had a sentence that made more sense.

"There," she stood up, quite proud of herself. "That was actually really easy."

Leon took the paper from her hand and read aloud the newly deciphered message, "Seasons The of the Order. Well, it makes *more* sense but, I still don't know what that is." He took the pencil from Eira and re-wrote the message. "There," he said, holding up the piece of paper. "The Order of the Seasons. That makes more sense to me." He looked around the room to see if anyone had heard of *the Order of the Seasons* before, but there was a universal look of confusion on the other's faces. They turned back to the books and tried to find anything on the Order of the Seasons. After going through all the books a second time, now looking for different information, someone finally found a small section hidden in one of the books titled *Our Land: History and Mystery*.

"Here it is," cried Clea. "The Order of the Seasons." Clea read aloud from the book and all listened to the story. "It began centuries ago with a group of wizards. One from Talvia, one from Kevatia, one from Kesa, and one from Syysia. A wizard for each of the four seasons and the four lands. They were entrusted with the well-being of their countries and together they formed the alliance known as the Order of the Seasons. For centuries, they took care of their lands, keeping the peace and defeating any threats that presented themselves. One, the wizard of the Winter Country, was credited with defeating the Blue Queen herself when she ravaged the land. He cast her into a diamond tomb forever and sent that diamond into the depths of the land." When Clea was done reading, everyone had a mutual look of astonishment on their faces.

"Where do you suppose these wizards are now?" asked Killian.

"It doesn't say much in the book and besides, this book is hundreds of years old. Who knows how reliable it is now?"

"Gideon wouldn't have left us this message if they didn't still exist," added Eira.

"Well, he didn't happen to mention where they were now, did he?" asked Theo.

"There's no more to the letter, no other clue?" pressed Leon.

"No, there's just a small cross under the first word of the scrambled message. The word that turned into *Seasons*, nothing else."

It appeared as though the group was back to where they had started. They had deciphered Gideon's clue about who can defeat the witch, but they were once again puzzled as to where to find him.

"You know," began Killian to Eira, "we could have saved all this trouble if you just married Dundan and murdered him on your wedding night." Killian chuckled, "Not the stabbing he was hoping for—am I right?" he nudged Leon. The group glared at him. "I mean, you could have—you're kind of a badass."

Killian got smacked again.

They asked Edmond if he knew anything about the Order of the Seasons and the four wizards, but he had never even heard of them before.

"I'm sorry, Your Majesty, I can't help you," started Edmond. "But I would try the library in town in the morning. Their collection is far more expansive than mine, and the librarian is the oldest man in the town, possibly the oldest in the land. He may know something."

The anticipation running through her body was making it difficult for Eira to sleep. *That's it,* she thought, sitting up in bed. *I may as well go see if there are any more books about the Order of the Seasons while I'm still awake.* As she made her way down the stairs and through the hall to where the library was, a dim light coming from the living room caught her attention. She changed her direction and walked slowly over to its doorway. Peering inside, she saw Leon sitting in a large chair with the glow of a lamp overhead. He was holding a small glass with some amber liquid in it Eira knew right away.

"Well, this seems familiar," joked Eira as she stood in the doorway. "So, you're celebrating our discovery?" she asked him as she walked into the room. He looked up and then at the glass, smiling with just one corner of his mouth.

"No, actually, just enjoying my uncle's collection of whiskey. And, thinking," he took a deep breath and raised the glass to his lips for another sip. Eira walked over and stood by the coffee table at his feet.

"Can I join you?" she asked, motioning to the table.

"Not if you're going to hit me again," he smiled from behind the rim of his glass.

She smiled and sat in front of him on the edge of the coffee table. Leon handed her the glass and she grasped it in her hand, tilting it toward her nose for a smell and then finally, very unlike her usual self, slammed her head back and downed it in one gulp. Her face instantly soured, and she handed the empty glass back to him.

"Well, I've never seen you do that before." He took the glass and started pouring more of the amber liquid inside it.

"How many of those have you had?" she questioned him.

"Tonight?" he responded with a smirk. "I've lost count."

She breathed a heavy sigh, "So...what are you thinking about?" she finally asked.

"What do you think?" he glanced at her, swirling the glass in his hand.

"Well, it could be anything from, 'damn this is good whiskey' to, 'how the hell are we going to defeat that witch?' to, 'I hope Eira can ever forgive me for what I did'."

Leon touched his nose at the latter comment to indicate she was right. "Eira," he began, "I can't even begin to tell you how sorry I am."

She took a deep breath, "Look, I know, but that doesn't make it any easier for me to forgive you."

"Just, please consider it from my perspective." He shot the last sip of whiskey and placed the empty glass on the side table next to the glass decanter; half full of the amber liquid. Then he leaned forward and took her hands in his, the warmth of them making Eira long for his touch. "I thought this was the only way, you have to believe me. There was no way we could defeat him with the few people we still had on our side in the castle. I figured I could leave you and maybe gather people who would fight or find someone who knew some way of defeating her and then I'd come back and we would work it out, but in the meantime, you would be safe."

"You didn't think that we would come up with some sort of plan? How long did you think it would take you to find someone who could help? You know we're better working together."

"I know that, but I couldn't see a way out for you. Not at that moment. I couldn't live in the same castle as you with him. And I knew you could take care of yourself. You've beaten me up enough times to prove it." She gave a soft laugh. He raised one of his hands to stroke her cheek, "I love you so much, Eira. You have to believe I did what I thought was best for you." He leaned forward, his forehead pressing against hers with his hand now moved to behind her neck. She was about to say something, but before she could think of the right response, his lips were on hers and she was caught in a moment of weakness, reminiscing about what they used to have. Leon leaned back in his chair, pulling her forward off the coffee table and into his lap. His hand slipped up her thigh, under her nightgown and up her back as she pressed into him. In those few moments, Eira had forgotten everything that had happened in the last few weeks, but all too soon, it came rushing back to her as she pulled away from him.

"I can't do this," she said, standing up. "I can't forgive you yet. You can't just kiss me and make it all go away. It doesn't work like that." She placed her hand over her mouth as a couple of solitary tears rolled down her cheek. Leon sank back into the chair as Eira turned and headed out of the room and back up the stairs.

When she left Leon's company and headed back to bed, a whole flurry of emotions and thoughts were racing through her mind. She still desperately wanted to know more about the four wizards and what Gideon's message meant, but now she was tortured by what she had let herself just do. Daylight could not come fast enough. She felt as though waiting for morning meant that she was letting her people down. For every minute she spent sleeping, Lord Dundan and the Blue Queen were ruling *her* country and forcing *her* people to bow to them, and who knows what else. The fact that she was now reunited with Leon also did not help her mind rest that night and she knew that he was most likely awake as well, thinking the same. She wanted to get out of bed and walk around, to try to clear her head but she worried that if she did, she might run into him and it was too soon after their ongoing quarrel and brief moment of unbridled passion to tell what might happen. There were more important things at stake now, so there she lay, letting her mind run rampant with thoughts of the Blue Queen and Lord Dundan until she tired herself out and the release of sleep came.

The next morning, Eira awoke to the bright springtime sun shining through the plantation-style windows in her grand bedroom. There was a new dress hanging on her bathroom door and she assumed that one of Lord Edmond's maids had left it for her. It was a flowing gown that looked like spring; if it could be turned into a textile, with flowers all over it. She headed down the circular stairs into the foyer, where Killian and Nell were waiting, ready to head into town. She was glad that Killian had volunteered to go with her this morning, for she was still not ready to be alone with Leon and it seemed the feeling was mutual when he gave little protest to Killian's offer the night before. Eira encouraged Nell to tag along as well.

They headed out on foot, mostly because the getup Eira was wearing demanded it. Riding would be somewhat of a challenge in that dress, and she had never really thought side saddle a good choice. Nell was dressed similarly to Eira. However, her dress was not as elaborate and seemed to resemble a more simplified version of Eira's. She enjoyed the leisurely walk in the shade of the large trees and the smell of lilacs and magnolias swirling in the springtime breeze. When they reached the library, it was a very old house that looked as if it would crumble into ruin at any moment. Not a promising sight. Inside it was filled to the rafters with bookshelves that left no room on the walls for anything else and Eira wondered how anyone could find information on anything they were looking for in there.

They were greeted by the librarian, a very kind old man named Maurice, who insisted that they sit down for a cup of tea first. Edmund was right; this man certainly was on the far side of middle-aged. The far, far side. She was impressed he was still walking around with only the help of a slender wooden cane he seemed to hold more for show than actual balance. He shuffled around in the back for a few minutes until he finally made his way out through the maze of books with a tray and four cups of tea. It was impressive how well he moved around the store considering she had difficulties not knocking over any books, and based on the thickness of the glasses Maurice wore, he could not see very well at all.

"Now, what can I do for you?" asked Maurice as he placed a cup of tea in front of Eira and then Killian and then Nell. "Sugar?" he asked next, and Eira nodded.

"Mr. Maurice," Eira began, "we were wondering if you know anything about the Order of the Seasons?"

"The Order of the Seasons?" asked Maurice. "I have not heard those words spoken in years." He then stood up from the table and wobbly wandered off to a bookshelf in the back. When he came back, he was holding a very antique-looking book and the dust in the air increased when he bumped into a stack of books and they fell to the floor, creating a rather large cloud of dust. He chuckled and sat down again.

"Organized chaos, I like to think of it," he said, referring to his version of the Dewey Decimal System. He opened the book and looked through the pages until he found what he was looking for.

"Now, we know about what the order is but, what we want to know is where to find them?" asked Killian.

"Find them?" questioned Maurice. "Now, why would you want to do such a thing?"

"We need to talk to the wizard of winter—it's extremely important," answered Eira.

"A matter of life and death," added Killian.

"You young people, always so dramatic. Well, I'm sorry but, no one knows where to find the four wizards. There is rumour around where they are but, I'm afraid I cannot remember. Most things go in one ear and out the other these days."

"Maybe this can help." Eira pulled out Gideon's letter with the secret message and held it up to the light for Maurice to see. "We figured out the first part of the message but it looks like there is also a cross under the word *Seasons*. Do you have any idea what that could mean?"

From outside the window of the library, a man peered in. It was clear their conversation was not only for the ears of the four sharing in it inside the safety of the book-lined walls. They continued just as well at the pace they were going, unaware of the silent listener outside. He pushed the window in slightly to allow more of the conversation within to travel outside and listened intently to what was said next.

"Of course," gasped Maurice. "The Seasons Cross."

"The Seasons what?" asked Nell.

"Cross. The Seasons Cross. It is where it was said that the wizards would meet. It is the exact point where all four of the countries that make up this land intersect. It is not an easy place to get to, however. I don't know of anyone that has ever ventured that far out and has actually made it there."

"How would someone get there—if they wanted to?" asked Eira.

"And why would someone want to?" asked Maurice as he leaned in closer to Eira. She just smiled and he leaned back in his seat again. "Look, I'm telling you," he glanced at Killian and Nell, "all of you—do not go there. You have no idea what it'll do to you. Trust me—do not go through that pass."

Well, obviously, they were going to go through it.

"Okay, but what if we really had to?" asked Killian. "If there was no other way around it?"

Maurice sighed, "Well, don't say I didn't warn you. It is a long journey, one you should not take on lightly. If you are sure you want to go there, then I believe I have a map you can follow." Maurice went back to a bookshelf filled with stacked rolls of parchment. He pulled one out and blew off the dust. "Follow the map *exactly*, for it is an easy journey to get lost on." Then he chuckled, "Although, sometimes I find you need to get a little lost before you find what you are looking for."

They said goodbye and headed back to the plantation house where they met the others who were waiting anxiously for any news.

"Of course," said Leon after Eira had explained what the symbol under the word had meant, "why didn't I see it before? I remember hearing stories about the Seasons Cross as a child, about the brave men who would venture out to find it and all the mysteries it holds...and they would never return. Honestly, I didn't think it was a real place."

"Well, I guess it is, and it's our best chance at getting Talvia back," said Eira.

"How long will this journey take?" asked Clea.

"Based on the map, it looks like a few weeks—a month, maybe," responded Killian.

"A month?" Eira was shocked. She did not like the thought of Talvia being ruled by Lord Dundan and the Wicked Witch of the Blue for months.

"There is one problem," added Killian.

"What?"

"We have to travel through the Quesnell Pass."

All but Eira and Nell gasped at the words that came from Killian's mouth.

"What's the Quesnell Pass?" asked Eira wearily.

"It is a dangerous road that links all four countries to one another. No one ever travels it, for it is wrought with perils no one wants to encounter. It has a strange magic within it that more people refer to as a sickness. It is easy to stray from the path and you may be lost forever," answered Leon.

"It's the only way to get to where the four seasons meet. We really have no other choice," said Clea after looking at the map Killian was holding.

"Well," said Killian, "What are we waiting for?"

Eira left the room for a moment. She had to think about the journey she was about to embark on. Despite the perils, she was going to go. She had to. She was now Queen of Talvia and she could not sit back and watch it crumble. If Gideon left them the clue, he must have known that they would have to travel through the Quesnell Pass and he would not send her on a journey she would not return from.

That wouldn't be helping Talvia at all. She was, however, having a slight panic attack out in the hall. She placed her hands on her knees and bent over, breathing heavily in and out.

"It's still strange to me," she uttered when Killian placed a hand on her shoulder. "Everything that has happened over this last year, and now I'm going on another journey to find a wizard to battle a witch. That's not normal," she smiled. "Well, maybe it is for here."

Killian gave a slight chuckle, "Well, if it makes you feel any better, it's not that normal for here either. We're all venturing into the unknown here—you're not alone, darling."

Eira and Killian walked back into the room and Eira headed over to where Nell was standing. "Are you sure you want to come with us? This is your chance to turn back now. I can't guarantee what will happen."

"I know, but I think I do," she smiled.

Eira hugged her friend and turned to the rest of the group, "Okay, then. I guess we have some packing to do."

They gathered their belongings and stayed their last night with Edmond. In the morning, they thanked him for his hospitality and made their way off his land and ventured into the unknown. It was truly unknown to all of them—not just Eira. For very few have ever made it through the Quesnell Pass to tell the tale of what lies within.

7

The timely drips from the ceiling of their cell were the only thing that let them know how much time had passed in their solitude. Drip. Drip. Drip. Every second, and when sixty of them had fallen to the floor and floated down the ever-growing stream on the cold stone working its way into the deeper, darker areas of the basement, they knew it was only fifty-nine more minutes until another hour had disappeared from their sentence. Charles and Gideon occupied a cell together, which did not seem bad at first, but as the days went on, it was becoming increasingly uncomfortable. They knew there were still people in the castle that were ultimately on their side, even though the Blue Queen's power was threatening them into doing things they would not normally do. Ceilidh was among the servants who were not taken prisoner and were still able to roam freely within the castle walls. She would sneak extra food to Charles and Gideon when she could and tell them what was going on above.

"I do hope my letter made it to them," began Gideon.

"I hope so too. They're our last hope of getting out of here," said Charles. "Are you sure they will be able to decipher the clue you left for them?"

"Eira is a smart girl. I'm sure she will solve it."

They could hear footsteps coming from down the hall and soon they saw Lord Dundan rounding the corner of the dungeon and making his way to their cell.

"Him," he said, pointing to Gideon. "Bring him to me." The guards unlocked the door and grabbed Gideon from inside. "I hear you have been in contact with the outside—that you sent a message to our dear little queen. Is that true?"

"No, my lord," replied Gideon.

"It is Your Majesty, now," forced Lord Dundan, bringing Gideon to his knees.

"I promise you...Your Majesty. I have not been in contact with anyone outside of my prison cell."

"You had better not be. If I find out that wretched girl is on her way back with some sort of army, you will suffer the consequences." He then threw Gideon back into the cell and locked the door. "It wouldn't matter, anyway. Any army she can come up with is no match for the new queen. Let her try, but I assure you, she will fail miserably."

****

At the entrance to the Quesnell Pass, the group sat astride their horses and stared at the great archway, towering stories above them. The large rock faces on either side were covered with moss, and towering statues of men rose from them. You could only see their torsos emerging from the rocks and their long hair and beards were carved right from the stone. They were turning green with age and as you followed the carvings from head to torso, their chests turned to what looked like scales and then disappeared into the rock.

"They say they're the guardians of the pass," said Theo as they passed the men looking down at them. "Torso of a man but the body of a great serpent. They are supposed to scare people away from venturing in."

"Huh, a good job they're doing," added Killian.

They headed into the unknown. Maurice had warned them that it was imperative they stay on the path and not to stray. The pass will try to get you lost with its various twists and turns, and routes that look faster or safer. The moss-covered stone walls towered above them and the mist left little visible. As they ventured deeper in, small ferns began to grow amidst the moss on the stone and looking toward the sky, Eira could see faint beams of daylight weaving through the tops of the stone walls like a jagged scribble. Water flowed down the rocks in small streams and pooled at their horse's hooves, disturbing the mist and causing it to rise around them. They squeezed through a particularly tight spot and when they emerged on the other side, the stone walls gave them a wider berth and the sunlight shone through from ahead and above, revealing every shade of green that covered their surroundings. Ahead, they could see the stone walls were beginning to part more and more.

"How long have we been walking?" asked Killian after about an hour in the pass.

"I don't know. It feels like forever," answered Clea.

"It hasn't been that long. It's the spell of the pass. You just think it's been longer," said Eira.

"How come you're not being affected by it?" asked Killian

"I'm not sure. Maybe it affects different people at different rates?"

"It's because you're royal," responded Leon. "You're immune to the effects of the pass."

"Dope," grinned Eira.

"We just need to stay on the path and the rest of us should be fine," added Leon. "Look at the horse's feet in front of you. I find it helps rather than staring into the twists and turns of the road ahead of us."

"So now we're just a bunch of idiots staring at horse's hooves? That's a good idea," added Killian.

"Then don't look at them—do what you want," Leon argued back. They began to quarrel with one another until Eira had enough and yelled for them to stop.

"Stop it. It's the pass that is making you two argue like this. Let's just stop for a moment and have something to drink." After a few moments and some water, the group was feeling better and were able to continue the journey, but it was not long before the rest of the non-royal group fell into the same pattern and were arguing with one another again. Nell also seemed unaffected by the pass. Perhaps it was because she was not born of this world.

When nightfall finally came, after what seemed like a day that would never end, wandering through the pass, they came to an outlet in the road where they decided to set up camp for the night. The next days and nights seemed to always play out the same with them wandering along the road, unsure of if they were going in the right direction, following what little sunlight they could see overhead through the treetops, and barely getting any sleep at night. The group was growing increasingly agitated with one another, especially the guys, and the journey was not going as planned. The nights were cold and the shivering of their bodies made it far more difficult to relax and get any rest.

"Are you cold?" Killian asked Eira one evening as they were setting up for the night. It was almost pitch black on the path and all the light they had was from the slivers of moonlight peeking through the trees and the fire Leon and Theo were preparing to make.

"A little, but I'll be okay," answered Eira.

"Here," said Killian as he removed his jacket and placed it around Eira's shoulders. This motion of gallantry did not bode well with Leon, who had just appeared behind them, carrying some logs for the fire.

"Oh, of course," he began. "Go to him when you're cold. Not your fiancé."

"He's my friend, Leon," answered Eira. "And who said I was your fiancée? You left me and still have never actually proposed to me."

"You know what I mean. I'm the one you're supposed to be with and go to when you need something."

"Get over yourself. I did go to you when I needed something; when I needed your help to find a way to get rid of Dundan, and you abandoned me," snapped Eira.

"Guys," yelled Nell. "Stop arguing," she said, grabbing the firewood from Leon. "We're all tired and hungry. We'll have a fire soon and then we'll be able to eat and rest."

"She's right. Come over here and help me with the tent," said Theo.

"I'm not tired," said Eira

"Good, then you can have the first watch," said Nell before she turned to bring the firewood to Killian. She was really embracing her role on this journey.

"I'll keep you company tonight—I'm not tired either," said Killian.

"Of course you're not. You just want to stay with her. Why didn't I see it before?" charged Leon as he approached Killian with his arms outstretched, ready to fight him.

"Enough!" yelled Eira as she pried the two apart. "Go help with the fire, Leon. This isn't like you."

"And you're taking his side, again. I can't believe this."

"I'm not taking anyone's side. Go help with the fire," she pointed toward where Nell was dropping the logs.

The only sound during dinner was the crackling of the fire breaking the cold air around them. When the fire began to die, the group made their way into their tents for the night. Eira and Killian stayed by the embers of the fire and kept watch.

"I'm sorry if I'm causing any tension between you and Leon," began Killian.

"No, it's not you. We've had tension since he left," responded Eira, pulling a blanket around her shoulders.

"Well, I hope you do understand that he didn't want to leave. Sometimes we act impulsively, but those impulses are usually coming from a place of deep feelings. He didn't mean to hurt you." Eira simply smiled in response as Killian stood and moved to get another log and placed it on the fire, then stirred it a bit with a stick, blowing on the embers so the log would catch.

The fire was burning bright and warm now and before long, Eira had fallen asleep. Killian walked slowly over to Leon's tent and opened the flap slightly and gently kicked him awake. Leon opened his eyes and sat up to peer out of the tent at Killian. All Killian did was nod over to where Eira was sleeping before walking off to his tent for the night. Leon rose and ruffled his hair as he walked over to the fire, ready for his turn to keep watch. He scooped her up and moved her to where he was sleeping and covered her over with his blanket, then made his way back to sit by the fire. Before long, Clea and Theo awoke for their watches and the sun began to rise over the barely visible horizon.

The journey that day went more smoothly than the last. Perhaps a good rest was all the group needed to get their clear heads back. It was clear that the pass was still causing them to struggle mentally, but it was less impactful in the morning and always grew more debilitating as the day went on and the more they had been wandering.

When they found their resting spot for the night, Killian was busy chopping wood for the fire and the rest were busy setting up tents and readying the food for dinner.

"What is he doing?" asked Clea to Eira and Nell while they watched Killian chop the firewood.

"Well, we know it's all for Nell," smirked Eira.

"Don't bring me into this."

"Put your shirt back on," yelled Theo to Killian. "That's not a requirement for chopping wood."

"Do you want to come over here and do it? Be my guest," Killian argued back. The pass was really causing tension between the group. Nell and Eira, being the only ones that didn't seem to be affected by it, were struggling to play peacekeepers.

"No one wants to see that," yelled Theo again.

"Really? No one?" Killian turned to where Eira, Nell, and Clea were standing. "Ladies?"

"Don't drag us into this," called Clea.

"Fine, whatever. It's done anyway."

Over the next few days and nights, Leon's anger toward Killian grew stronger. He had convinced himself that Eira no longer wanted him and had moved on to someone new. The day came when it was more than he could take when he saw Eira and Killian laughing about something as they rode side by side. When they dismounted for a rest, he made his move.

"I knew it," Leon called out to the two of them. "How could you? You were my friend and as soon as I was out of the picture, you made your move."

"What are you talking about?" asked Killian as he backed away from Leon's advance on him.

"You want her. I can't believe I didn't see it earlier."

"Leon, you're being ridiculous," said Eira.

"Yeah—I don't want her. She's yours, believe me, I know that."

"What is that supposed to mean?" asked Leon.

"You know, just that Leon gets everything. You grew up in a palace and played with princes, and get to marry a princess and what do I get?"

"Just admit that you love her," pushed Leon.

"Of course I love her—because you do, dumbass," Killian yelled back. "You would walk through fire for her so, so would I. That's just how this works."

"Guys," interrupted Theo. "You need to stop this before one of you says something you'll regret."

"Yeah. Enough—both of you," added Clea.

"Stay out of this. This is between me and the wannabe king," stated Killian.

Leon clenched, "Oh, you know what—Lorelai should have married Max." An expression of utter shock grew on Killian's face. "There, I said it. Her and Luke don't deserve each other. Max was way better for her, and treated her much better. There wouldn't have been all the lying and stuff."

Killian gasped, "You take that back!"

"Nope. She's stupid and when someone proposes with a thousand flowers, you marry that guy. Do you know how much that would have cost him? Although, I'm assuming Kirk would have given him a discount for that many—but still. You don't just turn down a guy who makes that sort of gesture."

"That's it," said Killian and he lunged at Leon and the two were caught up in a wrestling match. There they were, throwing punches at each other left and right with no regard for where the path was.

"Guys," yelled Eira. "You need to stop!" But it was too late. The two had wrestled themselves off of the path and tumbled down a hill into the brush. The moment they fell off the path and landed in the bushes below, it was as if a curse was lifted off them.

"What happened?" asked Killian as he sat up. Leon looked around puzzled and it took him a moment to get his bearings. They could hear Eira and the others calling to them from above.

"Oh no," said Leon, "we fell off the path. We have to get back to it quickly."

They had been warned to never stray from the path, no matter how tempting something on the other side looked. The heavy foliage was making it impossible for them to make their way back. Suddenly, they heard a noise in the distance; cracking branches as if something large was moving through the forest. A flock of birds fled to the skies, and Leon and Killian sprang to their feet. They tried their best to scramble up the embankment, but it was no use.

"Hurry," yelled Eira. They continued to try to make their way back up to the path, but it was far more difficult going back up than rolling down. When the two had just about reached the top, Theo held a hand out for Killian, who was slightly ahead of Leon. Eira and Clea reached out for Leon and the two helped him over the edge and back onto the path. As soon as he was securely standing back on the path, Eira could not stop herself from embracing him with a big hug. She was looking up into his eyes, taking in his smile, when suddenly her gaze shifted to the side, looking back to where the two had fallen off the path.

"Eira?" asked Leon, pushing her ever so slightly away from him to get a better look at the expression on her face.

"Did that tree just move?" she asked, looking at a collection of trees just past the embankment the guys had fallen down.

Leon turned around to look. "I don't think so. We're back on the path now—we're safe," Leon assured her.

Eira looked again and then asked, even though she had the feeling she already knew the answer, "Do trees have eyes in this land?"

"Not usually," answered Killian as the group stared into the distance at a large set of eyes staring back at them. They could not make out the shape of what the eyes belonged to. It simply looked like a forest of trees.

Suddenly, the owner of the eyes emerged. What looked like a large group of trees began to grow until it was towering above the treetops and revealed itself in the shape of a large beast resembling something from the Jurassic era.

"What is that?" asked Eira.

"That would be a Carnifer," answered Leon.

"What's a Carnifer?"

"That," pointed Leon.

The beast moved toward them, running faster on his massive hind legs made from two tree trunks, the roots coming out like toes and destroying everything in their path. A high-pitched roar radiated from its mouth as it grew closer. The group was instantly crippled over, clutching their ears.

"Quick," called Theo as he ran back to the camp to grab his sword. The others followed behind him.

"Eira," called Leon. "Get the horses." He pointed to where they were pulling at their reins and bucking to try to set themselves free, but by the time Eira had reached them, the horses had broken free and were running in the direction from where they came.

She looked back at Leon as if to ask, *Now what?* He ran up to her and handed her a sword.

"You don't seriously think we can defeat that thing."

"Come on, it's just a bunch of twigs," he shrugged.

The Carnifer tore up the embankment and onto the path in front of the group. It tore through their campsite as the group threw everything they had at it.

"Take that, beasty," called Killian as he chopped at its legs with an axe. "Nothing to it. Just like chopping down a tree."

"A tree that's moving and trying to kill you," responded Theo.

Killian turned to see Nell running from the Carnifer's tail swinging toward her. He ran and tackled her to the ground, rolling them out of the way just as its tail sailed overhead.

"Thanks," she smiled up at him.

"Go hide," he pointed down the path. "We'll find you after." She nodded and ran off, careful not to actually leave the path.

Clea and Leon were firing arrows at it, to no avail. They either passed right through the gaps between the branches or simply stuck in the beast with little impact on its ability to attack them. The beast's massive intertwined vine tail swung around toward Eira. She quickly dropped to the ground and rolled under it, just barely clearing it. When she managed to get back on her feet, she stood looking at her friends trying to ward off the monster. Trees were falling as the Carnifer struck against them and nothing seemed to cause it any pain.

"How are we supposed to beat a giant tree?" thought Eira. Suddenly, she had a realization. "Leon," she yelled.

He turned to where her voice was coming from and almost had his head chopped off by the Carnifer's tail.

"Honey, not a good time," he yelled back.

"No," she called back. "You were right—it's just a bunch of twigs."

"What are you talking about?"

"We need to light it."

"What?"

"Light it up."

"Nice," called Killian. "I've got you," he said, pulling his axe from the cut he made in its tail. He reached into his pocket and pulled out a box of matches and tossed them toward her. She moved forward and caught them with ease, then made her way to the mangled campsite and found their blankets and tents stomped into the ground by the Carnifer's massive feet. She pulled out a blanket and shook it off.

"Eira," Leon ran past her, quickly firing arrows into the Carnifer. He tossed her a small metal shape, which she opened quickly to reveal a knife. She cut the blanket into small pieces and wrapped them around her's and Clea's arrows, then lit them.

"Thanks," said Clea, taking the arrows and placing them in her bow. The two fired flaming arrow after flaming arrow into the Carnifer. When the first arrow caught, the beast screamed in pain.

"Nice thinking," called Leon. "It's working."

"I wouldn't say that so soon," called Theo, nodding toward the Carnifer managing to snuff out some of the flames on a nearby tree whose leaves were damp from the morning mist in the air. There were just enough water droplets to shake onto the Carnifer's body.

"More arrows?" called Killian.

Eira looked back at the empty pile. "There aren't any," she replied.

Unexpectedly, the sound of hoofbeats began to echo through the air. The group turned to where the sound was coming from and saw Harwin galloping toward them. He ran right up to the Carnifer and stomped the ground in front of it. The Carnifer's demeanour changed almost instantly. It began backing off and heading for where it came. Harwin followed until it was down, off the path and heading back into the forest.

"Harwin," called Leon. "Good boy," he said, petting his forelock. "Who knew Carnifers were afraid of unicorns?"

"Please, Leon. Everyone knows that," jeered Eira.

"Unicorns are very ancient and mystical creatures. They have many powers unknown to people, and I'm glad this is one of them," added Killian.

The group looked around at the mess the battle had made.

"Well, I guess we're moving forward on foot," said Clea, looking at the shards of wood on the ground from the post where the horses were tied.

"I guess so," nodded Eira. *Great, another journey mostly on foot.*

Harwin stuck around for a few moments to make sure the group was safe, and then left again for home as the group journeyed on. They wanted to get a safe distance away from the Carnifer, just in case. Nell appeared again once the chaos was over.

"You sure you're still up for this?" Eira joked, hugging her friend.

"I think it's a little too late for me to turn back now."

"Hey, um," Killian leaned into Leon, "you were joking about what you said about Lorelai, right?"

Leon simply sighed and rolled his eyes.

The next couple of days travelling down the path went smoothly. They were no longer being affected by the pass's magic, and the trees were beginning to show more light between them as they grew farther and farther apart. When there were hardly any trees left, the sun was shining and they were walking on a clear road with the mountains surrounding them. It looked as if they had wandered into a rainforest and the temperature was getting warmer and warmer the farther they walked. The plants were turning into more tropical ones and the air was humid.

"What's happening?" asked Eira.

"We must be heading into the summer part of the pass. The Quesnell Pass goes through all four countries, remember?" answered Leon.

They wandered along the road through the tropical rainforest for a few days until it seemed the rainforest was slowly disappearing, and a new temperate region was presenting itself—fading into one another. They were pulling themselves through the humidity at a sluggish pace when a tropical breeze blew through and with it, came sand. Eira looked down at her feet when she felt the fine grit hitting her arms and face like a gentle exfoliation. Following the direction where the breeze had come from, at the edge of the rainforest, she pulled back a few large palm leaves that were hiding the change in scenery and found a vast desert. Desolate and hot, exactly like what she thought the Sahara Desert would look like, if she ever had the chance to see it in person and she supposed now she wouldn't need to.

"We have to go through there?" asked Eira, wary of what the heat would do to the spirits of the group.

"I guess so," answered Leon, standing behind her holding back some of the foliage sheltering them in the meantime from the blazing heat that awaited them. "It's far too hot to travel during the day, though. Our best hope of making it through this part of the pass without dying of heat stroke is to leave at sundown and travel through the night."

"Good thinking, buddy," called Killian from behind. He placed a hand on Leon's shoulder. "We'll rest here until sundown. It'll be a rough journey ahead."

The sudden pitter-patter of raindrops hitting the canopy of leaves above them caught the group's attention.

"Good, rain," said Theo. "We should fill up with water before we leave." He took out his canteen and used one of the giant leaves to funnel the sky's salvation into it, then he took a drink. "Better than any water we'll find out there," he motioned to the desert with the hand holding his canteen. Eira turned to take another look into the desert. With the sun high in the sky, a blast of hot air swept in and kissed her cheeks. She didn't want to have to wait for sundown, however, she knew it would be best. The pass was designed to kill them and it surely would if they headed forward now.

****

"My lord, my lord," called a man as he ran into the great hall of the castle in Trillium Nivale.

"What is it?" questioned Lord Dundan as he sat entitled upon Eira's throne.

"She's figured it out. Eira, she is going to find the wizard who can defeat—"

A tall woman walked out from behind the throne. She wore a cobalt gown that complimented her golden bronze skin. Her hair flowed like a burgundy waterfall, cascading down and over her shoulders and breasts and the now black as the coal it originated from, Diamond of Azul, was placed so delicately around her neck. She stared at the man with eyes that pierced like ice.

"Defeat *me*, you mean."

"Your Majesty," bowed the man, "I did not see you there."

"Continue," said Lord Dundan, "What is she doing?"

"I overheard her talking to the old man in the library in Kelby. She was asking all these questions about the Order of the Seasons and the Seasons Cross."

"Why should I care about any of that? Come back when you have some real information."

"Now, now, Dundan," silenced the Blue Queen. "There is no need for hostility. This is useful information and you would know that, if you knew anything at all," she raised her voice and stood over him as he slunk into the throne. "The Seasons Cross is where she will find the very man who defeated me the first time," said the Blue Queen. "But the only way to get there is through the Quesnell Pass. She is only proving her foolishness if she decides to venture in there."

"Even if she were crazy enough to venture into the Quesnell Pass, there is no way she will succeed," scoffed Lord Dundan.

"But what if she does, my lord?"

"Then we will be ready for her when she returns."

8

"Dundan!" her voice bellowed through the halls of the castle. The sheer shrillness of it made all the servants cringe at the sound while they were accomplishing their daily tasks. Lord Dundan ran from the ballroom toward the voice. "Dundan, get in here," the voice called again. He finally pushed his way through the large double doors, huffing from the exercise he had just received running down the corridors.

"What is it, Your Majesty?" he asked as he turned to shut both doors.

"There you are. What took you so long?" Ophelessa rose from her position lounging on her chaise in her sitting room, pondering her mundane thoughts and what she was going to do now that she was ruler of Talvia. "Well, it doesn't matter now. I've been thinking, and I believe it is time I meet my people."

"Don't you mean *our* people?" Lord Dundan responded, frustrated with her ignorance regarding his role in the situation.

"Do not patronize me," she protested. "I am aware that it was you who gave me my newfound autocracy." She walked slowly over to him, her long gown swishing at her sides, making every movement more dramatic than the last. She raised a hand to his cheek, "Oh, darling. You do know how utterly grateful I am. Give it time. This will be our kingdom soon enough. Now don't you think it is important the people meet their new queen?" she smiled. "Ready the carriage. We're going into town. And find that quiet girl. What's her name? Kimmy? Cassie?"

"Ceilidh, Your Majesty?" Lord Dundan responded

She waved her hand, "Whatever, just find her and bring her here. I need to look my best for the people."

Lord Dundan hurried out of Ophelessa's chambers and headed down the hall in search of Ceilidh. He knew exactly where she would be and headed for the dungeon. Below in the depths of the castle Ceilidh was attending to her friends; Gideon and others who were captured and placed down there for the time being. She snuck off to there every day to bring them extra food and inform them of what was going on inside the castle.

"Ceilidh. You need to stop coming down here," said Gideon as she passed a piece of bread through the bars to him and then another for Charles. "You are going to get yourself in trouble. What if she finds you? She will lock you up with us—or worse."

"I'm already locked up—can't you see that?"

The thunder of footsteps came down the hall of the dungeon, and Lord Dundan rounded the corner. Ceilidh jumped and turned her back to the cell.

"I thought I would find you down here," he said, marching toward her. He took her arm and pulled her away from the cell. "She wants to see you, and I don't think it is a good idea to keep her waiting." He thrust her arm from his hand and motioned her in the direction to leave. She curtsied to him in slight thanks for not getting her in trouble and hurried down the hall and up the winding staircase, ascending from the dungeon. Lord Dundan turned to Gideon and Charles, sitting in their cell. He pointed to Gideon, "You, the librarian, come with me." He removed the keys from the hook on the wall next to the cell and unlocked the door.

"Well, that's just downgrading," he responded as he stood and made his way out of the cell.

Three times she knocked on the large double doors before being called inside. Ceilidh cracked the door slightly and peeked in around the side of the door. "Lord Dundan said you wanted to see me, Your Majesty?"

"Yes, Kelsey. Come in, my dear."

"Um, it's Ceilidh, Your Majesty," she curtsied. Ophelessa did not look pleased to be corrected.

"Right, well Ceilidh. I am going to take a little trip into town, you know, to meet the people. And I need to look my best. You can start with my nails and then my hair." She had changed into a long silk robe and was sitting in the armchair in front of the vanity, fixated on her reflection in the mirror. Ceilidh nodded and walked toward her, opening the drawers of nail polish and hair tools, and got to work.

Lord Dundan led Gideon to the library. When they arrived, Lord Dundan went over to the large table at the centre of the room. There were papers of all sorts scattered about and various books left open to mark pages of importance. Gideon cringed slightly at the disarray of his beautiful collection.

"Over here," Dundan called, "what do you make of this?" he asked, pointing to a page in a book. Gideon looked closer and saw the remains of an old recipe written down. It was difficult to make out, but if one tried hard enough, the worn out ink could be deciphered into the words that once lay there.

"And why would you need an obedience potion? Everyone is already doing everything you want."

"Everyone except one."

"So, the great Ophelessa is going back on her vow?" pried Gideon.

"She pretends that I still have control, but I am starting to question it. I need to take matters into my own hands. She wants this kingdom as much as I do, but it belongs to *my* family."

"It belongs to Eira," responded Gideon, "and she will get it back. You have no idea who you are dealing with. She may be young, but she has more power over this land than anyone ever will. And besides, you're getting what you deserve," he smirked.

"Do not irritate me. Where will your little queen be when you are facing execution? She hasn't been back in weeks, and who knows if she will ever come back," challenged Lord Dundan.

"She will be back, but by then, I'm sure Ophelessa will have complete control over you. This potion isn't going to work on a sorceress such as her. She will detect it before she even takes a sip of her drink. There is a reason she has only ever been defeated once before. It takes someone with great power to do that."

She was doing an excellent job of pretending to be happy doing the task asked of her, "There you are, Your Majesty," said Ceilidh as she finished pinning, pulling, and curling Ophelessa's hair into an extravagant up do. "How is that?"

"I suppose it will have to do," responded Ophelessa, rising from the armchair in front of the mirror and gliding over to the dressing screen in the corner of the room where her newly made gown was waiting for her to be laced into. She walked with her hands at her side, long fingers outstretched to ensure not to ruin her nail polish. "Now, help me into my dress," she called to Ceilidh. Ceilidh hurried right over and strapped Ophelessa's bust and the rest of her into the gown. While she was lacing up the back of the dress, she noticed the clasp of the necklace she was wearing looked as though it might break and fall from her neck at any moment.

"Your Majesty," she gasped, "your necklace looks as though it may need some repairing. I can have it sent to the jeweller in town for you if you like?"

"No," interrupted Ophelessa all too quickly raising a hand to touch the jewel around her neck.

"I am sorry, Your Majesty," responded Ceilidh, tying the corset and stepping out from behind Ophelessa. "I just thought a queen would want to look her best. The jewels could be cleaned as well. I could have it there and back in less than a day if you are so worried about parting with it?"

"It's just special, is all. Family heirloom, you know."

"You should at least have the clasp looked at. I would not want it falling off and breaking or getting lost," added Ceilidh.

"Yes," Ophelessa pondered, rubbing the diamond between her fingers. "Perhaps you are right. I will think about it."

Ceilidh curtsied, "Is there anything else I can do for you?"

"No, that will be all. You can leave now." Ceilidh curtsied again and exited, leaving Ophelessa contemplating the idea of parting with her necklace, even if it would only be for a day.

The people in the town of Huurre did not welcome their new queen as well as Ophelessa had expected. She did not know what their problem was. She was, or so she thought, everything anyone would want in a queen. Beautiful and powerful. She had the power to make anyone do anything she wished of them, meaning she could make Talvia the most prosperous of the countries. However, the people knew the chance of that wealth trickling down to them was practically unheard of. Her presence in the town was announced, but the people merely looked up for a moment and when the announcement was over, they returned to their work.

"This is not how it is supposed to go," said Ophelessa, sitting comfortably in her fur lined carriage to shield from the cold. "Order the guards to drag the people into the centre of town if need be. I will address them and they will adore me."

Lord Dundan sighed and knocked on the carriage behind where he was sitting to signal the driver to stop. He stepped out and ordered the guards to call—and force— everyone into the centre of town. When all the people were unpleasantly standing in the centre of town, the royal carriage pulled up in front of them and halted. The door swung open and a foot landed on the step, followed by a gown, and then Ophelessa herself.

"Well, well. Isn't this a charming little group," she said, taking a look at the people standing before her. The expressions on their faces were less than mediocre. "Now, is this any way to greet your queen?"

"You're not *our* queen," someone called from within the crowd. Ophelessa and her guards looked for where the comment came from but could not determine who made it.

"Am I not? Then why am I riding in the royal carriage and why did I come all the way down here to meet my people? I am your queen, and you're all going to have to get used to it. Poor little Eira is not coming back, no matter how you hope. She is gone. No one knows where. Besides, you'll all find in time how accommodating I can be—if you don't piss me off. Everyone had better obey me and call me their queen, or there will be hell to pay. Now, I believe it is customary to bow to your queen." She raised her right hand and gave a flick of her wrist. All the people were forced into a bow and then she raised her hand again and they were freed. "That's better. Now, I have a lot of important things to do, so I best be off," and she got back into her carriage.

9

Even as the sun began its descent in the sky, the heat of the desert was almost unbearable. Their only salvation was knowing it would soon be night, however, that was sure to bring problems of its own. Even in a desert, the temperatures at night can resemble that of Talvia. They could see no salvation of the Autumn Country in the distance and had long lost track of the time they had spent wandering in this wasteland. There were no plants or any sign of life for miles. Patches of dry desert trees could be found every so often, but the bark was bleached white from the sun and the branches laying in the sand looked more like a graveyard than wind broken branches. All they could do was continue wandering in the direction they hoped would soon bring escape from the part of the pass that was clearly designed to kill any that made it this far in. Their water was running low and in a couple of days, there would be none to sustain them.

"Do you guys hear that?" asked Eira as she stopped in her tracks and signalled for the group to do the same.

"Hear what?" asked Clea.

The group stopped and listened again. "It sounds like humming," said Theo.

"Humming?" responded Killian. "Now what would be humming out here?"

"I don't know, but it sounds like it's getting louder," Leon added.

The group stood still and listened to the only thing that had broken the silence in hours. The humming grew louder and louder until it was all they could hear surrounding them. In the distance, they could see the outlines of more dunes, the same as the one they were walking across. They looked out as the dunes began to look as though they were shifting.

"Over there," pointed Eira, "look. It looks like that sand dune is moving."

"That's because it is," exclaimed Leon. "The sand is shifting from the wind. That's what's making the humming sound."

Without warning, a gust of wind, with the force of a hurricane, crashed against them and the sand beneath their feet began to shift and give way. The group fell to their backs and started to slide and roll down the shifting avalanche of sand. Eira turned and twisted during her descent, trying to stop herself from falling, but every attempt she made was thwarted by the rushing particles of sand surrounding her.

"Eira," she could hear a call coming from beside her. It was Leon, reaching out a hand for her. She tried her hardest to grab it, but the fall was too fast. The wind was still pushing against her and sandblasting every inch of her body. Luckily for them, there was no more sand falling from the top of the dunes. It was only the sand that took them out from their feet that was racing to the bottom with them, along for the ride atop it. She felt a weight sweep in beside her and pull her in. It was Leon who had managed to roll in the direction of her fall and grab hold of her before they ended up farther apart than any of them would like. The rest of the group were trying to stay together as well, but with little luck. They were falling for a good five minutes when the wind seemed to suddenly halt, as if it were turned off by a switch. Along with it, the humming ceased as well. However, it remained in their ears for some time after. Eira and Leon continued to roll down the remainder of the dune in a tangle until the flat earth broke their fall. With a thud, they separated from each other and all that could be heard was the coughing up of sand and the heaving breaths of relief that their ordeal had ended.

"Are you okay?" asked Leon, dragging himself over to Eira. He lay beside her, leaning over her with a hand to her cheek.

"Yeah," she coughed in response. He let out a sigh of relief and fell on his back beside her. Eira sat up and scanned their surroundings, trying to identify any signs of their friends. One by one, she could see people sitting up in the distance. She and Leon slowly made their way to their feet, along with the rest of the group, and meandered over to them.

"Is everyone alright?" asked Eira.

"Yup," assured Killian. "Not my first time tumbling down something," he winked. She gave him a slight smile.

"How about you guys?" she looked at Clea and Theo.

"Could be better," answered Clea, brushing the sand off and out of every inch of her.

"Agreed," added Theo, doing the same.

"Where's Nell?" Eira asked after determining they were down a person.

"I'm alright," called Nell from a few feet over. She was laying so perfectly flat on the ground, it was difficult to see her in the darkness. Killian wandered over and helped her up, brushing the sand from every inch of her body—a little too thoroughly. "Thanks, I'm good," she finally said, brushing his hands off of her bottom.

"Well," started Eira. "I guess we should keep moving if everyone is okay. We have to make it through here before the sun rises and it gets too hot to survive."

The group nodded, and they began their journey again. As they wandered for longer and longer, the sky seemed to get darker and darker. It was still never a complete abyss of blackness swirling above their heads however, any light in the sky seemed to be fading more and more. Perhaps it was the result of the clouds rolling in. The moon was no longer lighting up the path or the desert surroundings for them.

The sudden illumination of the sky took everyone by surprise. A bolt of lightning sailed down behind the sand dunes in the distance, creating a glowing crack dividing the heavens. There was no rain or any sense that a sudden storm was coming. Just a single flash of light that signalled they should seek shelter, and fast. The air was muggy and warm as more clouds rolled in creating a grey wash against the once-clear night sky. All the stars hid from the oncoming electrical pulse that radiated through the air. Then the abrupt sound of a distant rumbling grew louder and another flash of white light followed.

"That's not good," said Killian, looking toward the flashes growing closer with every roll of thunder.

They halted in their tracks and waited for another sign that the storm was growing closer. The wind blew again, a wind they were all too familiar with now, and they knew they desperately needed shelter.

"Look," called Leon over the howling wind, "the caves over there."

They ran for the safety of the rocks and made it just as the rain began to spill from the skies.

"What are we supposed to do now?" asked Eira. "We can't keep moving in this storm, but if we wait it out, it may be morning before we can head out again."

"I know," responded Leon. "But I think this is our only option right now. It's far too dangerous to be the tallest things wandering through the desert with that lightning above us. Let's just try to get some rest, and hopefully the storm will be done before daybreak," said Leon. "If not, we might have to just wait out the day here."

It was difficult to get any sleep that night with the pounding sky above them. Each crash of thunder was like a sudden shock to the system that sent the ground into spasm. A sudden rogue bolt of lightning struck one of the trees growing from the side of the rocks near the cave and sent a branch crashing down. The rain came down harder than any storm Eira had ever witnessed in her mere twenty-two years, creating rivers flowing through the sand. The only good thing the storm brought was more water for them to fill their canteens and quench the thirst they had been battling for some time now.

"Hey," greeted Eira as she sat down next to Nell. Most of the group was still awake, but all were pretending they weren't in hopes of finding some sleep. Nell didn't bother, though. She sat up in the entrance of the cave and her figure sitting there was what urged Eira to go and see what her friend was up to. "How are you doing?"

"Oh, you know—fine. I don't know how you get used to this almost dying thing."

"Unfortunately, you do. But you haven't been in any real danger. We've got you—especially Killian," she nudged her.

"Don't even," Nell pushed back.

"Come on. What is with you? I think you want him just as badly as he wants you. You just don't want to admit it. I mean, you couldn't stay away from him the night of my party, and you decided to come with us into this pass knowing full well it could kill you."

"I don't know," sighed Nell. "It's more complicated than that."

"It doesn't have to be—you're just making up excuses. Look, this is all weird, I get it, but I can guarantee you he wouldn't think twice about leaving this world and moving to yours for you. You can just date in the meantime. It's not like it's difficult to travel back and forth—it's quite convenient, actually."

"Yeah, it really is," she joked. "Okay, maybe, when all of this is over. I'll think about it. So, if I'm going to take the leap and try with Killian, when are you going to forgive Leon? Because I'll only *start* to think about forgiving him, when you actually do."

Eira sighed, "I don't know, and maybe a small part of me already has, but I just can't think of that right now. My kingdom is being taken over by the worst possible person and I have more important things to deal with first. Leon and I's relationship can wait until all of this is over."

"Can it, though? I wouldn't waste any time, you never know what will happen. He almost died last time, and what if something happens again before you get to tell him how you feel?" Eira glared at her. "Okay, yes, I heard it. I should take my own advice, right?"

The storm eventually passed and when they emerged from the cave in the early morning, it was clear what damage the storm had done. A few of the trees around had taken the brunt of the lightning's force and the sand still had trails of a once rushing river flowing through it. It was early morning light they were greeted with and luckily it was still cool enough to start their journey. The sun would be at its hottest in only a few hours though, so they knew they had to move fast.

They continued through the desert and it was not long before they began to feel the oncoming heat that would only intensify as the day went on. It would also not be long before the dry desert claimed all the water that had been flowing beside them in some sort of riverbed that only sees its potential after a heavy rainstorm. It was now midday, and the group was growing weary. They foolishly drank most of their water, assuming they would be out of this desert pass soon and Autumn would present itself, however that seemed hardly the case. As quickly as the heat stole every bit of energy they had, the landscape ahead of them began to change.

"What's that, in the distance?" asked Clea. All that could be seen in the distance was the heat waves radiating off the sand, but then there was something new. Grass was peeking out through the arched ground and a cooler breeze suddenly blew their way. The group ran toward it while more and more grass began to fill the empty patches in the ground. The cool green grass felt like a welcomed hug after what they had been through. Eira embraced the ground and rolled around, taking in the smell of the fresh grass. The rest of the group admired the change also, running grass through their fingers and looking at the wildflowers growing.

"Maybe this means we're almost out of Summer," said Eira.

"I hope so," added Clea.

"I'm not so sure," began Leon, with a hand to his brow, looking off into the distance. "This grass is a welcomed change, but I don't see any indication we're almost done with Summer. It's still sweltering out here, and if we don't find water soon, we're not going to make it."

"Wow, thanks for the optimism," said Theo with a clap on Leon's shoulder.

"Well, do you see a way out?" asked Leon.

"Not yet, but there has to be one soon. If the desert is done and we're now in these grasslands, it shouldn't be long before we come across some water. These plants are growing somehow. There's water somewhere."

The group looked at their surroundings in some sort of futile attempt to see water flowing.

"Well," began Eira. "I guess the only thing we can do is keep moving."

They reluctantly hopped to it and began their seemingly never-ending journey again. It was true that they now seemed to be in a grassland part of the pass, but it was clear this was not Autumn and that they were still hopelessly in Summer. All of their canteens were down to the last few sips of water, and it seemed they were no closer to being freed from the high temperature.

"Ahh," Killian called out in exasperation, "I wasn't built for this heat."

Well, you're going to love Australia, then, Nell's expression said as she glanced at Eira.

"Keep it together. We have to be getting close to the end," assured Theo.

"I don't know. I'm not sure how much longer of this I can take."

"Killian, you'll be fine. Have a sip of water," said Clea, pointing to his canteen attached to his belt.

"There's not much left. I may need to save it."

Clea shrugged as if to say, *it's up to you.*

The next half hour was spent listening to Killian complain about the heat. "This is ridiculous—I'm melting out here. Can't you see it? I used to be taller." Leon gave a small chuckle under his breath.

"Stop being dramatic. It's really not that bad," said Leon.

"What, how are you not sweating through your shirt?"

"I'm just not. I guess the heat isn't really bothering me."

"Huh? I wonder if it has anything to do with the dragon?" Eira asked. It was hard to forget what had happened with Leon and the dragon, even though the scar Sirona had left him with was beginning to fade slightly. It was no longer the bright red it was the days and months after he was given it.

"Maybe, who knows," shrugged Leon.

"I wish I had dragon power right now," mumbled Killian.

"Just drink your water, Killian. If you need more later, you can have mine," said a quite frustrated Eira.

"That's fine, darling. You're more important than I am. Nothing happens if I die."

Eira simply rolled her eyes at his hysterics. Then something caught her attention. They looked like large figures making their way across the plains, but none in the group could make out what they could be until they grew closer.

"They're elephants," gasped Theo. The group stood there in shock. All were surprised to see any life in this harsh place. Minutes went by and the group continued to stare plain-faced at the herd moving toward them. Perhaps it was the heat or the shock of it all, but none could bring themselves to move from their spots. The elephants walked right past them and still the group simply stared at them and watched as the herd moved past.

"I wonder where they're going?" asked Eira.

"Probably to some sort of oasis they know about," answered Leon. It took a moment for the group to realize the significance of what had just been said, but when they did, they charged after the elephants, calling for them to wait—as if elephants would stop and listen. However, as Eira had learned many times over, Talvia and its neighbouring countries are a magical place and, sure enough, the elephants stopped. It was as if they were sent here to rescue the group by someone watching over them.

"Oh, thank you," called Killian, grabbing his canteen and gulping down his last few sips of water. "Ahhh."

Standing before the graceful giants, the group peered up at them, wondering what to do next. Eira had never ridden an elephant before but it was something she had always dreamed of doing, although she had thought she might do it someday in her own world when she travelled to Africa or some other place.

Riding the elephants was not the difficult part, it was getting on. They were far too large to simply climb on, no matter how determined Killian was, but the elephants were nice enough to give them a hand, in the form of a trunk, to help hoist them onto their backs. All were safely travelling atop their elephant in no time, with Killian bringing up the rear on the calf of the group. Killian was not too impressed, however the young calf seemed quite pleased with himself that he was helping and strode past the adults, head high with great prominence until he got too excited and charged off into the distance carrying a bouncing and swearing Killian along with him.

Eira swayed back and forth, straddling the elephant just behind its head. They travelled along like this for quite some time until the sun was starting to lower in the sky and the sweltering heat would soon turn to a bone-chilling cold. Something rose out of the sand dunes in the distance, but the sun was blinding their view of what exactly it could be. The elephants seemed to be heading straight for it, and as they drew closer, the sun managed to position itself directly behind the structure and its outline was revealed to be a large sandstone city.

They were soon at the city's large stone gates and the elephants made their way through with pride, as if they were carrying a rather significant load. The city certainly was an oasis amidst the desert but, not the kind they had imagined. The elephants travelled through the bazaar where vendors were selling their fruits and pottery. Children were playing in the streets and staring at the elephant riders as they passed by.

"I had no idea the Quesnell Pass was inhabited," said Theo. "It was said to be a place where people became intoxicated by its magical presence and were ultimately consumed by it. Not a place where people could thrive."

"Well, I guess we were wrong," added Leon.

The elephants took them right up to the palace gates. The whole journey through the village in the shadows of the great palace reminded Eira of the scene in *Aladdin* when he travels to the palace with the Genie, and there's a big musical number, of course. This, however, was not as theatrical. The two-story intricately carved wooden doors pushed inward to reveal the white marble palace. It rose before them like something out of a storybook; the grand palace of the sultan with towers made of marble and domed roofs made of solid gold. It was emulating something out of *Arabian Nights*. The elephants delivered them to the front doors and men wearing long white tunics with deep blue vests over top and white pants to match came out to lead the elephants away. The gold buttons went right up to the base of their necks, stopping at the collar that went all the way around. Finally, topping them off, were turbans of the same blue as their vests. If Eira did not know any better, she would have sworn she was somewhere in the Middle East of her old world. A bellowing voice came dancing through the wind and they turned to see who it belonged to.

"No one comes into my palace armed," the voice proclaimed as the guards took their weapons. A shorter, rounder man appeared out of the palace doors with outstretched arms, welcoming them. He was also wearing a long white tunic and pants, however his were trimmed with gold and there was intricate gold embroidery on the green vest he was wearing that was open at the front. His hair was dark underneath his turban and his beard was kept neat.

"I don't trust him," whispered Killian to Theo as he handed over his sword and every other small piece of weaponry hidden on his person.

"Welcome to the Palace of Alzahra. We have been expecting you, Queen Eira," said the man.

Eira's eyes widened at the mention of her name, "You have?" was all she could think of saying.

"Yes, the elephants were sent to get you. The desert is no place for someone to be wandering. Especially someone as important as you."

10

Killian found it quite uncomfortable sitting with his legs crossed in the dining room of the sultan. He certainly enjoyed the food, but was not enjoying the manner in which he had to consume it. Eira was admiring the gilded lattice of the shutters on the windows around the room and the colourful lamps that hung from the ceiling when her attention was dragged elsewhere.

"My people have lived here for many centuries now. It is said that long ago, a man and his family were convicted of a terrible crime and sentenced to exile through the pass. It is said that none make it through the pass alive but, this man was clever." He reached for the small golden bowl filled with sugared dates in front of his place at the head of the table. "He never intended to try to make it through the pass," he popped the date into his mouth, "but to live out the rest of his life within it. He, his wife and three children started a new life in the pass and over the centuries our humble village grew as they welcomed the other exiles. None can indeed make it through the pass, but if you choose to stay here, it can be a pleasant place to live."

"Are there any other villages in the pass?" asked Eira.

"None that we know of. The pass is no place to wander through. We have lived here for centuries and here we remain, never wandering farther than our borders." His gaze shifted upward as a new presence entered the room. "Ah, Lina," he greeted the young woman standing in the doorway with an outstretched arm motioning for her to come and join everyone at the table. She strode toward the sultan and as she walked past, she did so with the utmost of grace. Simultaneously, the men looked up from their meals and their jaws dropped at the glimpse of her beauty. Her tall, slender figure was draped in a silk sari of purples and blues with her long dark hair twisting its way down her back. She was about the same age as Eira and when she walked past, Eira could hear the click of heels and glanced to the floor to see the golden shoes held on with jewelled snakes wrapping their way around her ankles. She kissed the sultan on the side of his head and took the empty floor pillow next to him, folding her legs to the side as to not ruin her immaculate attire.

"This is my daughter, Princess Lina," announced the sultan. "I would like to present to you, Queen Eira of Talvia."

Lina turned to her and smiled, bowing her head, "It is an honour to meet you. I have heard many stories of the wonders that lie outside the pass but have never had the chance to meet anyone from there."

"Well, we would not be here if it weren't for your father. We would still be wandering the desert, hopelessly lost."

"Yes, I heard he sent his elephants to retrieve you."

"Horses would have been more practical if you ask me," puffed Killian through a mouthful of yellow-coloured rice and flat bread.

"Lina," began the sultan, "perhaps after dinner these gentlemen would like a tour of the palace." The sultan turned to look at Killian, Theo, and Leon, "What do you say?" he asked the men.

"Yes," coughed Theo. Then he swallowed, took a breath and a sip of wine, and when he was composed, he turned his head back toward Lina, "I for one would love a tour."

"I bet you would," added Clea under her breath.

"I would also like a tour," added Leon. Lina nodded and smiled to them in agreement at their request and Eira could not help but roll her eyes.

"It's okay, Lina, I'll come along and keep an eye on these two," joked Killian as he outstretched both his arms, embracing Theo and Leon from either side of him. She smiled at him.

"How wonderful. After dinner then, we will show you where you'll be staying. Now, Your Majesty," he turned to Eira, "there are important matters I would like to discuss with you. Don't think I let you into my home without any sort of..." He paused for a moment searching for the right word, "Intentions of my own."

"What do you mean?" asked Eira warily, taking a sip from the jewelled chalice in front of her.

"We have lived here in this land for centuries and my people are starting to suffer." The sultan leaned in closer over the massive wooden table, "When I heard you were making your way through the pass, I took it as an opportunity to make an alliance between our kingdoms."

Eira's eyes narrowed, *I feel like I've heard this before.* "What kind of alliance?" the words trailed warily from her lips.

"The kind that involves our families becoming one," smiled the sultan as he sat upright again, his face beaming with a grin stretched across the whole of it.

"Really? Because I don't have any family. I have a brother but, I don't know where he is and while your daughter is beautiful, I don't think you will get him to marry her."

"I am not talking about Lina." The sultan leaned an elbow on one of his knees casually and rested his cheek on the back of his hand. Eira knew exactly what he meant and seeing as Lina was the only member of his family she had met, and she did not know if he was married...

Oh, for fuck's sake. "You can't mean—"

"But you're so old?" blurted Killian.

"Not me!" he shot back at him. "My son, Sami. He is in need of a wife, and you would make a perfect match."

"Oh, thank gods," Eira sighed. "I mean, no!"

"It is time for my people to get out of this land and make a new life."

"You can't be serious?" She stood and faced him, "I am not just some bargaining tool that can be married off as people please. Why do people keep thinking the only way to get what they want from me is to force a marriage? There are other ways, and why on earth would you think I would agree to this?"

The sultan motioned a hand to the guards at the door and suddenly, like dominoes, the surrounding doors shut and the guards pulled their swords from their sheaths. The guards were much larger than any of them, with their muscular biceps on display under their vests. Definitely not someone you'd want to go up against.

"Oh, come on," Eira called out in frustration.

"I'm sorry but, you really have no choice if you want to make it out of the pass alive with your companions still breathing. I will give you until morning to decide." He motioned to the guard at the door to take Eira. He moved to grab her, but Leon stepped in between them.

"Wait, you can't do this."

"I think I can," replied the sultan, standing from his seat. "You will never make it out of here by yourselves."

Another guard grabbed Eira from behind, and the one in front of Leon took hold of him. The rest of the group surrendered willingly, knowing they did not stand any chance fighting their way out of this one. They passed Lina standing in the hallway, on the way to their chambers for the night, looking despairingly apologetic for what had happened. It was clear she did not know anything of her father's true plans, but it was too late. The damage had been done.

"We would have been really happy together," said Theo as he passed her.

They were locked in the palace with two guards outside each of their doors and more below their windows. There was no opportunity to escape. When Eira finally convinced the sultan to let all of them together so she could discuss the arrangement with her *advisors*, they were still all at a loss about what to do.

"What are we supposed to do?" Eira asked Leon, pacing back and forth across the room.

"I don't know. Marrying the guy seems like your only option right now."

That's not funny, was what the look Eira shot him screamed.

"Okay, okay. I'm sorry. You're right, it's not funny, but...it kind of is. What is it with you and people wanting to marry you? I really don't get it."

Eira chucked a pillow at him. "Well, maybe you should stop dragging your feet. Apparently I'm a hot commodity." She was not in the mood for his sense of humour and while that was one of the things she loved about him and she knew he was just trying to make her laugh, she really didn't have the patience for it now.

"What are the chances we can fight our way out?" she finally asked to the rest of the group who were discussing their own thoughts about the situation.

"Well, seeing as he has about a hundred beefy swordsmen out there and we have...Killian. I don't think that's going to work." There was that sense of humour again, and Eira could not help but smile just a little this time.

"Hey," called Killian. "You know I could take them all with my bare hands."

"Our best bet is to try to make a deal with him in the morning. Talvia's wealth is coming back since you took the throne. There must be something he will want. Everyone has a price," added Clea.

"Alright, alright, fine," interjected Theo, putting his hands up to pacify the group. "I'll marry the princess. I mean, for you, Eira."

"Gee, thanks for your heroic sacrifice," she responded.

Theo nodded a, *You're welcome,* back to her.

"But I don't think he'll go for it. He wants more than a farm boy—no offence," added Eira.

"Hey, I helped save Talvia from a dragon," defended Theo.

"And you did a great job," smiled Eira, "but he wants out of this exile. I don't think there is anything we can truly give him."

"Well, I'm out then," said Theo as he made his way to the door to head to his room for the night. Killian, Clea, and Nell followed.

"What now?" asked Eira.

"I honestly don't know," Leon sighed. "Maybe a good night's rest will be the cure for this predicament." He placed his hands on her shoulders with a comforting grip. "You know if there was a way I could get you out of this, I would do it."

"I do," she replied softly. Leon nodded with a shy smile. He could not help but think about those two little innocent words she had just said and how he wished she was saying them for another reason, in another situation entirely.

Eira noticed some men brushing horses inside the palace gardens as she was led across the balcony hallway to where the sultan was waiting the next morning. It looked to her as if they were readying them for some sort of event; braiding their manes and tails in a decorative fashion and painting symbols in reds and blues on their haunches. They were all beautiful purebred Arabian horses, built for running in the desert. Where they had come from, in the pass, she did not know, but they were certainly a prize for any horse lover.

"Have you come to a decision, Your Majesty?" asked the sultan when she walked into the same dining room where she had rather enjoyed her time the night before, until she was presented with an indecent proposal. There was a new face in the room this time. A tall man she could only assume was his son. He stood there with all the pretentious grace of a kid who grew up in the lap of luxury. He was dressed in fine dark crimson robes trimmed with gold and while he was very handsome with his dark soul-searching eyes and neatly combed hair, there was something artificial about him that made Eira turn her nose up at him. To her, he was the younger version of Lord Dundan, a usurper, whom she was in the process of dealing with back home.

"Not exactly," she answered, making her way over to where he stood. Theo, Leon, Killian, Clea, and Nell were all led to the room as well and lined up against the back wall, watching the interaction unfold. "Can I interest you in Theo instead?" she smiled, motioning to him standing behind her.

The sultan looked at him disappointedly and uttered, "He's not his type."

"Okay, then." Eira began. "I came to make a deal with you. There must be something you want that I can give you, other than my lineage?" His son leaned over and whispered in his father's ear without breaking eye contact with her. There was something about the way that he stared at her that made Eira wonder if he was truly invested in this arrangement the way his father was.

"I'm sorry, Your Majesty, but there is nothing you can offer that would compare to the freedom your marriage would bring myself and my people."

"Are you sure? Talvia is a place unlike what you are accustomed to. Your people would have to go from living in this desert to living in a snow-covered freezer. I doubt your people would take to that change so easily."

"Maybe not, but they will appreciate no longer being in exile. Our resources are running dry and my people will not survive much longer in this desert."

"What if I can promise you that your people can continue to live their lives the way they have known for centuries? We can find a way to send you what you need."

"How? By sending messengers and delivery men into the pass? They will not make it a day in here and you know it."

"We can find a way if you just give me the chance," she tried to assure him.

His son was being particularly quiet the whole time, watching the two of them go back and forth with their arguments. A loud whinny from one of the horses outside broke the silence, and the sultan turned toward his son and smiled.

"My son is one of the best horse racers of my people. Did you know that?"

"Naturally," smiled Eira.

"Of course you didn't, but it is true." Eira was not sure why the sultan had changed the subject so effortlessly, as though he had lost all interest in their negotiations.

"I'm sorry. Can you catch me up here?" Eira was still trying to find her place in this new conversation.

"There is a race in two days; the Onyx Race. I will make a deal with you. Enter one of your companions in the race and whoever wins gets the girl, so to speak. If my son wins, you marry him. If you win, you are free to be on your way. This is my new deal. Take it or leave it. The choice is yours."

"I'll do it," interrupted Killian. "I can race across the desert. Nothing to it."

"You were just complaining about the heat yesterday," said Theo. "No, I'll go."

"Shhh," hushed Eira. "What exactly does this race entail?"

Finally she heard the sultan's son speak for the first time, "It is a gruelling seven-day journey through the desert. You will be tested against the elements and only the strong survive."

She paused a moment, "I can't answer you right now."

"I understand. My offer expires in one hour. I will be back then." The sultan motioned at his guards to follow him and his son out. The doors closed behind them and Eira knew the guards were standing on the other side of them.

"I'll still do it," shrugged Theo.

"Are you kidding me?" Eira turned to him. "It is a week-long journey in blistering heat with only the water you can carry. I cannot ask any of you to do this."

"I'll race him," said Leon after taking a deep breath. "How bad can it be?"

"Do you really want to find that out?" replied Eira.

"It seems like our only option, Eira," said Clea.

Eira scanned the faces of her friends, looking for someone to come up with another idea—any idea. Finally, she took a breath and looked at Leon, "Okay, you can do this. At least it will give us some time to think of another plan—if you don't win."

"Thanks for your faith, hun," he smiled with a classic note of sarcasm.

"That's not what I meant. You know that they're not going to let you win."

"Alright, my man," Theo patted Leon on the back. "He's got this. If any of us have a shot of succeeding, it's Leon."

"Thanks, buddy." Leon patted his hand over Theo's.

"Well, now that this is settled, I'm going to get something to eat. Anyone else?" announced Killian, and Clea, Theo, and Nell followed, leaving Eira alone with Leon again. It was almost as if her friends kept planning it that way.

The four walked down the hall with their four guards trailing after them.

"So," began Clea, "when do you think those two will finally put all of this behind them and make up?"

"Well, if Leon is really going to race, she doesn't have much time. Eira will finally forgive him before the race. It's the right thing to do," responded Theo.

"No way," assured Killian. "Sure, Leon may die out there, but Eira is far more upset than she lets on. And she's incredibly stubborn—we know this. Only if he wins, will she *maybe* begin to forgive him. These days apart from him while he's risking his life, will surely do the trick."

"No way. She will definitely forgive him before. She will never let him go out there without letting him know how much she cares."

"Well, you know, you guys could bet on it," added Clea, not being able to resist adding fuel to this fire. The guys looked at each other.

"You're on. If she doesn't forgive him before the race, I win," said Killian.

"Deal," Theo shook Killian's hand forcefully. "But she will."

"Are you sure you want to do this?" Eira asked while Leon's gaze was still on the door their friends had just walked out of, and he turned to give her attention.

"I don't have much of a choice, do I?" He turned toward the door and moved to leave. She wanted to call after him but stopped herself and simply watched as the door shut behind him, leaving her alone with only her thoughts for company.

Later that afternoon, Eira was allowed to wander the palace gardens—with two guards following closely behind her. She saw Lina sitting on the grass watching a couple of lion cubs chase each other around a tree and play fight with each other.

"They were found just on the outskirts of our borders, barely a week old, dying from heat exhaustion. One of my father's guards brought them back here, and we nursed them back to health. We'll release them back once they are old enough. The lions who live in the pass are well adapted to the heat and know how to survive out there. They'll be good hunters in the future." She smiled, watching one of the cubs pin her sister down and bite her ear. Then a butterfly caught the little cub's eyes, and she chased it off into the taller grass. The other lion cub got to her feet and trotted with baby-like steps over to Eira.

"What are their names?" asked Eira running her fingers through the soft fur.

"That one is Asha," Lina said, pointing to the butterfly hunter. "And this one is Maali."

"Hi Maali," she whispered to the cub with both hands on the sides of her furry face. "Hey, Lina, can you tell me more about this race?"

Lina took a deep breath and with a sigh, she told Eira every dreadful thing she knew about the race. "If it is not the heat of the desert that kills them, it will be the other men, for they would stop at nothing to be the victor. The first across the finish line receives riches beyond belief and a better life for his family. Many of the men have nothing else to lose, so they enter the race on the chance they can change their fate. Death is a risk they're willing to take."

"Do you think Leon has any chance at all of winning?" Eira asked with hope in her eyes.

"My brother is a skilled rider, and he has competed in the races for three years now. He has not lost one yet."

"Is there any way your father would reconsider this deal?"

"No. My father is a stubborn man and I don't think he is going to back down on this one. He knows Sami will win. To him, he is not gambling."

"Then you need to help us find a way out of here," pleaded Eira. "Please, you know this palace. There has to be a way for us to escape if it comes down to it. We can use the two days we still have before the race as time to plan. My own kingdom is in peril, and I have to get back home."

Lina paused a moment and looked around to see what the guards were up to, making sure they were not so close as to overhear. Finally, she took a breath and let it out slowly, as if debating something in her mind, "Alright, I will help you but, don't give up on your Leon too easily. He may just surprise you."

With the sun setting over the pass, it was Eira's last chance to talk to Leon before the race tomorrow. She knew she had to or she would regret it. This was not some fairytale or sweeping epic romance movie where you know the guy can't possibly die because they are meant to be together. This was real life and there was a very good chance of her never getting the chance to do this again. The deserts in her world can reach temperatures of fifty degrees Celsius, and this was a magical place. She got a glimpse of the desert and she could not bear the thought of him willingly travelling through it. The only problem with her desire, was getting over to him. Everyone was in their own room to keep any communication to a minimum and they were on a twenty-four-hour lockdown, with personal guards on watch. Leon's room wasn't exactly far, it was right next door to hers, but it may as well have been on the other side of the palace. The only thing not guarded was her balcony, and that would be due to the fact it was four stories up, with no possibility of escape. When standing on it, she could see into Leon's room through his window, but unfortunately, he did not have a balcony, only a small balconette, a small stone railing on the outside of this window, perhaps to stop people from falling out. It was barely big enough for a single person to stand on. Nevertheless, it was her only chance.

She hurried out to her balcony and looked to see if Leon was there. Sure enough, the window was open, and Leon had just emerged from a steam-filled bathroom, making his way through his evening routine. His attire left something to be desired; wearing nothing but a towel wrapped around his waist. He was moving toward his clothes folded neatly on the bed when Eira called out to him. Just as he was holding up his shirt, he heard her call and turned toward the window.

"What are you doing?" he asked, now standing in front of the window with his hands on his hips. The distance between them was not that far, only a couple of feet maybe, however, the distance below them was an acrophobe's worst nightmare.

"I need to talk to you."

"Okay," he responded with a pause, indicating he was waiting for her to start.

"Not like this. I'm coming over." She started to climb up her balcony railing, so she could hop over to his.

"Wait, Eira," he yelled in his loudest whisper, looking around to make sure no one could see them. "Are you crazy?" He stepped out onto the ledge as far as he could and held his arms out for her. Eira had made it to where she was straddling her railing with one hand on the stone of Leon's railing and another on the stone of the wall. She leaned forward to place both hands on Leon's railing, but this whole escapade seemed a lot easier in her head. Eira stayed there for a moment, not sure how to move next.

"Now what?" asked Leon. With a quick movement, Eira swung her leg that was still in the safety of her balcony over the rail and beside the other one. She now had her hands on Leon's railing, but her feet were still on her balcony. Eira moved one leg across the void between their balconies and then the other. She was now standing on the other side of Leon's window. Pulling one leg over the railing, Eira was now straddling it. She moved her right hand to his shoulder and then moved her other. His hands were firmly grasping her waist. Now all she had to do was swing her other leg over—no problem. Problem. Leon helped to pull her forward, but her foot got stuck between one of the spindles and when she finally loosened it she fell over the railing, knocking Leon backward into his room with her lying on top of him.

"Well, that wasn't so bad," she said, staring him in the eyes, still lying on top of him.

"Easy for you to say—you had me to land on." He pushed her up and off of him, then made it to his feet, adjusting his towel and rubbing his back, which had just become far too familiar with the terracotta tile floor.

"Sorry, are you okay?" Eira asked.

"I'll be alright."

The two looked at each other for a moment, Eira being a bit thrown off by his towel.

"You wanted to talk?" he finally broke the silence.

"Yes." She took a breath as if she was checking back in from a daydream.

"Okay, I'll just go get changed." He moved for his clothes and carried them into the bathroom. He soon emerged again from the bathroom, fully clothed this time. "Okay, I'm all yours," he smiled.

"Right, um," she suddenly could not think of the words, "I just wanted to make sure you're okay and that this race thing tomorrow isn't causing you too much...stress. You know, you don't have to do it and while I appreciate you wanting to do this for me, I don't want you to be doing this purely because you think it'll make me forgive you or win me back in any sort of way. It's a really sucky situation we have found ourselves in and, you know, it is what it is and if you didn't do it, I'm sure someone else would have. Clea seemed like she was willing to go and I mean I think that's really commendable that she was willing to hang out in the desert for a week after what we experienced, it is not nice out there, and I feel like this race is designed to kill you, and I just feel bad for those horses, because it's so hot out there and they're the ones doing all the running and—"

"Eira," Leon cut her off, "you're rambling."

"Yep," she replied, rocking back and forth from toes to heels.

"Look, I get that you're worried about me, but you don't have to be." He moved toward the dresser and took the pitcher of water sitting atop it and poured himself a glass. Eira took a few steps closer.

"I know I don't have to be, but I can't help it. You always do this. You make it seem like everything you do for me isn't a big deal and that it's just your job to do it. Why can't you let me be worried about you, and care about the fact that you're risking your life for me?" Her temper was growing and her voice started to rise.

"The guards are going to hear you—be quiet." He turned back to the dresser and began filling his glass again, but he paused, resting both his hands on its surface. He leaned over the dresser as if he was thinking. Eira stood behind him and placed a hand on his shoulder, but he didn't move. "Look, Eira, I have to do this, and I have to act like it's not a big deal because if I start to acknowledge the fact that I might die, and I might leave you alone in all of this..." He paused for a moment with his back still turned to her and took another breath, "I have to do this because I have to prove to myself that I'm worthy of you again."

"You were never not," she said, pushing his hand off the dresser and sliding into the space between himself and the dresser. He stood up and looked deep into her eyes, "I'm going to win this thing because there's one thing you're forgetting about."

"What?"

"That I love you, and there's no way I'm not winning this thing."

"Love can't exactly stop you from dying, and you're racing against a guy who has lived and rode here his whole life."

"Yeah, but he hasn't had you for any of it, so he really doesn't have a reason to win as badly as I do."

Aww.

Eira gasped as Leon's arm wrapped around her and his other hand went behind her head, fingers tangling in her hair, pulling her lips towards his. He kissed her fiercely and then broke away, devouring her with his eyes while his arms rested on either side of her supporting his weight on the dresser. He kept her gaze, forehead pressed to hers as if to seek permission for what he was doing. She pushed him back slightly, wrapping her arms around his neck, "Why'd you stop?"

He stood upright, pulling her with him into another kiss, easily lifting her onto the dresser. She wrapped her legs around him and embraced everything that was happening. She didn't realize how much she had missed the feeling of his lips on hers—until now. Soon he was carrying her over to the bed where he laid back on it, pulling her with him. She looked into his deep hazel eyes and watched as they darkened with desire. She needed him more than ever and he certainly shared the feeling. He then rolled himself on top of her and didn't even think about stopping this time.

Eira stood on her balcony, looking over at Leon in the moonlight. He was still standing in his window, making sure she was safely back where she needed to be. He could see on her face that she was beginning to get emotional.

She could feel the tears welling up, and he had known her long enough to recognize the signs. He gave her a calming smile and leaned as far out over the railing as he could. She did the same and they were soon face to face. He kissed her again and took a deep breath, "I made the mistake once of not fighting for you and I'm not going to do it again. I'm going to win this race. You have my word." And Leon's word was as good to her as anything. He had proven to her many times that when he gives his word to something he always comes through, just like the day he promised to stay by her side and help her to the Hoarfrost Mountains where a dragon used to lay.

11

He was as black as the gemstone that gave him his name. A purebred Arabian stallion. He was the first to win the great race across the desert decades before, and thus the race became known as the Onyx Race after its first victor. The race was not an easy feat, even to the most skilled and knowledgeable in the ways of the desert. Leon had never really endured this type of heat and sand, even growing up in a snowless Talvia. This was where Sami had an advantage—even if Sirona had given Leon some sort of ability to withstand the heat.

Eira had been awoken early by the maids who were ready to turn her into an Arabian princess. They pulled at her hair and scrubbed her skin as she sat in a bath drizzled with essential oils. They worked oil into her skin and through her hair to make it soft and shiny, then curled it and did her make-up. The sultan had insisted upon it, most likely so his son could see she could look the part of a presentable bride when he surely won the race. She was now a prize for the victor, and she prayed it was Leon, for she had stayed up most of the night trying to think of some way out of the race. She was dressed in a beautiful pink, royal blue, and gold sari given to her by Lina as a peace offering for what her father had done to them, but at that very moment it felt more like a humiliating costume she was forced to wear.

The people had gathered in the stands above the starting line. All the horses and their riders were readying themselves. The horses beat at the steaming earth below with their hooves and the dust rose around their ankles. Eira was being led to the stands when she spotted Leon getting ready. She tried to make a break for it but was pulled back by one of the sultan's guards.

"Hey, let me go."

"Where do you think you're going?" he asked.

She forced her arms from his grasp, "You could at least let me say goodbye."

Suddenly, the sultan appeared behind them, "Let her go. It will be the last time she sees him alive." Eira was breathing deeply as she stared at the sultan, then turned back to the guard and stared at him. He stepped back, giving her permission to leave.

"Are you ready?" Eira asked Leon, walking up beside him and his horse. "I guess so," answered Leon, tucking another water sack into the saddle bags against the deep brown side of his stallion. The men were starting to take their places at the starting line. "I think I have to go now," he turned to her.

"Just be careful. Don't risk your life trying to win. If it comes down to it, just make it back here. We'll figure something out in the end." She touched a hand to his cheek and looked deep into his hazel eyes and then kissed him. "I love you."

Killian reluctantly handed over a small pouch of coins to Theo, who was smiling after seeing Eira kiss Leon from the stands where they were watching—a sure sign of forgiveness. Clea rolled her eyes at the boys' immaturity and focussed back on the race.

"I hope you're ready for this, winter boy?" said Sami as he rode up beside Eira and Leon. Leon looked up at him, literally sitting on his high horse. He let go of Eira and mounted his horse, gathering the reins in his hands and holding the stallion at the starting line.

"I hope you're ready to see what a real rider looks like?" responded Leon.

"We will see about that. It's a long journey, with plenty of time to decide who truly is the better rider."

Eira made her way through the lineup of horses and back to the guard who was standing, arms crossed, waiting for her. She was then led to her seat in the stands. Eleven men were competing altogether. She was sitting between Clea and Lina in the sultan's private booth. It was draped with colourful fabrics to shade him from the sun and servants fanning him with long palm fronds and serving drinks. The sultan stood and addressed the crowd, wishing all the participants the best of luck.

While he was distracted with his duties, Lina leaned over and whispered to Eira, "Don't worry about Leon," she said, "I think he will be alright. He is a skilled rider. I can tell by the way he sits just above the saddle, readying himself for when the horse launches itself into a gallop."

"You can tell all of that?"

"Yes, but I also know something else," she smiled, looking out into the crowd as to not draw the attention of prying eyes. "I have given him the second fastest horse in my father's collection. My brother, of course, has the fastest. My father thinks he has given Leon his slowest stallion but the two are identical except for the small white mark on his left front leg. I covered it with dye and marked the other stallion's leg with white."

"You switched them?" whispered Eira.

Bang! The sound of the firework ricocheted through the air and startled Eira in her seat. The horses galloped off from the starting line and into the desert beyond.

Leon's horse was racing forward as fast as he could. He was second only to Sami who took the lead. After the display of running horses for the enjoyment of the cheering crowd was done, Leon slowed his horse to a walk just like the others. It was a long journey and the only time there was a need to run the horse was at the start and before the finish.

The gardens in the Palace of Alzahra were beautiful, but provided little relief from the terrors going through Eira's mind. She sat there watching the peacocks strut across the lawn and the various servants fanning the sultan who sat in the shade of his tent across from her. She was a captive in his paradise until Leon returned, and the days could not go by fast enough.

Lina was doing a good job meeting with them in secrecy, planning an escape for them if they should need one. Their best bet would be to leave during the night over the back wall of the garden. The guards rarely watch over there and if they were distracted by something, such as Lina, Eira and the group would have the opportunity to make their escape. She was filling her time with stealing and packing away what supplies they would need. Lina brought tins of food that would last until they cleared the pass and Eira placed them in the bags she had hidden under the bed in her room. Now all she could do was wait the seven tortuous days until the race was over.

****

"You should set up camp, winter boy," said the prince. "It will be getting dark soon and this desert is not a place you want to be at night without shelter."

"I'm familiar with the desert. How do you think we got here?" Leon had been travelling the road through the desert all day. The other competitors were still within view and they all wandered along, taking their own paths. A campground was made where they all set up their canvas tents and tied their horses for the night. "And believe me, I've been through far worse than this."

The prince's tent was set up next to his, and they looked almost identical. All the men had small, simple tents, just big enough for one person. They could not risk carrying anything heavier on their horses. Sami began to make a small fire and took out a bottle of what looked like some sort of wine. He sat down and held the bottle out to Leon, offering him some.

"What's that for?" asked Leon. "Have you poisoned it?"

"No," he answered, pouring himself a cup and drinking from it. "It is a peace offering."

"And why would I want that?"

"Because I don't want to marry the Queen of Talvia just as much as you don't want me to."

Leon thought for a moment, looking at Sami sitting there in the glow of the fire and then finally moved and sat next to him, taking an empty cup and pouring himself a drink from the bottle. "If you don't want to marry her, then why are you out here?"

"I cannot refuse my father's wishes and he wishes that we end our exile through a marriage alliance. This race is the only way we can all get what we want. If you win, you get to leave, and the only way you will win is with my help."

"And why should I trust you?"

"Because I saw you today with her before the start of the race. You truly love her, and how much you love her is how much I love Sania."

"Who's Sania?" smiled Leon.

"The girl I would rather marry, but she will not provide any sort of relief from this exile, at least not for my father." He held his cup up to Leon and then took a sip, "Believe me when I tell you that this race is serious. Men die out here and none of these men can be trusted."

"Again, then why should I trust you?" pushed Leon.

"I don't think you really have a choice."

Leon glanced around at the other competitors, watching him and Sami with disdain in their eyes. Something was telling him to trust Sami, at least for the time being.

"What were you doing talking to the prince?" asked one of the other men early the next morning when Leon was readying his horse.

"Nothing," replied Leon. "We were just talking. He wanted to know more about Talvia, where I'm from. You know, I don't think he's ever seen snow," he joked.

"If you think I'm going to let some foreigner take my victory, you are mistaken," threatened the man.

"I'm not trying to take anyone's victory. You can take first place. I just have to beat him," he motioned to Sami watering his horse.

The first day and night of the journey was behind him and Leon was beginning to feel the effects of the desert sun already—Sirona must not have had as much of an effect on him as he thought. He was drifting in and out of consciousness while his horse continued, following the path the horses ahead of him were making.

"You alright?" asked the prince, riding up beside him and handing him a bottle of water. Leon took the bottle and gulped down a few mouthfuls of water.

"Yeah, I'm fine. Thanks," he replied.

"You're going to have to do better than this if you want to make it another day out here, let alone another six."

"I'll be fine. It's weird though, the desert heat didn't seem to affect me when we were stuck in the pass. I'm kind of surprised it is taking its toll on me this soon."

Sami looked at the water bottle in Leon's saddle bags. "Hand me your bottle, the one you've been drinking out of." Leon did as asked and tossed it over. Sami opened it and took a sniff. "Yeah, I thought as much," then he poured the water out. "You can't drink this—it's poisoned."

"What? How do you know?"

"I'm trained to detect this poison. I can catch the faint smell, something you'd never be able to as an outsider."

"Okay, well, thanks. But what am I supposed to do now? I'm down a bottle of water and you said the oasis is still a day away."

"You can keep that in the meantime," Sami said, motioning to his bottle of water still in Leon's hands, "But you're going to have to be careful with rationing the rest of your water until we reach the oasis."

"And what do we have here?" asked the same man from the morning riding up beside them. "Working with the prince, are you?" The man rode in front of Leon, cutting him off. "I told you, I am not going to let you take my victory, and now you're working with the prince. What chance do any of us have now?" He drew his sword and placed its tip at the end of Leon's nose.

"Look, he was just offering me some water, that's all," said Leon, placing his hands in the air. "Probably because *someone* poisoned mine."

"What are you insinuating?" pressed the man.

"What's going on here?" asked another man, riding up to the three that were now in a standstill.

"This boy is working with the prince. There is no way any of us will win the race if he has help from the sultan's son himself."

"Just relax and put down your sword, Hassan," said the man.

"What did you tell me?" Hassan turned his attention from Leon to the man who had just joined them. "Do not tell me what to do," and he swung his sword around his head at the other man who drew his sword. Leon watched as the two swords clanged in the air and the men dismounted their horses, ready for a fight. Leon and Sami followed suit, trying to break the two up, but it was no use. The man had turned his attention back to Leon and was backing him through the sand. Leon had no choice but to draw his own sword and fight.

Swords were clanging left and right as some of the other competitors caught up with the leaders and joined in, taking different sides. These men fought ruthlessly, either because of what the heat was doing to their minds or because of the way they were taught to fight. Either way, they were skilled and Leon was not fairing so well.

"Leon, behind you," called Sami just before a large man would have run his sword right through him. Leon quickly clashed swords with the assailant, knocking his sword to the ground. "We can't waste our energy on this fight—we have to get out of here," shouted Sami.

"Get back to the horses," called Leon. "I hope you're ready to race." They fought their way back to their horses and kicked them into a gallop, managing to escape the fighting, racing deeper into the desert.

It was dark by the time Leon and Sami made their way into the caves in the mountains. It would provide them better shelter from the other competitors than pitching their tents in the wide-open desert.

"Tomorrow we will circle around behind these mountains and end up behind the palace. Then it is a straight ride to the finish line," said Sami.

"Do you think your father will keep his word if I win?" asked Leon.

"I'm not sure. I would like to believe my father to be an honourable man when it comes to his word but, this whole situation is not like him at all. I do not know what will come of your victory."

****

Eira tapped her fingers over and over again on the desk in her room. She was growing impatient with all the waiting and wondering. She moved over to the balcony and placed her hands on the railing and looked below. Eira did not notice the guard standing beside the balcony door until he coughed and she turned to see a brooding man with his arms folded and a sword hanging by his side watching her. He smiled briefly and Eira turned back to the sky, that was twinkling with millions of tiny lights. The moon was full that night and she knew that somewhere out there, Leon was looking up at the same moon.

12

The next morning, Eira awoke from a rather stressful sleep. Her dreams were terrorized by visions of Leon's body being left in the desert after the men from the race had killed him. She tried to shake it off with a warm bath. *It was just a dream, he is going to be alright. It was just a dream.*

When she was finished getting dressed, a knock came at her door. She figured it was going to be one of the sultan's maids, wanting to help ready her for the day, but she was surprised to see Nell standing on the other side.

"Good morning," she sounded strangely chipper.

"Thank gods you're here. I need to do something today, anything, to take my mind off of the race," said Eira.

"Well, I am ready to be your distraction, then. What should we do? We can't exactly leave the palace, but I'm sure we can find something to take our minds off of everything."

Eira frowned, "Yeah."

"Okay, no problem. How about we go see what everyone else is up to? Maybe Clea can think of something."

"Yeah, I guess," Eira motioned for Nell to head into the hall and she followed.

They found Clea, Killian, and Theo in the gardens. They were sitting in the gazebo, enjoying some iced tea. Killian and Theo looked positively enamoured with the foliage around them—a sure sign that they were bored out of their minds. At least Clea was reading Eira's book from earlier, so she was entertained for the time being.

"Hi," smiled Eira as they stepped into the gazebo.

"Good, you're here," smiled Killian. "Who would win in a fight against that guard over there?" He pointed to a rather large man standing a few feet away from the group. He was all muscle and looked like he was made of stone. "Me or Theo?"

"I'm not answering that," replied Eira.

"So you think me too, then?"

"No, I think he'd kill both of you without even trying." Clea smirked from behind her book. "Anyway, does anyone have any ideas of something to do today? I seriously need to get my mind off of the race," asked Eira as she took the empty seat beside Theo.

Nell tried to sit in the empty seat beside Clea but managed to trip over the table and take out a potted plant with her. She jumped to her feet and brushed herself off while the group stared at her clumsiness. "Are you okay?" asked Eira.

"Yeah."

"You could teach her some fighting. She's definitely going to end up being a liability if we end up in something—which, given the history of this group, is likely," said Killian.

"Yeah, that'd be fun," smiled Eira at Nell.

"No," Nell replied.

"Why not? I mean, you don't need to learn how to kill a guy with a sword, but some self-defence might not be a bad idea." She turned to Killian, "Killian can do it."

"What?" He sat upright from fiddling with a leaf on the vines that covered the gazebo, "I said you."

"Oh, come on," pleaded Eira.

"No."

"Why not?"

"Because she's going to complain the whole time that it's too much work."

"No she won't."

"Yes I will," added Nell.

"Come on," begged Eira again.

"Look, I might be a little clumsy, but I don't need it," added Nell.

"Yes you do," smirked Killian. "I just don't want to be the one to teach you."

"Oh yeah? Come at me," she motioned to herself. "I've seen *Miss Congeniality*, I can make you fall to your knees."

A devilish smirk grew on Killian's face, "Well, we all know that, Nell, but this is different."

Her face was not amused. She stood from her chair, "Shut up. Just try to attack me from behind."

"Why from behind?" asked Killian.

"Because that's all I know."

"Well, that's not going to help you much. What if someone comes at you from the front?"

"Then I'll turn around."

"Okay guys," Eira interrupted and Nell sat back down. "Fine, Theo can teach you."

"Yeah, and I'll keep my shirt on the whole time," Theo smirked at Killian.

"Um, no," replied Nell.

"How about Clea?" asked Eira.

"Better, but still no."

"Me?"

"Eira, I love you too much to put you in that position. I'm not a pleasant person to be around when forced to do physical activity."

"Fine, I'll do it," sighed Killian. "I can handle her bitchiness for one afternoon."

Nell glared at Killian, "Fine. But I'm only doing this for you," she turned to Eira. "To help you take your mind off of everything."

The sultan's training room was in the basement of the palace. It was the coolest place in the palace to ensure no overheating while training. The guards still trained in the desert to become acclimatized to it, but the initial training started below the palace. The group stood at the top of the winding staircase and stared into the abyss.

"I'm not going down there," said Nell.

"It'll be fine," assured Killian. "It's not that many steps."

"Oh, no. Going down is fine, there's just no way I'm walking back up all of those."

"I'll carry you," groaned Killian.

"Yeah, I second that. I don't want to walk back up all of these steps either," added Eira.

"You guys are so annoying, it's bad enough I have to deal with the two of you on this journey. Eira I can handle, but you two together are a nightmare. And why am I always finding bobby pins in all of my stuff? It's ridiculous." Eira and Nell chuckled. "You guys are doing this on purpose, aren't you?"

"Well, I mean, you made such a big fuss about it the one time you found a bobby pin in your bag, we thought it'd be funny," said Eira.

Killian let out an exasperated sigh and stomped down the stairs. "You guys coming or not?" he called from the bottom.

The rest reluctantly headed down the stairs to meet Killian.

They all took turns teaching Nell some moves, and Killian tried his best not to get completely frustrated with everything. Nell wasn't exactly the best student—as she had warned, but her complaining was next level. Killian was rather impressed with Nell's *Miss Congeniality* move though and it did, in fact, bring him to his knees.

"Okay," he groaned while on the floor, "I guess you can take care of yourself if attacked from behind."

"Yeah, and I was holding back. I didn't want to actually hurt you."

Eira took Clea and Theo to *help* her get some water for everyone—funny how that worked out—and left Killian and Nell to keep training.

"You want to keep going?" asked Killian.

"Not really," replied Nell.

"Good," he said, slumping against the wall. "You know, I hope you don't want kids, because you might have just made that a little difficult," he joked, holding his groin.

"Sorry," she smiled, sitting down beside him.

"Are you ever going to tell Eira? She's trying really hard to get us back together."

"I will eventually. I just don't think it's the time. Especially with everything that's happening with Leon."

"Yeah, I get that, but you know it's killing me keeping this from them. Leon is basically my brother, and Eira's like the sister I never had. When my mom died and it was just me, Leon took me in and I can't ever repay him enough for everything he's done."

"I know, we will tell them...when all of this is over. I didn't really hurt you that bad, did I?" Nell motioned to Killian.

"I'll be fine."

"Good," she stood over him, staring down into his deep eyes. "Because if I know Eira, she's not walking back down all those steps. We do have a bit," she gave him a sultry smile.

"Oh, yeah, no—I'm totally better now." He jumped to his feet and she pushed him against the wall, only for him to pick her up and turn, pressing her back against the wall with her legs wrapped tightly around his waist.

It's a good thing the door to the basement made a rather loud noise to announce the presence of someone.

"Are you guys done yet?" called Eira. "I'm not walking back down and up all those steps again."

Killian broke free from Nell's lips and smiled with his forehead pressed against hers. He released her from the wall and she stood, looking up at him. "Ugh, I don't think I can walk up all those steps," groaned Nell.

"Come on," Killian sighed and hoisted Nell over his shoulder.

"Oh, you weren't joking about carrying me."

"Believe me, this is the lesser of two evils. I'd rather carry you than listen to your complaining the whole way."

Five days later, the servants shuffled into Eira's room in the mid-afternoon, to prepare Eira for her presentation to the victor of the race. It was the same routine as the morning of the race, and Eira endured every bit of it as she hoped it was the last time. It was a royal blue and orange sari this time, waiting for her on the bed. She put on the parts she could figure out, but the maids helped with the rest. Eira would be enjoying her time in this utopia if it were not for the sultan's plan and her eagerness to get back to her own people that needed her.

Lina had proven herself to be a worthy friend and while she was being held captive there, they were all being treated like royalty. Eira walked out onto the hallway balcony and met Clea and Nell, who had also been dressed to look like the girls of the village. Theo was wearing a green tunic and Killian's was a bright aubergine.

"What, you got green?" he said to Theo. "Why would they put me in purple?"

Theo laughed, "Yes, but you wear it so well. It really brings out your eyes."

"Not a word of this to anyone, and never mention my eyes again."

"You guys look good," greeted Eira as they met the men in the hall.

"I know, right? It really brings out my eyes," smiled Killian.

They were all led to the same stands where they had watched the start of the race three days ago. The sun was dipping in the sky and the racers would be nearing the finish line within an hour. It was a grand event, even more than the start. Belly dancers were swinging coloured scarves around and vendors were out selling their food. All the villagers had come to see who this year's victor would be. There was stirring all around them, talking about if the boy from the winter land would make it across the finish line. Loudly, a bell rang out from above as the watchman called that he could see something in the distance. Everyone turned to watch, to see who the rider could be.

****

"There," pointed the prince, "do you see that tower in the distance? That is the finish line. My father cannot think that I let you win, so I will be ahead of you until the last couple of strides and then you pull ahead. Do you understand that?"

"Yes," nodded Leon. He could see the tower in the distance and was ready to run straight for it. That day had been difficult. They had run out of water and he was suffering from a bit of heat stroke, but he knew if he pushed on just a little farther, Eira would be waiting for him at the finish line. They were only two of five men left in the race. Sami had not lied that this race and desert kills most of the men competing.

"Okay then, let's go." Sami kicked his horse forward and Leon followed. The two raced across the last leg of the desert just as planned. Sami was slightly ahead and to the spectators watching it would look as though they were in fact competing with one another. As they drew closer, the tall tower was growing larger and larger and Leon could see stands and the colourful flags the people were waving. A distant murmur on the wind soon grew into distinctive cheering, and then he could see it—the finish line. He looked over to Sami who gave him a slight nod and Leon pushed his horse to move faster and pulled ahead.

"No," shouted the sultan. "Sami, push harder. Make that horse fly." The realization of defeat was growing in the sultan's eyes as he watched Leon cross the finish line. A split second later, his son crossed the line, but it was clear who the victor was.

Eira cheered with her friends and ran as fast as she could down to the finish line. Before she got there, the ritual had already begun of draping the victor in flower necklaces and pouring water infused with various oils over him and the horse. She leaped into him and nearly tackled him to the ground, but he managed to hold the both of them upright, and spun Eira around in the air. The sultan marched after her with his guards with Lina following behind.

"It seems that you have managed to make a fool of me," said the Sultan grabbing his son by the arm. "How could you lose?"

"I'm sorry, Father, I did my best."

The sultan turned to Leon and Eira, "I guess I must keep my promise to you. You and your friends are free to go."

"Thank you," said Eira, and she was just about to leave when the sultan's gaze moved past her to the stallion pawing at the ground behind Leon.

"What is this?" he asked, moving over to the horse and pointing at the white spot on his leg that had been revealed when the water was poured over him. "This is not the horse I sent you out with. You cheated."

"What?" asked Leon, knowing nothing of what Lina had done. "No I didn't. This is the horse you gave me."

"This is not the horse I told them to give you."

"No, you intentionally gave him the slowest horse you have. If you ask me, Sultan, you cheated," said Eira.

"Father, please," started Lina, "let them go. He won the race."

The sultan was not in a generous mood despite the pleas from his daughter. "Guards," he called to the men. "Take them."

Leon drew his sword and pushed Eira behind him as the guards approached. Clea, Theo, Nell, and Killian stood from the stands. They turned to head down to where Leon and Eira were, but four guards blocked their way. Looking around for an escape route, Clea unravelled her skirt leaving just the tight shorts she had on underneath, and climbed up on the railing and jumped into the stands below. Killian and Theo fought the guards until they were able to free themselves from the balcony. Theo ran out into the fight while Killian grabbed Nell and also ripped the skirt from her.

"You've been wanting to do that all day, haven't you?" she grinned.

"Yeah, but under different circumstances," he raised his brows, then grabbed her hand and dragged her into the crowds with him. He punched one of the guards out of his way and joined Theo and Leon.

Clea tossed a sword to Eira and the three of them began the fight below. They were outnumbered, even when Killian and Theo joined the party.

The sultan grabbed Lina and rushed off to the palace. "Father. Father, please," pleaded Lina as she tried to release her wrist from his grip. "You have to let them go. They have done nothing wrong."

"Except decide to venture through the pass. No one comes out of it alive."

"Please, it is my fault. I switched the horses. They knew nothing of it until the race had already begun."

"You did what?" he stopped in his tracks. "Get in the palace," he forced her arm from his grasp, "I'll deal with you later."

Eira managed to escape and ran back through the palace halls. There weren't many guards that she met on the way, for they were all called to fight outside. She got back to her room and grabbed the bags she had hidden for when they would make their escape. The next seasons in the pass were autumn and winter, meaning everyone would need their warmer clothing. Eira grabbed them in a haste and then ran back outside to where the fighting continued. She looked around and saw Leon and Theo against two guards while Clea and Killian were holding off their own. She quickly spotted Nell and ran to her, grabbing her hand and pulling her with her. There were people scattered everywhere and men falling to the ground left and right.

"We can't hold them off," shouted Theo to Leon, "there are too many of them."

"We have to leave," shouted Clea. A panic had spread through the race crowd and people filled the streets. Sami was fighting with them but, even his help was not doing them much good.

"Get to the horses," called Leon. "Eira, go," he shouted to her. She ripped off the part of the sari that was impeding her movement and threw herself up over one of the racehorses. Clea did the same, and soon they had all managed to find a horse. They still had to fight their way out of the village with people panicking all through the bazaar streets and the guards after them.

Eira slowed her horse to look back at where Theo and Leon should be coming from. They weren't there. The fighting continued inside the village on horseback and Theo was in a heated battle with one of the guards when Leon shouted to him,

"Theo, we have to go. Make for the gate." He turned for a split second to hear Leon's request, but it was a second too long to take his eyes off of the guard. A piercing pain radiated from his gut as the guard's blade ran through him. The guard pulled the dagger from Theo's abdomen and was about to finish him off when his sword was stopped mid-air by Leon's. "Go," he shouted, "I've got this." Theo clutched his waist where the sword had pierced him and found the strength to push his horse on, racing through the streets towards the gate.

"Close the gate," ordered one of the guards. Theo quickly kicked his horse and managed to escape, with the gate closing tight behind them.

Eira, Killian, and Clea stopped their horses once they felt enough space had been gained between them and the sultan's guards. Looking out to the village they had just escaped from.

"Where are they?" asked Eira.

"They'll come, darling, don't worry," answered Killian. Nell gave her a reassuring smile from her place, sitting in front of Killian. Sure enough, she could see the two of them riding out of the village and into the desert toward them.

"Come on," called Clea, turning her horse around and kicking it forward. They raced through the desert and it took them little time to see the entrance to Autumn ahead of them. They passed from sand to gravel and slowed their horses on the path as swirls of red and orange leaves flew around them. Leon and Theo had caught up to them and slowed their horses when they entered the safety of the new season, but this part of the pass could not repair the damage that was already done. When the horse had slowed enough, Theo could not hold on any longer and fell to the ground in pain.

"No," screamed Eira. "What happened?" She flung herself from her horse and rushed to his side, her knees slamming into the earth beside him. He was clutching his wound and bleeding profusely. No words were coming from him as the tears streamed down Eira's cheeks.

"Why are you guys just standing there? Do something!" Eira sobbed.

They looked at the severity of Theo's wound. "There's nothing we can do," said Killian. "Not out here, I'm afraid."

Leon bent down to comfort her as her tears watered down the blood coming from Theo's body. Killian, Clea, and Nell stood there in silence. There was truly nothing any of them could do, stranded in the Quesnell Pass. She grabbed Leon's sword and franticly ripped a sizeable piece off his tunic and tried putting pressure on the wound, remembering everything she had learned from watching various medical dramas, but it didn't seem to be doing anything. Theo raised a hand with all the strength he had left and put his hand over Eira's. "It's no use," he whispered, and that was it. His eyes closed and his body went limp.

As her cries echoed through the air, a familiar sound grew upon the horizon. A response to the Queen of Talvia's sorrow-filled cries. A call coming back at her that she had heard only a couple of times before. It was the cry of the great snowy owls. Killian and Leon turned their gaze toward the sky. Eira turned her head to the sky as well and wiped the tears from her eyes. An owl swooped and landed in front of them, staring with its wise eyes at the group, moving its head from side to side. Eira moved closer to it and reached a hand out and the owl met it with its massive beak. She walked around behind it and climbed on its back. Clea and Leon followed, and the owl soared into the sky with them just as another swooped down and picked up the unconscious Theo in its talons and carefully took off. Another owl hovered low and Killian and Nell jumped onto its back, just as the others had done. The sun was setting, and the air was clear from high above the treetops. They were still in the shelter of the mountains climbing high above them, surrounding the pass. They did not know where the owls were taking them but, when the owls come, it is usually to help.

13

The owls landed in what was clear to be the Talvian part of the Quesnell Pass. As the world grew whiter and the soft flakes of snow fell onto Eira's face, the owls soared into a sheltered part of the mountain only they knew the entrance to. A hidden cave in the side of the mountain range that bordered the pass. They were in what looked like an almost ceiling-less cave—a crystal ballroom. The mountains climbed high around them, creating a shelter, but they could still see a few stars above, shining through the cracks between the towering crystal spires and snow-covered evergreens making their way up the sides of the cave and down from the ceiling. Moonlight reflected through the crystals and created an enchanting glow, so bright there was no need for any light. The whole cave sparkled, and all around were hundreds of great snowy owls perched on the various shelves of the mountainside and on the steadfast branches of the mighty conifer towering above them right up the middle of the cave, almost poking through the small skylight at the top. Each pine needle was delicately frosted, yet its strength was unwavering.

"Where are we?" asked Eira, in awe of it all.

"I don't know," answered Leon.

The group walked in further to take in all the wonder. "This is incredible," said Clea.

"Yes, and messy. Watch your step," added Killian. Then he noticed Nell, wide-eyed and standing behind everyone, "Hey, you okay?" She looked like she was going to throw up.

"Nell, what's wrong?" asked Eira, moving closer to her and Killian.

"I have to go home, Eira," Nell said, her panicked voice wavering. "I don't think I can do this," she stared into Eira's eyes. "I mean, that was a real war, a real battle. I'm not a warrior princess like you. I thought I could do this, but I need to get out of here. I mean, there was a guy missing an arm back there. And I'm Australian—we usually just walk off things like that, but I don't know."

"Hey, hey. Okay," Eira said putting her hands on Nell's shoulders, "we'll get you out of here, I promise."

"And Theo's dying," she cried into her friend's shoulder.

"I know. It's going to be okay." She turned to Killian and motioned for him to switch places with her and she turned Nell into his arms. Eira looked all around but could not see Theo or the owl that had carried him. "Where is Theo anyway?" she asked.

"I don't know. The owl must have taken him somewhere else," said Leon.

"Indeed, he did," said a voice. From behind an owl, a man walked out. He was an old man with a salt-and-pepper beard and shoulder-length grey-brown hair. "My name is Alareison, but everyone calls me Al. I am the caretaker of these owls and I have taken good care of your friend. He will be himself again in a few days' time. The power of the Frostfire root works fast."

"Where are we?" asked Clea.

"You are in the Land of the Owls," replied Al.

"I don't believe it," gasped Leon. "No one has ever seen where the owls live before. The owls appear and disappear, and no one knows where they actually come from."

"Can I see him?" asked Eira.

"Of course," said Al. "Right this way," and he led her to where Theo was resting. He was still unconscious, but his wound already looked better. She knelt beside him and stroked his hair, only now beginning to feel the chill of the snow on her bare arms.

"Now, how did you manage to get this far into the pass?" asked Al.

"We are on our way to the Seasons Cross to find the Order of the Seasons," replied Eira.

"The what?" asked Al, shocked at what he had just heard. "You won't find that around here I'm afraid. No such order or place exists, believe me."

"That can't be true—we've come all this way," pleaded Eira. "How are we supposed to defeat the Blue Queen now?"

"What did you say?" asked Al. The colour drained from his face. "I have heard that name before, in a time I would wish never to go back to. Is she truly back?"

"Yes. She's been released and has taken control of Talvia," said Eira.

"And who are you to be dealing with all of this?"

"This is Eira, Queen of Talvia," added Killian joining the two. "She has come all this way to try to reclaim her kingdom."

"If it was truly her kingdom, she would not have lost it to the Blue Queen in the first place."

Rude.

"She was tricked, and you don't know her. She is a great queen, the best we have seen in decades!" Clea defended.

"You mean the only one you have seen in decades. I know the history of this land more so than any of you," said Al as the group watched him intently tending to Theo's wound. When he was done, he turned and faced the group, "Well, it doesn't matter, anyway. The Blue Queen cannot be defeated. The wizard who trapped her the first time does not exist anymore. And, I suppose that is who you are looking for, which is why you ended up in this gods forsaken pass."

"How do you know that? How can you be so sure?" Eira argued, beginning to become quite furious with the man who was saving Theo's life.

"He does not exist. He was defeated long ago," yelled Al and he turned away from Eira to attend to his owls.

"You're him, aren't you?" she asked.

"I don't know what you are talking about."

"Yes, you do," repeated Eira. "You're the winter wizard. That's why the owls took us here and not simply out of the pass to seek help elsewhere."

"I told you, the man you are looking for does not exist anymore. He has slowly evolved into a new life, caring for those who keep the balance of this land in check. He is not the great wizard he once was. The Order fell long ago, and I am all that is left. I care for the owls now, that is all."

"No, please, you have to help us. You defeated her once. You are the only one who knows how."

"I can't. Besides, it was centuries ago that I defeated her."

"Can't or won't? You were entrusted with the well-being of this country and now she is dying. Will you not come to her aid?" said Eira.

"Ophelessa is a powerful sorceress and her power is only growing stronger and stronger every day she is out of her imprisonment. You will need all the help you can get to defeat her, and I will not be enough. I am sorry. Your friend will be well soon enough. You're all welcome to stay here until then, but after that you should all be on your way."

Eira was livid with him. After everything she had been through, she could not believe it was all for nothing. She changed into warmer clothes, removing the once beautiful sari that had now been stained with Theo's blood. Al left the group that night to make camp under the stars in the shelter of the owl's home. None of them got much sleep that night, Eira especially, knowing that their journey had come to an end and was not the success they had hoped it would be. She sat on her bent legs beside Theo's bed and watched as he breathed in and out, so softly, so peacefully, knowing nothing of their failure. He was still in a blissful state of hope. He looked different from when they started their journey into the pass. Now his hair was messy, and his facial hair had grown, but somehow he looked just the same. All she wanted was for him to wake.

"You should get some sleep. He'll be alright." She turned to see Leon standing behind her.

"I know...I just—I'm not tired."

"I'll sit with him if you want," said Leon, sitting on the ground beside her. She leaned her head against his shoulder and let the tear fall into his shirt. "Go get some sleep. I'll let you know if he wakes," smiled Leon, kissing her on the cheek.

"Thank you," she sighed, looking into his eyes and kissing him.

When the morning sun shone in, Theo awoke. The owls were all a flutter, having their breakfast, and one in particular seemed to like Killian's more than his own.

"Get away from me you mangy vertebrate."

"Just ignore it, Killian," said Clea.

The owl bopped Killian on the head with its beak. "And how do you suppose I do that?" He turned and tossed a handful of food over his shoulder and the bird flew happily after it in an instant. "There you go, you maddening feather ball. That'll keep you happy for a while. Stupid owls," he muttered under his breath, lifting another spoonful into his mouth, "would make a few nice throw pillows though."

It was quite a sight to wake up to if you didn't know you had fallen asleep there. "Where am I?" asked Theo, sauntering over to where the group sat having breakfast.

"You're awake," Eira breathed a sigh of relief, rushing over to him. She moved to embrace him but he backed away slightly.

"Ah," he winced when she touched his side.

"Sorry," she said, stepping away from him, assuming it was a reflex from the pain, "does it still hurt?"

He didn't answer right away, just looked at her as if he was trying to place her in his mind, then he glanced at his surroundings again, "Sorry, where am I?" he asked again.

"The Land of the Owls. They brought you here after you got hurt. You almost died. Do you not remember anything?"

"Um, not really." He ran a hand through his hair and looked at Eira again, "Who are you?"

Eira didn't respond, just looked back at the group as if to ask them for help. Glancing around, Theo caught the eye of someone, "Leon, thank the gods, someone I recognize."

"Theo, you don't recognize any of these people?" asked Leon moving closer to him.

"Well, other than Killian—should I?"

"Theo," started Leon, "what do you remember then?"

"I don't know. The last thing I remember was we were getting ready for your bachelor par—"

Leon's eyes widened and Killian jumped in, "You mean the one we were planning a couple of months ago for when, you know, those two finally get hitched because that's Eira, his fiancée, sort of...we think." Killian leaned into Eira, "We're all still a little iffy on your guys' relationship. Leon's never been married." Eira's teeth clenched and she turned to Leon, and Nell gave Killian a similar look. "What? I'm not lying. He didn't actually get married."

Leon felt it was best to ignore Eira for the time being, "You think it's seven years ago?" he asked.

"What are you talking about? It *is* seven years ago, or, now. I don't know." He touched his forehead. Eira had stormed off, "And that's Eira?" he said, pointing in the direction she was headed. "She's not even supposed to be here."

Suddenly Eira came storming back with Al jogging quickly behind her. "Fix him, he can't remember anything," she pushed.

"Ah," breathed Al calmly, "yes, I have seen this before. It is a side effect of the Frostfire root. He should be himself soon enough. The quickest I've seen the effects wear off is a few hours, the longest...a month."

"A month!" cried Eira. "We can't have him like this for a month."

"Can someone please tell me how we ended up here?" interrupted Theo.

"We were in the Quesnell Pass and—" started Killian.

"What? Whose idiotic idea was it to go in there?" asked Theo.

"Well...you didn't seem to oppose the idea," added Killian.

Theo turned back to the rest of the group and then to one of the few people he knew, "Okay, seriously, what is going on here?" he asked Leon.

"Well, it's a long story."

"Maybe if we fill him in on it, it'll spark his memory," suggested Clea. Theo looked at her and Clea could sense what he was thinking, "I'm Clea, by the way. That's Nell," she pointed.

Killian took a deep breath and turned around as if to compose himself before a speech. He turned around and then began, "It all began a little over a year ago on Eira's twenty-first birthday. She found herself in Talvia, brought back by an ancient magic. Leon found her and brought her to the castle and while she was pretty insistent at first that she didn't want to help us because of some rebelliousness against being told her whole life who she was supposed to be, she finally did agree. Leon introduced her to us, and this god," he rolled his eyes, "we won't go there. We didn't know Clea yet, and after a couple of days, Eira agreed to go on the journey to the Hoarfrost Mountains with us—which was a little on the nose, if you ask me. I mean, was she not going to give into her destiny and defeat the dragon? Anyway, we travelled to Huurre where Leon ran into Arlo and he took us on his ship—"

"Ahem," interrupted Clea.

"Oh yeah, we also met her there. Anyway, it turns out Arlo is a pirate now and we were captured, but luckily we escaped and managed to get to the shores of Evervell where we travelled for a bit, but then Eira got you guys kidnapped, but don't worry, yours truly managed to get you out of it, so you're—"

"Ahem," interrupted Leon this time.

"What? I'm the one that actually got you guys out of there."

"Yeah, but if Boreas hadn't followed us and realized we had been kidnapped, who knows what would have happened?"

"Fine."

"Wait," said Theo, holding up his hand, "who's Boreas?"

"Oh, the god of winter, he was with us too," smiled Clea.

"Guys, come on, can you let me finish telling this story? Thank you. Anyway...so it was a group effort, and we managed to escape. We then found ourselves in the Valley of the Ethereal with the Wintren-elves and Lord Evian. We stayed for their massive party thing and frankly, I don't remember most of it, but at the end, these too finally fell for each other," he put his arms around Eira and Leon, "and we headed into the rest of the valley. Then Eira and Leon got separated from us, which was probably for the best because it gave them the chance to work through their issues and let their love for one another grow deeper and deeper—I'm just assuming, I don't really know what happened between you two, I wasn't there. Anyway, we eventually met you guys in Glasera, and lo-and-behold, that is where Clea is from. We dealt with the leader of the city who was kind of a dick, hoarding the city's riches for himself and eventually we tried to escape but got caught in the foothills of the mountains so Leon made the heart-wrenching decision to let Eira go up the mountain without us to try to defeat the dragon—which was poor judgement on your part, I'm going to say it," he glanced at Leon. "So Eira, obviously, did something to piss off the dragon because before we knew it, she was descending on the city wreaking all the kinds of havoc you would expect from a dragon. Then Eira comes back and she knows the dragon's weakness and we go with her back up the mountain to defeat the dragon, but before we go Lord Evian gives her this cool sword made from a dragon scale, but she decides not to hurt the dragon. Then Leon gets stabbed—and I would like to point out that two out of the three of us," he motioned to him, Theo, and Leon, "have been stabbed since we met you," he looked to Eira, "and I'm not liking my odds. Anyway, you and I take down the men who did it, but Leon's lying on the ground and Eira's screaming and there's really nothing we can do. But then, the dragon saves his life—I know, crazy, right? Anyway, the dragon leaves and the snow comes back and everyone's happy—yay! Leon and Eira are all like, 'I love you', and 'I love you too'." He started to make kissing noises and rubbing his hands on his shoulders.

"Don't ever do that again," said Leon.

Killian continued, "Okay, so then Eira is crowned queen and a year goes by, then after her birthday this dude shows up claiming he's the rightful heir to the Talvian throne and he has the Diamond of Azul and threatens to release the Blue Queen if she doesn't hand over the throne. Well, Eira ain't a fool—she's like, 'hell no, I'm not giving you my crown, you're going to have to do better than that, stupid head'."

"I didn't say that," Eira whispered to Leon.

"So then he does. He's got bottled moonlight and is going to release the Blue Queen unless Eira marries him and makes him king. So then Leon is all like, 'there's no other way, I'm not going to marry you anymore', so he leaves, which frankly we're all still a little mad about. I mean you gave up kind of quickly," he turned to Leon. "But then we find out that he actually left to get help but made it seem like he abandoned her, so Lord Dundan would think she was distraught and that she was really going to marry him. Which she almost did, but then instead of signing a marriage license, he signed a document of regicide and was arrested. But obviously, that's not where the story ends. We go to find Leon and when we do, we find out that Dundan escaped and did in fact release the Blue Queen, who has now taken over all of Talvia, but luckily Gideon sent us a secret message to come and find this owl guy who healed you, but to find him we had to travel through the Quesnell Pass where we were kidnapped by this sultan guy who also wanted to marry Eira off to her son, and Leon was all like, 'hell no, I'm going to be the only one who marries her', so he competed in this crazy race thing through the desert and won, but then the sultan thought he cheated so a battle broke out and we managed to escape but you got stabbed. We were convinced it was the end for you, buddy, but then these owls brought us here and you lived. And now you're all caught up."

"Okay, that was a lot of information to get in three minutes," said Theo.

"Did anything ring a bell?" asked Killian.

"Nope."

"Well, that's okay, maybe just take some time to process everything and let us know in a bit," said Clea.

Theo wandered off to process, leaving the rest of the group to kill time on their own.

Eira spent the whole day alone, hanging out with the owls. She found that they were pretty good company; listening to her ranting and trying to work through everything. Eventually, she fell asleep on the hay padding the floor and before long she awoke to the moon high in the sky, radiating its beams into the cave. She got up and headed back to where the rest of the group were probably fast asleep—they were. She saw Clea, Killian, Nell, and Theo all fast asleep on the floor of the cave where Al had made them some comfortable beds with extra blankets and hay. Leon however, was nowhere to be seen. She scanned her surroundings, trying to see where he was. Then she saw the figure of a man sitting on a small ledge that opened the cave to the outside world. She knew it was him by the way he was sitting. She hesitated for a moment, wondering if she should go over there, but finally got up the courage to go and interrupt him from whatever he was thinking about.

"Hi," she said sheepishly. He looked up and smiled, but didn't say anything. "Do you mind if I join you? I slept all afternoon and I'm not really tired now."

"Sure," he smiled.

"I wanted to say I'm not upset about earlier, but you do need to tell Killian and Theo that they need to work on not blurting out your past secrets around me," she joked.

"Yeah, they really suck at that. It's not a secret though, it just never came up. It's not like I was actively hiding it from you. We never really asked each other about our pasts. But I'm sorry you had to find out about it like that. The reason I never told you was because it was seven years ago and a *big* mistake. Like Killian said, it ended almost as quickly as it started."

"Was she your girlfriend?"

"Well, I wasn't exactly in the habit of proposing to women I don't know," he joked, "but honestly, she wasn't really. I mean I guess some people would say that, but we were more friends that—never mind," Eira rolled her eyes. "Anyway, we never really stayed together long enough to be more, and she just happened to be the one around when I was being stupid. I was young and had just had a huge fight with my dad about the duty to Talvia I had to uphold. I hadn't even met you yet and was sick of being told that marrying you was the only future I was allowed to have. So, I wanted to show him that I was in charge of my own future. It obviously didn't work out. I didn't love her or want to be married and she felt the same. My dad didn't realize that being groomed for something and wanting that something are two different things."

"Hmm, I kind of know that feeling," she smiled.

"Yeah. In all honesty, Eira, I haven't thought about her since we broke up. Especially when you came into my life. As much as my dad annoys me sometimes, and don't ever tell him I said this—he was right."

"About what?"

"That you are the only future I would ever want." She let out a groan and smiled as he leaned in and kissed her.

When the sun rose, Leon and Eira had fallen asleep on the ledge and awoke to the screech of the owls in the cave. They wandered back into the cave and found the rest of the group eating breakfast.

"Well, he seems back to normal," announced Killian.

Eira smiled, "How are you feeling?" she asked Theo.

"A little sore. I'm much better, though."

"Good."

"Well, maybe now Leon can see if he can manage to persuade bird boy over there to help us along on this journey," said Killian, nodding to Alareison throwing meat to the owls.

"Wait," said Eira, "none of you tried to convince him to help us? What were you all doing yesterday?"

"We were trying to get Theo's memory back—you're welcome, by the way," said Killian.

"Why me?" asked Leon.

"Because you're the one who manages to convince people to do things. I don't know how you do it—it's kind of annoying, honestly."

Leon rolled his eyes, "I'll do my best," said Leon looking at the owls, "but he doesn't seem willing to help."

Leon tried to plead with Alareison, but his efforts were no more successful than Eira's had been. She sat watching the two debate as their arms moved up and down in conversation.

"If anyone has a chance of convincing him, it's Leon," said Killian, sitting beside Eira. "He can be very persuasive at times."

"Yeah, tell me about it," said Eira.

Nell joined as well, and they all watched the silent scene play out in front of them, for they were too far away to hear what the two were saying. From the looks of it, their best guess was that Leon was losing the battle.

With little luck, Leon made his way back over to where the group was waiting to hear the bad news they had known all along was coming. Al was a very kind old man, but Eira could tell he could be as stubborn as a mule by the way he talked. He was old and wise and knew the ways of the world and was not willing to accept someone else's reality in place of his own.

"What are we supposed to do now?" asked Eira to Leon later that day as they were packing to leave their refuge.

"I wish I knew. If I had just stuck with you in the first place and trusted that we could find a way out, none of this would have happened."

"It's not your fault. Well...not entirely," she joked, trying to make light of the situation.

"Well, we can't just head home and live our life under Ophelessa's and Dundan's dictatorship. I am technically still the queen. If we go back, they're going to have to do something to get rid of me for Dundan to formally take over, and the people—"

"The people are under Ophelessa's spell. Few of them are still on your side, not enough to revolt or anything like that. Besides, even if they were all on your side, no one is going to go against the Blue Queen."

"Well, she can't just kill everyone. What good is it being a ruler and having all that power with no one to rule?"

"Our best bet is to get our allies, the neighbouring countries, and try to outnumber her efforts. Everyone has a weakness—we just need to find hers."

They left it at that for the night and hoped morning would bring some revelation. Al was feeding his owls and overheard their conversation. In his mind, Eira was going into a battle she would never win so it was better to just not fight at all, but as he learned that night from the group, you fight to fight. There is always a chance you can win when you have more of a need to.

The time Theo needed to heal had passed, and they had outstayed their short welcome in the Land of the Owls. All agreed it was time to be moving on. To where—they did not know. It seemed the journey was over for them. Perhaps they would simply head home.

"I have changed my mind," announced Al, meeting them at the entrance to the owl's secret home. "I am an old man and I may not have many years left. I have decided there is no better way to live them out than fighting once again—to give you a chance to make Talvia all it deserves to be once again. I have to warn you though, this will be like no battle you have seen before. You thought you were out of the woods when you defeated that dragon but, I'm afraid your greatest battle is about to begin; the battle for Talvia—for your throne."

"I would gladly go up against Sirona again," joked Eira. "This chick seems like she has some issues."

Al reached into his pocket and pulled out a small silver whistle. It was long and skinny and he handed it to Eira, "Here. If you are ever in need, just blow the whistle and we'll be there to help our queen."

"Thank you," smiled Eira.

"I hope you are ready," said Al.

"I'm always ready," replied Eira.

"Good, because we are going to need some help first."

The owls dropped them off as far as they wished to go. The group headed out of the hidden valley and one by one they made their way through the long narrow pass until they could see light making its way through an opening in the distance. When they exited the other side, they were standing in Evervell forest, back in Talvia. In the distance, they could see Trillium Nivale and the castle rising above the forest with the morning sun.

"Ah," breathed Alareison, "I do love the smell of the fresh winter air. Well, we best be moving on," he added, heading in the direction that would lead them farther into the forest.

"Where are you going?" asked Eira. "Shouldn't we make our way back to the castle and get ready to fight?"

"I appreciate your faith in me," responded Alareison, "but, we are going to need more help than you think to defeat that witch." Eira stared at him, waiting for more and then he turned to head into the forest. "It is time we pay a visit to an old friend of mine. I believe you have met him before."

"You ever get that déjà vu feeling?" asked Killian.

The journey through Evervell felt a lot like the first time, although this time it was significantly colder and whiter. They walked for a day until they finally reached a part of the forest Eira began to recognize. When they reached a small opening in the foliage, she knew where they were. As the branches of the trees were pulled apart, what was revealed was a vision of golden branches lining a snowy path. They walked down the path for quite some time until they came to the grand gates of the kingdom of the Wintren-elves that Eira had dreamt about seeing again ever since she gazed upon them for the first time not long ago. It was just as Eira had remembered it; the woven root gates sprinkled with frost hiding the town nestled behind.

She was back in the Valley of the Ethereal, and Lord Evian was happy to see them again. They were glad to be welcomed in, and Killian was glad to be reunited with the hot springs.

"Welcome, friends of this realm," said Evian, as he held his arms open. "And...Alareison, my old friend," he was slightly taken aback at the sight of him. "I sense you are here for no great evening of reminiscing, though. There is something dire plaguing your mind."

"Yes, there is something dire on the mind—on all our minds," he responded.

"Well, come in and eat and drink and we will discuss this matter."

"Wow," said Nell as they walked into the halls of Lord Evian's palace. "You guys weren't kidding—this place is nice."

"Wait 'till you see the hot springs," added Killian.

Dinner was served on the terrace that evening with the snow softly falling and the roaring fires in the fireplaces keeping them warm. They all sat around a great round table under the archways draped in branches silvered by the frosts. Evian had called Olwen, High Lady of the fairies to join in the discussion.

"I understand that the day we had all feared is upon us," began Evian.

"Yes, Ophelessa has indeed been released and has taken control of the Talvian kingdom," said Alareison.

"Can you help us?" asked Eira

"I am afraid, my dear child, that I can do no more than you can, other than provide you with a greater number of soldiers," replied Evian. "Ophelessa has taken control of your armies along with an army Lord Dundan has spent years accumulating. We are gravely outnumbered."

"There must be something we can do? There has to be some hope of us being able to defeat her?"

"The hope we have lies within you, Your Majesty," replied Evian.

"We have sent a call for aid to our neighbouring countries," added Leon.

"Ophelessa cannot simply be defeated by brute force. She must be brought down by powers only one of us holds," Olwen motioned to Alareison. "You must trap her inside the diamond once more. It is the only way."

"Even if Alareison is able to contain her again, we must make sure she is destroyed for good this time," added Evian.

"How do we do that?" asked Leon.

"We must destroy the diamond after she is inside it, which is a task that is easier to say than accomplish. There is only one thing strong enough to break that diamond; another diamond."

"What?" questioned Eira, looking around the room for an answer.

"I know where your mind is going my friend but, that is an unknown journey," responded Alareison.

"Oh, well, you know," nodded Leon, "while were in the journeying mood..."

"What is he talking about?" asked Eira.

"There is a dagger, a dagger made of solid diamond that is strong enough to destroy the Diamond of Azul into a thousand pieces but, it is hidden, and the journey to it will be a long and arduous one," said Olwen.

"Typical," huffed Killian.

"Do you mean The King's Dagger?" asked Clea. Eira looked at her, wondering what she meant. "The King's Dagger is a story told to us as children about the greed of man. We all know it," she motioned to Leon, Theo, and Killian.

"I don't," replied Eira, and Nell gave a similar look of confusion.

"This is no children's book, though," began Clea. "This story has been passed down for generations. It is told, but none have written it down." Clea began to tell the tale of an ancient king and his most precious possession, "Once upon a time, the first Queen of Talvia had a dagger made for her husband, the king; a dagger carved from solid diamond. When the queen presented the dagger to the king and he gazed upon its splendour for the first time, he was instantly mesmerized by it. It became his most prized possession, and he thought himself invincible with the power it contained. The dagger was strong enough to pierce the toughest dragon's scales with the ease of slicing through softened butter. Everyone in the kingdom admired the dagger and when the king rode by with the dagger displayed on this belt for all to see, he felt as though he possessed all the power in the world. As time went on, the hypnotic effects the dagger had on the king were beginning to alter his mind. Its beauty was too much for him to let go of and he began spending his days cradling the dagger and caring only for its well-being. He became so tormented by his greed of the priceless dagger that he began to neglect his own family and duties to his kingdom."

"It was like that movie we watched," interrupted Leon, "with the ring and...Smuggle?" Eira chuckled and shook her head at him, then let Clea continue.

"One day, his kingdom was invaded by men from the North. When they took hold of the kingdom, they kidnapped the king's eldest son and held a ransom for him. They wanted the dagger. The king was horrified by their proposition and offered the men all the riches he had in the royal vault but, they only wanted the dagger. The king was not going to part with the dagger and his son was killed. When he saw the lifeless body of his son lying on the ground, he realized what the greed of the richness of the dagger had done to him. The king fled deep into the forest with the dagger until he came to a small lake hidden in the mountains. Exhausted by the journey and on the brink of death from the sorrow building in his heart, he fell to the ground by the water's edge. At that moment, a woman came walking across the water toward him—a figure as pure as the white snow. She was the guardian of the lake. The king told her what had happened and how he wished he had not been so greedy as to give up the life of his son. The woman told the king that if he tossed the dagger into the middle of the lake and never returned for it, she would bring his son back to life but, if he ever tried to get it back or showed that kind of greed again, she would take away the life she returned. The king agreed and threw the dagger into the middle of the lake. At that moment, he had a sense of relief wash over him. His heart was no longer filled with sorrow and he made the journey back to his kingdom where he found his son waiting for him. The king lived out his days with his family around him, providing him with all the riches a man needs in life. His eldest son became king after his death and ruled his kingdom for many years with the lessons he had learned from his father, never taking what he had for granted."

"When word had spread about the king throwing the dagger into a lake in the mountains, many tried to find the lake and retrieve the dagger for themselves, but none could ever find it," added Al. "The lake can only be found by those in a time of great need. The king was in great need of ridding himself from his greed and it is said that the guardian of the lake will only reveal the dagger to the one who will use it for their own selfless reasons. To this day, none has ever found the lake or the dagger. The world is not yet in need of that power."

"So, the dagger is real then?" asked Theo. "I thought it was just some story we were told as children to teach us about the dangers of greed?"

"Well, where do legends come from?" answered Olwen. "They were truth once, even if the truth of them has been long forgotten."

"I believe the world is once again in need of that power," said Evian.

A knock came at Eira's door later that evening. She shuffled across the stone floor to where the large wooden door was. Eira pulled open the door to reveal a smiling Nell on the other side. "Can I come in?" she asked.

"Sure," Eira answered, stepping aside and letting Nell in. The two sat on the couch in the seating area and Eira could see in Nell's eyes that something was worrying her. "What's up?" Eira asked.

Nell shrugged, "Not much, just wondering what's going to happen when I go home tomorrow. I don't like the thought of leaving you here to deal with all of this. Man, if I knew when I met you that one day I'd be hanging out in a magical land fighting a witch, I might have given you the cold shoulder," she joked.

Eira smiled, "Ah, come on. Think of how boring your life would have been then." The two friends shared a look they both knew had deep feelings behind it. "But really, how are you doing with all of this?"

"I don't know how to feel. I know I'm not cut out for this, but I can't help but feel like I'm abandoning you, and...what if I never see you again?"

"Nell, you're not abandoning me. I have everyone here to support me and fight with me. Let's face it, you'd be completely useless in a battle," Eira mocked, and Nell couldn't help but grin at her joke. "Although you did take Killian down in training. Not many can do that."

"I think he was just pretending." Nell sighed, "Look, Eira, you're my best friend and I love you so much. My life significantly improved when I met you and I can't bear the thought of something happening to you."

"I know, but this is my life now. Honestly, it was always my life—I was just running from it. I know you've never seen me fight, but I'm kind of good at it," Eira winked. "I'm so lucky to have a friend like you, and I know we will see each other again."

"I hope so. The shitty thing is, if you all die, I won't know. Finally, enough time will go by and I'll assume the worst, but—"

"Nell! Don't think that way."

"Sorry. I can't help it."

"Look, let's just talk about something else. Have a good old-fashioned Nell and Eira gab sesh about guys or whatever," Eira smiled.

"Yeah, okay. So, I guess you forgave Leon?"

"For the most part. I'm still slightly angry with him, but damn he's good at making me forget that," Eira grinned.

Nell chuckled, "Well, at least there's that."

They chatted for a long while, reminiscing and making plans for the future, when they were interrupted by Leon walking in. "Oh, hi," he said to Nell when the girls turned to look at him from their position on the couch. She stared daggers back at him, then smiled at Eira and strode out of the room. "Is she ever going to forgive me?" asked Leon, walking over to the couch.

Eira stood, "Eventually," she kissed him.

Nell made her way down the hall and knocked on another door. "Well, well, well. Couldn't stay away, huh?" asked Killian as he leaned against the doorframe.

"I just left Eira and I'm leaving tomorrow, so I figured I should say goodbye," replied Nell.

"A proper goodbye, or...?" She gave him a smirk and he reached a hand out and pulled her inside. The door clicked shut as he pushed her against the other side of it. He gripped the back of her thighs and swiftly lifted her up, her legs wrapping around his waist. He moved a hand to her head and tangled his fingers in her hair, pulling her lips to his. Killian's broad chest pushed into her and she could feel every inch of him pressed against her, his warmth radiating onto her body.

He didn't stop there, though. He wasted no time moving them over to the bed and throwing her onto it. "Gods I missed you," he breathed as he took in every curve of her, sprawled on the bed. He crawled over her and captured her lips in another embrace, then moved to her neck, devouring it with kisses. "You have no idea how much it's been killing me to not be able to have you."

Nell smirked, "Well, I'm here now. What do you want to do to me?"

He moved to look at her face; a devilish grin growing on his. "I don't know if you can handle everything I want to do to you."

"Try me."

His desire for her was obvious as he pressed against her. Their eagerness for this pleasure was only intensifying as Killian kneeled on the bed, pulling Nell up with him. She tore his shirt from him and he had hers off before she could reach for the button on his pants. Every taught muscle of his abs was only drawing Nell's gaze lower until she had no choice but to throw him back on the bed and remove the piece of clothing keeping her from what she desired. He sat against the headboard and pulled her on top of him, reaching for her neck and bringing her lips to his once again and kissing her with all the passion he had in him.

When the bed was sufficiently in disarray, and they were completely and utterly satisfied, Nell nestled into Killian's arms and drew small circles with her finger on his chest. "You're not going to do something stupid like die on me, right?" she quietly asked.

Killian smiled, "Not a chance," and kissed the top of her head.

Eira could barely sleep that night. She awoke early in the dawn of the next morning after drifting in and out of a difficult slumber for the last couple of hours. She left a peacefully slumbering Leon and stood on the balcony looking out over the Wintren-elves' kingdom and to the luminescent moon casting a white wash onto her surroundings and the world below.

"Do you really believe she can find it?" Eira heard Alareison ask Lord Evian. She leaned carefully over the balcony, for the voices were coming from below.

"She is the only one who can," answered Evian. "She needs the dagger to save her people from the brutality Ophelessa has caused. The lake will only be revealed to her."

Eira stepped back from the balcony for a moment and thought about the words she had just heard coming from Lord Evian's lips. She knew what she felt in her heart was the right thing to do but it was difficult for her to put her faith in something that until today, only existed in legend. If the dagger did still exist, lying at the bottom of a hidden lake in the mountains, then she was going to try her best to find it.

Later that morning, Eira awoke again after managing a few more hours of sleep. Leon was gone already, so she had the opportunity to pack for the journey to the lake. When everything was crammed into her pack and it was almost bursting at the seams, she made her way down from her room in Evian's palace. She found everyone around the same table they were last night, discussing strategy and other aspects of war. Leon was leaning over the table with his sword leaning against his hip, and Eira could not help but smile at the sight of it. She always liked the way he looked when he was dressed, with his sword at his side. Leon looked up when she walked into the room.

"You're packed already?" he asked. "Are you planning on leaving us?"

"Yes," answered Eira. "I'm going to find the King's Dagger. It is our only hope of defeating Ophelessa for good." They all stared up at her unsure of how to respond. "Here," she said, handing a sealed letter to Leon, "Send this to Trillium Nivale. It is a final plea for negotiations with Lord Dundan and Ophelessa. If they do not agree to the terms outlined, which I suspect they won't, then we will be ready for a battle." Leon took the note from her hand, still looking quite perplexed.

"Eira, do you know what you are doing? Ophelessa's soldiers are marching into the fields below Trillium Nivale. There is no way back to the kingdom without a battle. She is not going to let anyone through without a fight. They're just waiting for us to try."

"Send the message for her to back down. We'll give them one last chance and then we will meet their armies on the borders of Trillium Nivale and we will be ready to fight."

"How will we do that?" asked Killian. "We are greatly outnumbered."

"We have the Valley of the Ethereal on our side," Eira shot a smile to Lord Evian who nodded in reply, "and we have our allies from the neighbouring lands. We just might be able to pull this off. Give me three days to come back with the dagger and if I'm not back by then, start without me."

"Just start a war without you?" asked Theo. "You're our queen!"

"It is the only option we have. You don't need me to trap Ophelessa inside the diamond again. Three days, that is all I'm asking."

"It will take them longer than that just to take the message to Trillium Nivale and return with Lord Dundan and the Blue Queen's reply," added Leon. "And don't think you're going to find this dagger by yourself."

"Not if you hurry, and I need you here to fight," answered Eira.

"I'm going with you and that is final." Eira gave a slight smile at his response, for she was hoping he would say that. Leon turned to Alareison and Lord Evian, "Now, how do we find this thing?"

"That is where I may be able to help you," said Lord Evian as he stood from the table and started walking toward the doorway. They followed closely behind him until they came to a hidden outdoor room; a room that looked as though it had once been indoors, but all that stood now were the ruins. It was filled with odd objects and artifacts Eira did not recognize at all, covered with the snow falling around them. There were a few books, but everything looked very mystical in nature and the snow never seemed to melt when it landed on an object. At the back of the room there was another door, but it did not lead into another room. It was away from the wall and simply sitting in its doorframe. "I find the fastest way to travel is through here." He opened the door and to Eira, it looked like all that was there was what she had expected to be on the other side, as if the door led nowhere. Eira smiled.

"While it will not lead you to the lake itself," began Evian, "I suspect it will get you close. And," he turned to Nell, "I will get you back you your world."

After Leon had packed all they would need for the journey in the saddlebags of one of Lord Evian's horses, the two stood side by side staring at the vines and the rest of the garden behind the open door.

"Please be careful," said Nell, embracing her friend in a hug. "I'll see you again after all of this, right?"

"Of course," Eira smiled back. She then turned to hug the rest of her friends.

"Be careful, darling," smiled Killian. "And don't do anything I wouldn't do," he turned to Leon.

Leon took Eira by the hand and led her through the doorway. When they stepped through, they did not hit the vines but were back somewhere in Evervell forest, in the mountains to the north. Eira turned around to see the door was still there, but only for a moment. Her view into the room in Lord Evian's garden and the faces of her friends faded out of sight as the door closed from the other side and they were left somewhere in the mountains towering over Talvia.

Eira assumed that with her being the queen, and needing the dagger for selfless reasons, finding the lake would not be as difficult as it was turning out to be. With all the other magical passages and whatnot in Talvia, she hoped that if she continued in a direction that felt right, she would eventually stumble upon it. However, that did not seem to be the case. She led Leon through the forest, up, down, and around the mountain, hoping she would find some clue, but truthfully, she had no idea where she was going. Finally, she had to sit down and think.

"Have you finally decided to stop leading me around in circles?" Leon smiled.

"Because you know where this lake is?" Eira responded with a prickly tone to her voice.

"No but, I don't think just wandering around aimlessly is the best way to find it." He sat down beside her, "Getting ourselves lost along with the lake isn't going to solve anyone's problems." Just then, Eira raised her head in a manner conclusive with someone having an epiphany. "What?" asked Leon.

"That's just what we need," she stood up and started looking round.

"What is?"

"To be lost. Sometimes you need to be sufficiently lost before you can find what you're looking for."

"I hate to break it to you but, I think we've been sufficiently lost for about an hour."

****

Killian rode as fast as he could back to the borders of Trillium Nivale with Eira's message safely stowed in his jacket pocket. The speed of the elven horses was matched only by one—Harwin. When he was closing in on the fields, he could see Lord Dundan's armies rising from beyond the lake. From the distance, it looked like the field was littered with figures and as he rode closer, he could see the camps where the soldiers were waiting for orders to fight. Luckily, with only him and his horse, he could ride in unnoticed and unharmed.

The horse's hooves clacked over the cobblestone of the large bridge connecting Trillium Nivale castle with the rest of the kingdom, and Killian pushed his way through the doors with a guard on either side of him. He entered the grand hall and noticed a familiar face watching him from behind one of the columns. It was Ceilidh. She was carrying a tray of food back to the kitchen when she noticed him and stopped to share a smile wrought with hopelessness.

"This man comes with word from the queen," said one of the guards to Lord Dundan and Ophelessa who were sitting atop their stolen thrones.

"I am the queen!" snapped the blue witch.

"I'm sorry, Your Majesty," said the guard, backing away. "A message from the former queen."

Ophelessa stepped down from her pedestal and walked over to Killian, snatching the message from his hand, "So, your precious little queen thinks she still has power over me?" She made her way over to the fireplace and tossed the message inside watching the fire catch its new fuel and engulf it into a mess of flames and ashes. "Well, that is something, isn't it? You tell her that if she wants her kingdom back, she is going to have to pry it from my cold dead hands. We are ready for war, is she?"

Killian looked to Lord Dundan who was standing behind Ophelessa. He looked as though he was shocked at the cruelty Ophelessa displayed. He tried to give off a sense that he still held some of the power in the kingdom but it was clear to Killian that the Blue Queen was less doing his bidding, and more taking over the kingdom for herself.

Killian made his way back to the Valley of the Ethereal just as fast as he had made it back to Trillium Nivale to deliver Ophelessa's message of impending war and informed them of what they were up against.

"They have an army like we never imagined, ready and waiting in the foothills of Trillium Nivale," said Killian. He looked around at who he was addressing. "Eira is not back yet?"

"I'm afraid not, which means we must start without her. Our allies have received our call for aid and will be on our borders within a day. We must gather our troops and make for the fields on the Western shores of Lake Isas. That is where we will set up camp and meet our allies," said Lord Evian. "I will wait here until Eira returns, and if she doesn't in the next few days, then I will head out and meet you in the fields."

They gathered all they would need for the journey and made their way out of the Valley of the Ethereal and into Evervell forest. The procession of elven soldiers marched through the forest in their golden armour. When they made it across the massive lake, they set up camp in the fields and waited for help to come. It did not take the fairies long to join them, riding the great polar bears of the North. They were in their human form; ready to fight. Within another day, the allies from the Spring and Autumn Countries added their numbers to the group and before long, they had a number large enough to stand a chance against the army waiting for them on the other side.

In marched the Syysian guard astride their horses and great horned beasts that resembled large moose, but far less clumsy looking. These animals were bread for speed and stamina in war. They were larger than a horse, standing at least twenty-five hands high, and muscular for bowling down the enemy like a bull with their large horns. The army was dressed in the colours of fall; red, copper, and gold. They carried their flags high above the marching horses, bearing their crest. It was a shield with a wolf's head crowned with golden branches and copper leaves.

Next was the Kevatian army with their horses and warriors dressed in shades of lavender with silver armour that displayed embellishments in yellow and rose gold. They carried their flags high as well, displaying their shield. Their banners were yellow with their crest in the centre; a single bird coming from the twists of flowers and leaves surrounding it. The shield itself was yellow with the design in silver.

When the captain of the Syysian guard joined, he greeted the others, introducing himself as Captain Gherrard. He was a large man with golden brown hair and a look that none in battle would want to be up against. When the man leading the Kevatian army dismounted his horse, a large gasp came from Killian, for this man was none other than his cousin, Lord Arlen.

"Arlen!" he greeted his cousin with a hug and a whack at his backside. "Look at you, I see you have come to fight for the best country around, and wearing lilac, no less," Killian laughed. Arlen looked a bit like Killian with the same auburn hair and muscular build, however he was far taller than his cousin, towering a few inches above him. Killian was already tall, so this guy seemed enormous next to him.

"If this were the best country around, it wouldn't need us to fight for it," responded Arlen.

"At least we don't look like a bunch of tulips riding around. You can get away with that in the Spring Country. This is the Winter Country. We're tough here."

"You're not even from here. And you think we're not tough, eh? Just 'cause we have a few baby animals running around? I'll tell you one thing; real men wear pastels." They were just about to start a tussle when they were interrupted by Theo.

"Guys!" he called out to them. "There is no need to start this now."

"Who does he think he is, saying I'm not a real man? I have no problem getting in touch with my feminine side," Killian said to Theo as they walked away together.

"Oh, we know," agreed Theo.

"I'll show him. Do you have anything pink to wear? Baby blue, maybe?"

That night, all the captains from the various armies met with Killian, Theo, and Clea in the safety of the large elven tent, set up far back from the front lines and where the soldiers were setting up their camps. The unbroken field below Trillium Nivale was alit with the light coming from various camps of both armies. From afar, it looked as though the fields were sprawled with fireflies, glowing in the still darkness. The conversation coming from the elves' palace of a tent was growing more and more heated as the night went on. The inside of Lord Evian's tent did not look as one would expect a modest shelter for the battlegrounds would look. This encampment was set up by the Wintren-elves and they really knew how to camp. All tents on the inside were almost like small apartments equipped with beds and washing basins in an elaborate manner. The elvish one, which would be Lord Evian's as soon as he arrived, was bigger than Eira's apartment back in Adelaide. It contained different rooms and in the main area there was a large table where they pored over maps and strategized for the upcoming battle.

"Her armies expand across the entire countryside beneath Trillium Nivale. We will have to attack from various sides if we want the best chance of beating her armies," said Captain Gherrard.

"She will most likely remain in the castle until the fight is over. If we want a chance at putting her back inside that diamond, we need access to her and the diamond," said Arlen.

"She's wearing the diamond, as far as I know, but I don't know if she'll bring it onto the battlefield with her. Either way, we need to lure the Blue Queen from the castle and get her on the front lines. We cannot destroy her if she stays hiding in that castle," said Killian.

"How are we going to do that? She has an army to fight for her. She doesn't seem the type to come down and fight for herself and risk losing the throne," said Clea.

"Leave that to me," said Alareison. "I believe that is where I will be of the greatest use to you."

"What do you mean? You're going to destroy her, aren't you?" asked Killian.

"I will do my best but, I doubt Ophelessa will refuse the chance to defeat the one who imprisoned her so many years ago. She will be more than eager to exact her revenge."

"Then that's what we're going to do," said Theo. "We'll start the battle with you and once she sees we have you fighting on our side, she will move to the battlefield herself."

"And then you'll destroy her, right?" asked Killian.

"And then I will do my best to get your kingdom back," answered Alareison. "I will do my best."

16

When Eira was a little girl, her aunt Feya gave her a beautiful gift for her tenth birthday. It was a little silver bracelet with flower charms hanging from it. Nothing significant but, she loved it so much and cherished it not letting any of her friends borrow it. It was the closest she had ever come to receiving jewellery from a mother figure, and it meant the world to her. One day she was playing in the back fields and realized it had fallen off of her wrist. She had tiny wrists as a child and was usually very careful as to not let it slip off. She searched all around but could not find it. Crying, she made her way to Feya, devastated at her loss. Feya dried her tears and told her that nothing is ever completely lost—it knows where it is. If you retrace your steps, you will probably find it, and if not, give it time.

Things are often found when you're not looking for them. Eira never managed to find the bracelet until years later when she was getting ready to leave for Australia and discovered it had fallen into a crack in the floorboards beside her bed. She had long forgotten about the bracelet and it was far too small to fit her anymore, but the sight of it again made her smile and realize it was right there, under her feet, all along. For whatever reason, this event from her childhood popped into her mind as she and Leon were wandering through the woods.

The snow was falling heavily through the trees of Evervell. Eira and Leon had been walking for a day now without luck. Eira was so sure that if they got lost enough, the lake would appear to them, but it was difficult to tell if they were indeed lost or because they were trying to get themselves lost it was, in fact, impossible to. Then, thinking of the story from her past she thought that if the dagger was ready to be found, it would be. They simply needed to stop looking. The journey was getting to the both of them and Eira was beginning to feel that she was just out on a hopeless mission.

"Are you ready?" asked Leon, as he circled around her in the training room of the castle with sword in hand.

"Please, I was born ready," answered Eira. With a swift movement, she advanced on Leon and her sword clanged in the air against his. They were in battle now.

"You need to move your left foot more," said Leon, pointing to it with the tip of his sword, "like this."

"Stop stalling. You're just afraid I'm going to beat you again," smiled Eira.

"Hardly." She took a swing at his head and he ducked just in time with an expression of shock across his face, then swung his sword back at hers. He was fighting with more force now, like an actual opponent, and was backing her off of the mat. She swung around behind him and managed to get her position back. She lunged her sword at him but he knocked it out of her hand, grabbing her hand in his and spinning her around until she was dipped like in a dance and he was hovering over her.

"See, I told you, you couldn't beat me," he smiled.

"Maybe I wasn't trying to. You're hardly a threat."

"Marry me?" he said quickly and quietly and then dropped his sword and took her in both arms and kissed her.

"Yes," she answered and kissed him again, but when she looked up, she was no longer looking Leon in the face, but Lord Dundan.

Eira sat up inside her tent with her heart pounding as she awoke in a split second from the dream, trying to catch her breath, chest heavy and tight. The sun was just starting to shine through the bows of the evergreen towering above their camp. She took a couple of deep breaths and looked over at Leon, still fast asleep. Slipping on her boots and coat, she went outside to breathe the fresh winter air and clear her head.

When she stepped from the warmth of the tent, a brisk wave of morning air graced her face and as she breathed in, she could feel the cold tightening the inside of her nose. The sun was warm, however, and she stood there for a moment with arms crossed, pondering. She was not really thinking of anything in particular but also not staring absentmindedly into the distance. She was simply in the moment and wished she could stay in it, for in that moment she was not a queen, she was not on a quest to find something, she was not dealing with the thoughts of facing an upcoming battle, she was simply Eira, and that was who she wanted to be. A couple of tears began to stream down her face for a reason she could not figure out. Perhaps the momentary bliss brought on by the beginning of her dream was all that it took. She so desperately wanted things to go back to the way they were when she was play fighting with Leon in the castle.

Suddenly overwhelmed, she could not contain her feelings, and they came pouring out of her. She heard the flap of the tent opening behind her in the silence of the winter's air. She was always amazed at how sound travels in the serenity of Talvia. There is nothing to diminish the tranquillity of it all. All the sound you hear is that of the winter's air.

"Are you okay?" asked Leon, putting a blanket around her.

"I'm fine," said Eira, quickly wiping the tears from her cheeks.

"What's wrong?" pushed Leon.

"You're going to hate me," she replied.

"Try me."

"It's just that all of this is beginning to feel like we're wasting our time. I have no idea why all of you have so much faith in me. I just want to be home, back in my life—our life, not dealing with witches and magical daggers. Maybe you all would have been better off with your father staying as king. What kind of saviour am I that not even a year after I become queen, I lose my kingdom to a horrible oppressor? I think everyone would be better off if I never came back. I just want to be back in my apartment where my biggest problem in life was figuring out what to do with it. I'm not the person you need—I don't think I ever have been."

"Eira," whispered Leon, as he pulled her close and wrapped his arms around her. "We don't need a saviour, we need a queen, and you are a great one." She looked up into his kind hazel eyes and managed a small smile.

"What if I can't find the dagger?"

"Then we will find some other way to defeat her. Maybe it is time we turn back and get ready for the fight. We've been gone for two days now and Theo, Killian, and everyone are probably getting ready for a battle."

"Maybe it is time to stop looking. As long as we have Alareison, we don't need the dagger right away."

They packed up their camp and headed out in the direction they thought would lead them to Lake Isas. After walking for a couple of hours, it was discovered that they indeed had no idea where they were headed. The snow was starting to fall more heavily in large flakes and was almost blinding. As they walked farther, their sight was diminishing, and they were entering a whiteout. Suddenly, Lord Evian's horse gave out a great whinny and raised his front hooves into the air. Leon tried to grab hold of him again and calm him, but the horse was not interested in going where they were headed. Some of the items tied to the horse's back fell off and startled him more, sending him galloping back into the forest in the other direction.

After a few more moments, the snow faded around them and an image was unveiling itself in the distance. It looked to be more mountains, but as Eira and Leon walked toward them, they suddenly found themselves walking right out of where they had come from. When they stopped to get a better look at where they were, they were no longer in the snowy forest.

"Where did all the snow go?" asked Eira.

"I don't know," Leon replied. The two stood there in silence and looked around. They noticed a collection of large boulders and as they walked closer, they could see the shimmer of water coming from behind the giant stones. As they climbed up the boulders and down the other side, they discovered what looked like a small pond, rimmed with rocks, hiding its existence. The entire, snow-less area was small and round, just enough to encircle the pond, and they could still see the snow falling and the white trees in the distance.

"This doesn't look like any lake that would be in Talvia. This must be the one we're looking for. Isn't it funny how when you stop looking for something, it seems to just appear in front of you?" said Leon.

"Great. Well, how do we get the dagger?" asked Eira.

They peered into the crystal-clear water and could see right to the bottom. Scanning the water, Eira finally spotted the dagger lying amongst the rocks on the bottom. "There," she pointed, "I see it. I can't believe it."

"Great, let's go get it," said Leon as he removed his coat and made his way down to the shore of the lake.

"Wait!" called Eira. "This just seems strange to me. We're just going to dive into the water and get it. It seems too easy."

"Well, it wasn't easy finding his place. The lake will only be revealed to someone who needs it. We needed it, so here we are."

"Maybe you should let me go get it."

"Eira, for once will you just let me do something for you?"

"I do. I let you do that stupid race and look what happened." Leon didn't respond. "Fine," she complied. They walked together to the edge of the lake and Leon started to remove his shirt, boots, and pants, and make his way into the water.

"Is it cold?" asked Eira

"Nah, just like a bath," Leon's voice had sharpened in pitch. "In the middle of an iceberg."

He dove into the water and swam over to where the dagger was resting beneath his feet. Treading water, he stuck his head under a couple of times to judge the distance to the bottom and then took a deep breath and dove. The ice-cold water pierced his chest as he held his breath. He almost made it to the dagger the first time, but misjudged how deep it was and had to come up for air. With a larger intake of air filling his lungs, he dove again, this time making it to where the dagger lay. Reaching out his hand, he tried to pick up the dagger but every time he went for it, it was as if his fingers went right through and it remained unmoved, resting on the bottom of the lake. Breaching through the water's surface, he swam back to shore empty handed. He could not stay in the cold water for much longer.

"What happened?" asked Eira as she handed a blanket to the water-logged Leon. He wiped his face then wrapping it around himself for warmth he answered,

"I couldn't get it. Every time I reached for it my fingers went right through it, like it wasn't even there."

"Well, what are we supposed to do now?"

"Maybe you were right," sighed Leon. "Maybe you are the only one who can get it."

"Like Excalibur and King Arthur," stated Eira.

"Who?" asked Leon, looking at her through the drips coming off of his hair and running down his forehead.

"Never mind," she smiled.

"Look, Eira, that water is freezing. You can't stay in there for long," he said as Eira took her boots off. She moved toward the water when they heard a laugh.

"She won't be able to get it either," cackled a couple of ravens who had been watching the whole thing from high above in the trees surrounding the lake. "Stupid humans, only one of royal blood who needs the dagger for a selfless cause can free it from the bottom of the lake." They laughed again, "But go ahead and try."

Eira looked up at the two birds cackling away on their branch and gave them a small smile, wondering what they would do when she returned to the surface with the dagger in hand. She looked back to Leon, giving him a wink and then dove into the water. The water was indeed freezing, and she was having trouble making her way to the centre of the lake. When she was finally over the location of the dagger, she took the biggest breath she could and dove.

Descending into the icy abyss, she could feel the water getting colder around her as she got closer to the bottom. It was far deeper than she had expected from looking down into the clear water from atop the boulders. The water's refractive capabilities had done well to hide how deep the lake truly was. When she finally reached the dagger, it was still glittering in the water as if someone had only placed it there yesterday. The blade was carved from solid diamond and the handle and hilt were silver embossed with various gems. She knew now why the king in the story was so infatuated by it.

Quickly, she scooped it up and made her way back up to the surface. She burst through, gasping for air and stayed there, floating in the water for a moment until she caught her breath. She lifted the dagger out of the water and the ravens who were still watching intently silenced their laughter, shocked at the sight of it. One raven fell off the branch, fainting from surprise, while the other quickly swooped down and snatched the dagger out of her hand. The ravens had spent years looking down at the treasure they could never possess and wanted it desperately for themselves. He flew back up to his nest and dropped the dagger safely inside. Eira had made her way back to shore and was wrapping herself in a blanket as Leon tried to get the dagger back from the ravens.

"Give that back right now!" he called up to them from the base of the tree.

"No, it's mine," replied the raven.

"It's actually not, and we really need that dagger."

"Please give it back," pleaded Eira, but they still would not comply. "I order you to give back that dagger. I am the queen," she stomped her foot.

"They don't care—they're birds," said Leon.

"Great. What are we supposed to do now?"

Leon shrugged his shoulders, "I don't know. Wait for them to fall asleep and take it?"

"We can't wait that long, and how are we supposed to get up in that tree anyway? Maybe we can trade them for it? Do we have anything they might want instead?"

Eira and Leon went back over to their packs and rifled through them, looking for something a raven might want. Both came up empty-handed until Leon thought of something.

"Wait. I might have something." He pulled a small box out of a hidden pocket in his pack and walked over to the tree with it.

"What is that?" asked Eira as she followed behind him trying to peer over his shoulder. He opened the box to reveal a beautiful diamond ring. Eira gasped, "Is that what I think that is?"

"Yes," replied Leon.

"You can't give my engagement ring to a bird."

"I'll get you another one, and I think this is a little more important right now."

"Fine, but can I just see it for a moment?" Eira held the ring box in her hand, relishing over the beauty that was held within. Sighing, she handed it back to Leon and he coerced the ravens into trading the ring for the dagger.

When they turned around with dagger in hand to find their dry clothes, the lake had disappeared around them and they were once again standing in a snow-covered forest. The air temperature instantly dropped significantly and they could feel the icy chill penetrating their wet bodies.

"What happened?" asked Eira. "We're going to freeze out here?"

"I don't know," answered Leon, looking around. Their pile of clothes and bags were just where they had left them on the edge of the lake but, there was no lake to be seen anymore. He walked over and pulled his dry shirt over him and then placed another blanket around Eira. "I guess the lake really does just appear for as long as you need it. Don't worry. I'll make a fire and we'll be dry and warm in no time."

Somehow, Eira did not believe him. The snow was falling more heavily around them and she was sure that they would die of hypothermia if they did not find shelter and more dry clothes soon.

The tent they had with them did not provide much shelter to the blizzard increasing outside. They could not be around the fire and inside the tent at the same time and were forced to choose one. Leon helped Eira into the tent and quickly laid down a bed of blankets. He slowly sat her shaking body down. She was shivering so much she could not form any understandable words. Leon sat close to her and removed his shirt and hers, then held her close under the blankets trying to give her some of his body heat. It seemed to work for a while and when Eira could once again speak he left her to tend to the fire. Eira was getting increasingly tired though, a sign she knew as oncoming hypothermia, and as soon as Leon left, she could not seem to keep warm herself. She lay in the tent, covered by blankets, but her lips were starting to turn blue. Finally, she fell into a deep, blissful sleep, a release from the cold penetrating her body.

When Leon saw that Eira had fallen asleep, he tried to wake her, "Eira, Eira," he shook her but there was no response. "Eira, you need to wake up, honey." He held her in his arms and tried to get her to respond. She had a faint pulse that was slowly fading.

Then there came the crunching sound of footsteps on the snow from outside the tent. He looked up to see a figure approaching their camp. Leon laid Eira back down and took his sword, heading for the opening of the tent. When he threw back the flap, he saw a figure of white before him. He smiled and bundled up Eira, carrying her over to Harwin and placing her on his back.

Then they rode.

Eira awoke to a bright, warm sunlight pouring onto her face. She struggled to open her eyes and when they finally acclimatized to her new surroundings, she saw herself lying in a wooden four-post bed in a small cabin. She could see Leon sitting by the fireplace drinking a mug of something. Slowly, she moved her legs to the side of the bed and was able to push her body up and then finally stand. Taking the extra blanket from the bed and wrapping it around herself, she made her way over to the fire.

Leon looked up, "Hey," he greeted, "you're awake."

"Yeah," she replied, moving to the spot on the couch beside him. "Where are we?"

"A traveller's cabin."

"How did we get here?"

"Now that's an interesting story. You passed out and suddenly Harwin was there."

Eira smiled, "Does he ever do what you say?"

"Apparently not, but I'm thankful he came to find us, otherwise who knows what would have happened. Anyway, he led us here. It was a pretty rough night with you going in and out of consciousness, but finally your body temperature went up and your colour came back. You've been asleep ever since."

"Wow, I don't remember any of that."

"I wouldn't expect you to. How are you feeling now?" he asked.

"Good. Kind of tired still, but I think I've slept for long enough. I'm also kind of hungry."

"I figured you would be. Pancakes?"

"Yes, please," her expression lifted.

The pancakes tasted like the first food she was experiencing in days. She didn't realize how hungry she was until Leon started cooking. The smell wafted through the cabin and she could not get enough. Eira paused for a moment with her mouth full of food, as a new realization popped into her head.

"How long is it going to take us to get back from here?" she asked after swallowing.

"Not long. Apparently we're just on the borders of Evervell, near the mountains. There were some old maps in that desk over there." He moved his head toward a small wooden desk nestled in the corner of the cabin. "I spent most of the night using them to keep me awake. Also, with Harwin, we'll be back in no time. Once you're ready, of course."

"I'm ready now," said Eira, jumping to her feet.

"Eira," he patronized. "You passed out and almost died of hypothermia. I think you should rest a bit more before we go."

"Oh, please—I'm fine."

"While I love your tenacity, I'm putting my foot down. We're staying here another day at least."

"Fine," she smiled. "Then I need more pancakes."

After breakfast, Leon went outside to get more firewood while Eira enjoyed a relaxing, warm bath. She was feeling much better with a full stomach and with the warm water encompassing her body. When she was done, Leon still wasn't back yet, so she changed into some of her warmer clothes and decided to venture outside to look for him. She opened the door and found him right away, chopping wood by the side of the cabin. The cabin was nestled among the evergreen trees and she could see the mountains in the distance. The snow was sparkling in the sun, making her surroundings look like something from a guidebook; the quaint yet luxurious cabin nestled in the woods, secluded from civilization, perfect for a romantic getaway. However, this wasn't exactly that.

"Hey," she caught Leon right after he had swung the axe and two halves of the log went flying.

"Hey," he replied, putting the axe in the chopping stump and then moving over to collect the wood in his arms. Eira grabbed a few pieces, too. "Thanks. I think that should be enough for now." They made their way back to the front door when Leon's yawn caught Eira's attention.

"Did you get any sleep last night?" she asked as they made their way into the cabin and she closed the door behind them.

"Bits here and there, but not much," he responded, placing the logs in their holder by the fireplace.

"You should go sleep. I'm fine now. You need it."

"I'm fine," he responded like a typical man; brushing off how he truly feels.

"No, you're not. Your health is just as important as mine. Go rest. I can make the fire."

"Alright," he finally gave in and made his way over to the bed, taking off his shirt and pants and then crawling into the covers.

As Leon slept, Eira watched the fire dancing around the fireplace. She found some books on a shelf, but none seemed that interesting. She finally decided on a romantic novella with outrageous plot lines and utterly useless characters, but it was still more entertaining than the fire. The sun was setting, and she glanced over to Leon who was still sound asleep. A pleasant feeling washed over her. Being in this cabin with only him made her forget, for just a moment, that she was a queen and in the middle of a war to get her country back. It was like they were an ordinary couple with regular problems like paying the rent and whose parents they were going to visit for the holidays. Nothing else seemed to matter. She forgot what had happened to get them here in the first place and everything they had been through. It almost felt like a vacation, one she secretly wished would never end. Her daydream was broken, however, by the sound of Leon's voice,

"How long was I asleep for?" he asked, sitting up and running a hand through his hair.

"A few hours," she replied. The sun had only just started its descent in the sky, casting the surroundings with a grey glow. He got out of bed and reached for his shirt and pants, pulling them on and then making his way over to where Eira was sitting. He sat down and smiled at her, then looked over to the stove, which had a simmering pot on it. The aroma of stew was in the air.

"Did you make dinner?" he asked. She nodded in response.

"It should be ready now if you're hungry." She closed the book she was reading and walked over to the shelf to put it back. She turned to Leon, who was still sitting on the couch.

"Hey," he started when she looked at him, "what's wrong?" He knew her well enough by now that he could read the expressions on her face, even when she didn't think her face had any expression on it at all.

"Nothing," she replied like she always did. Leon just stared at her. "It's just nice here, is all. It feels like we're back, living a normal life. Like we're just on some weekend getaway. There's no war starting. I didn't almost have my thrown taken from me. You didn't leave. I didn't almost die. Everything. I just wish we could stay here."

He reached a hand out and pulled her down onto the couch with him, "I know. I wish that too and I almost forgot about everything going on also, but we'll get back to this place soon; where we don't have to worry about anything but each other."

His words had a way of calming her, but only temporarily. She knew that tonight, she could think that way, but in the morning, life would be back to the way it was, and she would have those worries again. But, for now, she was happy to be in their brief fantasy. They ate dinner and found a board game in the cabin that they played for a while; neither of them knowing if they were playing it correctly or not.

"Hey," announced Leon during the game, "I think I saw a bottle of wine in the cupboard. You want some?"

Eira smiled, "Sure." He got up and wandered over to the kitchen, coming back a moment later with two glasses and the bottle. He poured the glasses and handed one to Eira. "Thanks," she said, then took a sip. "Mmm, not bad."

"Yeah?" He took a sip. "It is pretty good," he agreed, examining the bottle. "Maybe we should have it at our wedding?" he joked.

"You know, you should really stop talking about our wedding as if we're engaged. You still haven't even asked."

"Hun, again, that's just a formality," he smiled, but it was a smile that had heavy thoughts behind it.

"Sure, whatever." She moved her piece on the game board, "Ha! I think I won."

"Why don't we get married?" he asked, sitting down beside her, completely ignoring her victory.

"What are you talking about?" she turned to him, confused by what he had just said.

"Marry me. Right here, right now."

She stared at him wondering if he was serious or merely playing some twisted prank on her. When he did not respond, she finally did, "Are you seriously proposing to me right now? We can't just get married—we're in the middle of nowhere."

"Actually, we're not that far from the Valley of the Ethereal. Lord Evian could do it. It would only be a minor detour." Eira was still in complete shock at what had just happened. With every new word Leon spoke, she was having a harder and harder time finding her own words. "Eira," Leon took her hands, "I know this isn't the wedding, or the proposal you were hoping for, but I can't go into this battle without knowing you're completely mine. This is going to be the biggest battle we've ever been through and I know I've been dragging my feet and bugging you probably a little too much about this whole marriage thing, but I'm serious. We've both almost died since you've been back. At this rate, we might not make it to a wedding." She smiled at his humour, even though she knew the risks they were taking with this fight could very well be the end of either of them. "I can't wait any longer and I promise that when this is all done, we'll do it the right way; a proper proposal with me down on one knee with an actual ring, and the big celebration with everyone but, for tonight...just marry me."

It was a simple ceremony, with only the four of them, but Eira couldn't imagine it any other way. Feya had done Eira's hair up in an elaborate braided crown around her head with flowers woven into it and the elves had given her a beautiful gown to wear and Leon a handsome suit—not unlike the attire they were dressed in when they first confessed their love for one another on Myrrvintrel. Feya was standing beside her and when Lord Evian had finished, her heart filled again to the fullness it had been craving for so long.

Leon stood in the doorway of their room after the ceremony. Eira turned to him, "What?" she asked, moving farther into the room.

"Nothing," he replied as he shut the door behind him. "It's just weird. The first time we were here you were pissing me off and still not wanting anything to do with me, and now you're my wife."

Wife. Hearing the word escape his lips made Eira happier than she had been in a while. Since before her birthday, since before any of this happened. She was beginning to think that she would never be happy again until all of this was over, but this brief reprieve from the terror and sorrow growing in her heart was all she needed to keep going. She walked back over to him, "Yeah, who could have predicted that?" she teased.

He took her in his arms, "Well, I always hoped it'd be this way. You just took a little convincing."

"Well, you can be pretty convincing."

"I know," he smiled.

"So, what now?" she grinned at him with a sultry twinkle in her eye.

"Well, I think for this to be official, we have to..."

She rolled her eyes, "As if you haven't been wanting to do that all night."

He pulled her even closer to him and captured her lips in a kiss. It was heavy with passion as they hadn't been alone together since the night before the Onyx Race nearly three weeks ago. He then led her over to the side of the bed and pulled her on top of him, tangling his fingers through her hair, slowly removing the flowers woven in and letting them fall on the bed around them. It didn't take them long to be tangled in the sheets and their clothes piled on the floor. Every kiss on her body was a soothing relief to the aching within. The feeling of Leon's embrace was curing all of Eira's trepidation about what was to come for her kingdom—at least for the time being.

When the sun rose in the morning, Eira was right where she wanted to be; in Leon's arms. She awoke to him gently running a finger up and down her nose. Then he kissed it.

"Good morning," he smiled when her eyes opened and she looked up at him.

"Good morning."

"We have to get going," he said in a solemn tone.

"I know," she replied, sitting up.

They packed up their things and met Harwin outside. Leon pulled himself up and over Harwin, who bobbed his head up and down as Leon shifted his weight atop his back. He took the reins to stop Harwin from taking off like a shot—something he would have done if Leon had let him. Eira pulled herself up and over Harwin as well, sitting behind Leon and wrapping her arms around him.

"Are you ready?" he asked.

"As ready as I'll ever be," she responded. Leon kicked Harwin's sides, letting the reins run a bit in his fingers to give the unicorn every bit of freedom he needed.

Harwin galloped through the forest all day. When the sunset light covered the land, they were almost out of the forest, but Harwin needed to rest. He had been running hard for hours, so they stopped for a moment and made a small fire to have some dinner. It was a cloudy evening, and the sky resembled a grey wash. There was no light peeking through anywhere and the gloom was setting in.

Eira climbed to the top of a boulder to get a better vantage point, and she could see Lake Isas in the distance through the trees. When they were almost finished dinner, they heard a loud thunder racing through the land and looked toward the sky. All the birds that were in the trees scattered and a dark cloud erupted into the sky and bled through the white of the other clouds.

"What was that?" asked Eira after the cataclysmic blast had ceased.

"I have no idea, but I don't think it's anything good." They both climbed back to the top of the boulder and looked out to the fields below Trillium Nivale.

"It looks like they're moving," said Leon, "I think the war has begun."

18

In a few hours, Eira and Leon had made it to the centre of the lake and by nightfall they would be at the camp. They could see the size of the camp that Theo, Killian, and the others had set up. The number of soldiers at came to their aid gave Eira a new sense of hope brewing from deep within herself, even though the day was grey and grim.

They could hear the drums of war and every pounding beat was a pounding beat in her heart, mimicking every second ticking by that she was not there to help fight, that she did not know how many of her brave men and women were sacrificing their lives because of her.

Alareison led the troops to the middle of the field atop a white stallion that blended seamlessly into the white surroundings. Beside him were Theo, Clea, and Killian who was wearing a bright pink tunic underneath his leather armour, grinning haughtily at Arlen who was astride his horse beside Killian.

He grinned, "Mine's still bigger," said Arlen.

"What did you say about my horse?" answered Killian.

"You want to tell me what that was about?" asked Clea, leaning over to Theo.

"Don't bother," replied Theo, shaking his head. "His cousin drives him crazy, and it's best not to get between them."

There they sat, astride their horses pawing at the snowy ground and biting their bridles, ready to charge at the oncoming army. Without a moment to waste, the war was upon them. It happened so quickly, none really knew the official starting point, but someone charged forward and another charged toward them from the opposing side and it began. The brave men and women who had gathered to fight for Eira, were doing just that. But fighting their friends and neighbours was another thing entirely. Other people from the very towns and villages some were from had been seduced by Ophelessa's power and forced to fight. The battle was proving to take its toll. Her spell over the people had to be silenced and the only one who could stop its power was Ophelessa herself, by her own accord or by her death. It was clear that this battle was not going to reveal a victor so easily.

Ophelessa and Lord Dundan watched mindfully from the castle's balcony. They watched as their troops lowered slowly in number—but so did Eira's. Ophelessa gritted her teeth as she peered out over the fields below.

"An interesting turn of events, Your Majesty," said Lord Dundan. "It appears as if they did manage to find the very man that imprisoned you the first time."

"I can see that, you dimwitted oaf," sneered Ophelessa. "But I can also see that our little queen is not in their company."

"She did not return with them. Word has spread from the battlefield that she did not arrive with the others. That is good though, is it not?"

"And how is that good for us?" asked Ophelessa. "All of this will be for nothing if she lives."

"We can drive her out. Perhaps she is in hiding."

"She's not hiding! She has too much affection for these people and this land to do that," said Ophelessa.

"Well, how am I supposed to be king now? You promised me you would get rid of her."

Ophelessa walked slowly over to Lord Dundan and grasped his shirt in her hands, "Listen to me, I am queen of this little country now and you do what I say. I will make you king if I so choose, but until then, you had better stay on my good side, if you know what's good for you."

He forced himself free and stood straight. "Without me, you would not even be here. You should be thanking me for all I have given you."

"All you gave me was my freedom—which is why I haven't disposed of you yet."

"You're right, I did give you your freedom, and you swore an oath to whoever did. You and I both know that you cannot break that oath. Don't forget who is really in charge here."

Lord Dundan turned and disappeared out of the room. Ophelessa sauntered slowly over to the balcony and peered at the events unfolding below, "Believe me, I know who is in charge. You just haven't figured it out yet."

The battle waged on and the sky was growing darker by every passing hour. Ophelessa's anger in the inability of her soldiers to defeat Eira's army was increasing and showing more and more with every blast of dark anger she shot into the sky from her position on the balcony. The sky grew so dark that the time of day could no longer be determined. At high noon, it looked as if it was the dead of night, with only traces of light peeking through the storm clouds above.

With the battlefield now covered in a black haze, it was becoming increasingly difficult for the soldiers to see each other and distinguish friend from foe. Suddenly, Alareison stopped in the middle of his fight and stood still, staring at the sky. The battle continued around him, but none could harm him any longer. It was as if he had a force around himself, that he was in the middle of the battlefield, observing it all unfold around him, but all he could do was watch. He then raised both hands and his sword to the sky. Thrusting his sword into the ground a moment later, it shook the snow-laden field. With a blast of light, the sky returned to the daylight hidden behind the looming clouds. The air stood still in that moment and both armies halted as they watched the snow lift from the ground and swirl around.

Alareison had summoned the great snow ghosts to aid him in defeating Ophelessa's army. The snow swirled in the wind, coming together to take on the form of hundreds of men. The soldiers appeared out of the flurry, looking like wisps of warriors that once fought on the very battlefield where Ophelessa's and Eira's armies now stood. They wielded their icy blades but could not be pierced themselves. With a single touch of the ice-fashioned blades, Ophelessa's soldiers were frozen solid and their bodies fell like statues, paralysed from fighting any longer. The snow continued to fly around the battlefield, bringing more snow ghosts to fight for the Queen of Talvia—the rightful queen.

The snow engulfed the soldiers, this time taking on one last form. A great lion arose from the misty flakes, his mane a blizzard swirling around his face. The lion paced back and forth, watching his prey and with a mighty roar that echoed through the silence, the soldiers that were frozen awoke and dropped their weapons, surrendering to the mighty beast.

The victory was short-lived, however. From the balcony of the castle in Trillium Nivale, the Blue Queen looked out to the scene below. Her fury was building, and she could not leave her victory to the strength of the army she had built any longer. She stormed from the balcony and headed down the halls, casting aside any guards she met on the way in her anger.

"Where are you going?" asked Lord Dundan.

"To take care of things myself. Ready everyone for a grand party tonight. I believe we will be celebrating our victory."

She charged onto the front lines sending a blast of darkness into the sky to announce her presence. It was her and Alareison in the middle of the battle now. They threw everything they had at each other, but neither was pulling ahead of the other. Both sides resumed fighting when Ophelessa's presence was made known. Her army picked up their weapons at her command—willingly or because of some spell, it was unclear—and charged at the opposing forces. With swords and magic flying through the air, the battle was now in full bloom. What had happened already was merely the appetizer. Alareison was fighting his hardest, but it was becoming clear to everyone fighting for Talvia that his strength was weakening and he was no longer a match for the wrath of the Blue Queen.

Ophelessa had brought him to his knees. She raised her hands and with one more blast that engulfed Alareison in a bright blue light, the fighting ceased. It was true that he had defeated her once before, but he was younger then. Her magic had grown over the decades, being trapped inside the diamond she now wore around her neck. There was no stopping its forceful vindictive nature. This type of magic does not give way until it has accomplished what it was meant to do. Only a power greater than its own can destroy it, and Alareison's power was no longer the great magic that it once was. She walked over to where he lay, battered and bruised from the fight. She pulled him up onto his feet and glared into his eyes that said more than words ever could. He was defeated, and he knew it.

"You really thought you could defeat me again, old man? My power has only grown in the years I spent trapped inside this diamond," she said, touching the jewel still laying so delicately against her skin. Alareison did not reply, he simply stood there knowing this battle could not be won. She leaned in close and said a few last words, "I. Am. Invincible."

She thrust him away from her as she strode off in the other direction. With all his might, Alareison threw every last ounce of magic he had at her, but she was too quick. Turning with lightning speed, she threw her magic back at him and he flew through the air landing hard on the icy ground. With a burst of snow erupting around where he hit, he was gone—disappearing into thin air as if he was never there at all. Eira's armies kept fighting with all the strength they possessed within, but now that the Blue Queen was undefeated, there was no hope. They soon had no choice but to fall back. Theo and Killian called the orders and they retreated to the safety of their camp on the borders of the battlegrounds.

The cheers and celebration could be seen from the windows of the castle that night. Ophelessa and Lord Dundan wasted no time in celebrating their victory and Eira's army mourned the loss of their own along with Alareison. Silence and the winter wind winding its way through the tents, was all that could be heard in the camp. There was no celebration for them that night. A new plan was needed to defeat the Blue Queen, and it was looking completely hopeless until a familiar face returned to their camp.

Pulling aside the flap to the tent where Theo, Killian, Clea, and the other captains from the other countries were toasting a brave man and trying to find a new way of defeating Ophelessa, the queen returned.

"Eira," said Clea, looking up from her glass. Eira could tell that there was an air about them that did not seem right. As she and Leon had rode through the camp, they could hear the terrible moans and cries of injured men and women being tended to, and the sorrowful cries of the people mourning the loss of their friends and family.

"What are you all doing? This is hardly a time to be toasting," said Eira.

"They are not toasting in celebration," started Evian in a solemn voice appearing behind Eira. "I'm afraid we have not all returned from our first battle with the Blue Queen."

Eira looked around the room, trying to identify the missing face. Everyone she knew was standing around the table—all but one.

"Where's Al?" she asked warily, already knowing the answer. Killian walked up to her slowly and placed a hand on her shoulder.

"He fell at the hands of the Blue Queen." Eira gasped and a few tears rolled down her cheeks, not only for the loss of a brave man but for the loss of hope that instantly set up camp in her heart. Without Al, there was no hope of defeating the Blue Queen and reclaiming her kingdom.

"So this was all for nothing then?" said Eira as she placed the dagger in the middle of the table for all to see.

They stared at its beauty for some time, sipping their drinks for Al until someone finally broke the silence,

"We can't just sit around here doing nothing," said Arlen. "We did not travel all this way to give up the fight, and there will still be another fight. Her troops have not moved off. They are ready to battle again."

"No," interrupted Eira as she stood up, "we're not fighting anymore. I'm not going to lose any more people. Thank you for travelling all this way and coming to our aid but, I think it is best if you go home now. We can't win this fight—not anymore." She took the dagger from the table and turned and walked out of the tent, defeated from within and not knowing how to find the light in her ever-darkening world.

Eira stood there in the darkness with the dagger in hand, memorizing every little detail of its blade and handle. She felt a hand on her shoulder and she knew who it was without turning around.

"It wasn't for nothing," began Leon. "We can still defeat her. We'll find a way."

"How? I let good people die while I was out looking for something we can't even use now." She swung the dagger above her head and threw it out into the cold darkness—probably not the best choice.

Leon grabbed her by the shoulders and twirled her around to face him, "Eira, we will find a way. No one is unbeatable, not even her. She has a weakness. We just need to find it." Just then, the flap of the tent was pulled aside and Evian stood there.

"I think I just did," he said. They all gathered around the table listening to Lord Evian as he spoke, "I kept thinking about when Ophelessa came onto the battlefield wearing the diamond, displaying it plain as day around her neck. Why would she risk bringing the diamond onto the battlefield when that is the very thing we need to trap her again?"

"She was wearing it when I went to the castle too," added Killian.

"Yes, exactly," continued Evian. "Why would she want to keep something so close to her that would be a reminder of her imprisonment? It is odd that she would wear around her neck the very item that contained her for centuries. She is wearing her prison as if she cannot part with it."

"Well, maybe she's sentimental?" mocked Killian.

"I doubt it. Someone like Ophelessa would have wanted to destroy it right away, after being freed to make sure she could never be imprisoned inside it again," said Lord Evian. "I believe that she cannot physically part with it. It was an ancient magic that trapped her inside of the diamond the first time and when you imprison a being inside of an object, they are tied to that object forever, even if they are set free. It becomes a part of them, a sort of life source. If we can get that diamond and destroy it, I believe she will die along with it. She does not have to be trapped inside for us to destroy it."

The group stood there in silence for a moment, thinking over Evian's recent revelation.

"Are you sure about this?" asked Theo. "Even if we could somehow manage to get that diamond from her, are you sure destroying it will destroy her?"

"I am afraid it is the only option we have available to us. I know what magic trapped her the first time and I know the rules that go along with it. I am fairly certain this will be the way we can beat her."

"And how do you suppose we get the diamond from her?" asked Killian. "Just walk up to her and ask to borrow it for the ball?"

"Well, it would pair nicely with your pink tunic," added Arlen.

Killian's eyes widened as he sucked in all his breath, but he was cut off before he could lay into Arlen. "Look," began Eira, "even if we somehow miraculously managed to get that diamond off of her neck, how are we going to destroy it?"

"Was it just me, or did we have sitting on this table only a few minutes ago, the very thing we need to destroy it? The dagger?" asked Clea.

Eira looked plainly at her for a second and then burst out of the tent franticly in search of the dagger she had thrown away only minutes ago. Leon raced after her and the two began rummaging through the snow in the darkness for the dagger. Killian, Theo, and Clea all followed after them and stood in the doorway watching the two walking slowly around, staring at the ground, carefully placing every footstep as to not accidentally step on the dagger.

"What are you two doing?" asked Theo.

"Looking for the dagger," answered Eira. The three shared a puzzled expression in the doorway and within a second, realized what she had meant and hurriedly joined the search. The light from the lanterns in their hands was not enough to light the ground and find the dagger.

"Why would you throw it away in the first place?" asked Killian. "Eira, I love you, but you sometimes need to think before you do things."

"Says the king of never thinking before you speak or do things," she retorted.

"Hey, it's endearing when I do it. It's a character trait!"

"Which direction did you throw it in again?" asked Theo, trying to stop the argument.

"That way," pointed Eira. Theo walked slowly in the direction where Eira was pointing, and it was not long before he felt something hard hit the bottom of his boot. He bent down and brushed the cold powder from the surface to reveal the dagger, lying peacefully in its snowy nest.

"Found it," he shouted and ran back toward the group, handing the dagger to Eira.

"Maybe I should hold on to this, darling," said Killian as he took the dagger from her hand and made his way back into the tent.

"You'll only lose it," said Arlen, as he snatched the dagger from Killian.

"I will take it," said Evian, appeasing the situation.

"That's probably a good idea," said Eira. "It will be safe here for the night."

Eira found her friends by the fire that night. Theo, Killian, Clea, and Leon were all warming themselves and catching up. Leon was telling them about how they got the dagger when she arrived. She sat down next to Leon and leaned into him as he put his arm around her.

"So I take it you two have officially made up, then?" asked Theo. "I mean, you did before the race, but then there was that weirdness about Leon almost getting married—hey I guess you guys have that in common now." Eira and Leon glared at him, "Still not ready to joke about it—okay."

"Anyway, yes—we certainly made up."

"Ew, gross—we don't need to know that," said Killian.

"What—no," said Leon. He looked to Eira for approval, "We sort of...got married."

"What?" gasped Killian and Theo, rising to their feet. They stood there with arms across their chests.

"Who was your best man?" asked Killian.

"Guys, come on."

"Don't tell me it was that damn unicorn—horses don't count."

Leon rolled his eyes, "It was just us—come on, guys. You know I would have wanted you both up there with me—it just didn't work out that way."

Theo and Killian continued to narrow their eyes at them for a moment, then smiled. "Alright, I guess we're happy for you or whatever," said Killian as he sat down and went back to reading Eira's book that Clea was now done with.

"We'll do it again after all of this—properly, and you will all be there, we promise," smiled Eira.

Eira found sleep easily that night with the hope that their new plan would bring the defeat the Blue Queen deserved. When morning broke through the clouds, the day was still as grey as the one that preceded it. Ophelessa's power was growing across the land and her soldiers were ready for another fight if it came to it.

"Right," said Evian as he looked at Leon bent over the table in his tent studying the maps sprawled across the top. "How do you suppose we steal a diamond?"

19

"And what about me, Ophelessa?" argued Lord Dundan. "I am supposed to be king of this land. It is what you promised me in exchange for your freedom. You are going back on your word!"

"Oh, darling," started Ophelessa with every sense of condescension in her voice. "Haven't you learned anything about powerful women? You don't get anywhere in life making promises you intend to keep. You were never going to be king—so stop whining about it and make yourself useful."

Lord Dundan was taken aback. He looked around the room to the guards who were now being motioned toward him. "This is absurd, Ophelessa! I am the one who gave you your freedom! You cannot do this!"

"And I am thankful for that, but sadly my use for you has worn out. But instead of simply disposing of you, I will have you thrown in the dungeon instead. I am a woman who remembers those who help me, and those who don't!" she said with a different sternness to her voice than the usual undertone. The guards advanced on him, and he had nowhere to go. They took him by the arms and dragged him off.

"Ophelessa, you'll regret this!"

"Regret is for the weak, my dear. It is not a word in my vocabulary."

****

The morning light spread across the sky with the ease of water trickling downstream. The sky was not full of the warm sunlight that Eira had grown to love however, it was still the cold grey that made you crave the days when yellows and oranges radiated from the atmosphere. Eira stepped out of her tent and made her way over to Lord Evian's lavish version of camping. Little did she know that Lord Evian and Leon had been up for most of the night concocting a plan to steal the diamond. They had almost come to a consensus when Eira entered the tent and interrupted their train of thought.

"Good morning," she said with a smile.

"Morning," they replied in unison without looking up from the maps and charts scattered on the table. Eira went over to a bowl of fruit that was on the sideboard by the tent door. She took a rather delicious-looking red apple from the bowl and bit into it. She then drifted over to the table and circled its perimeter, watching the two men and looking at the maps. Killian appeared from another flap in the tent, stretching his arms above his head and scratching his back.

"Right," he yawned, "what's for breakfast?" He then noticed that Eira was there, which seemed to startle him. "They've been at it all night," he said, joining Eira where she stood. Eira handed over the bowl of fruit and he stared plainly at it for a moment. "I was thinking more along the lines of bacon."

"If you two are going to keep up this conversation, do you mind doing it somewhere else?" interrupted Leon. Eira nodded her head toward the door to indicate to Killian to follow her outside. He obliged and when they were outside, they made their way over to where some of the other soldiers were starting fires for breakfast.

"What are they doing in there?" asked Eira.

"Looking over those maps of the landscape and the castle, trying to figure out a way to get the diamond. Personally, I think they're wasting their time. You'll have an easier time prying a pearl from an oyster encased in concrete."

They reached the breakfast fires. The glorious smell of sizzling bacon was all they could focus on. Lord Evian's chefs were hard at work feeding the soldiers and when breakfast was finished, they returned to Evian's tent where they found Theo and Clea waiting for them. Leon and Lord Evian were no closer to devising a plan to take the diamond, however.

"You should take a break," said Eira, placing a hand on Leon's shoulder. "Killian told me you've been up all night. You need to get some rest."

He sighed, "Maybe you're right. Staring at these maps isn't going to magically give us a solution to this problem."

She placed a plate on the table beside him, "Eat something and then go to bed. We can keep trying to figure this out."

"Alright," he said kissing Eira on the cheek. He then sat and dug into the food she had brought him. Eira turned to the maps Leon had been staring at all night.

"There's no point in you tormenting yourself with those maps too," began Killian. "If Leon hasn't found a way yet, then there's a good chance we won't either. This is one of those situations that just takes some time and a clear mind. And there's no better way to clear a mind and find a solution than simply doing nothing. It's my favourite thing to do," he chuckled.

They all agreed that Killian might just be right. Eira put the maps to the side and sat down on the couches with the rest of the group. They spent the next couple of hours laughing and talking about things that had nothing to do with the impending war, the Blue Queen, or the diamond. It was friendly conversation, and that simple pleasure was what they all needed.

Just then, two guards threw back the flap of the tent and marched inside. The guards stood on either side of a man, holding each of his arms at the elbow as his wrists were shackled together. They all turned in shock as they gazed at the man standing before them. Eira could barely contain her rage and before the guards or he could utter any words as to explain the reason behind his presence, she marched right up to him and thrust her fist into his gut. He instantly curled over in pain.

"Consider yourself lucky she got to you first," said Killian. "I doubt Leon would have only used his fist."

"Yes, well," coughed Lord Dundan, straightening up and speaking through heavy breaths. But before he could continue, Eira cut him off.

"What are you doing here?" she demanded.

"We found him just beyond the borders of our camp. He was making his way over here," replied one of the guards. Eira did not say anything, just turned back to Dundan waiting for a response.

"Well, whether you are going to believe it or not, I am here to lend my assistance." Eira still did not respond. She wanted to see where he was going with this. "The Blue Queen betrayed me and locked me in your dungeon. I managed to escape, and I am here to help you defeat her."

Killian let out a heavily sarcastic laugh, "That'll be the day; when she accepts your help. Even if you are telling the truth, you lost every right to be one of our allies."

Dundan turned to Eira and looked at her with an expression that reeked of desperation. "I can see now that forcing you to marry me may not have been the best course of action to take my place as rightful ruler over this land."

"You think?" whispered Theo into Killian's ear.

"Rightful?" questioned Eira.

"Anyway, it was the jewel that did it to me. Being in possession of it for so long, it began to sour my mind. It was the Blue Queen using her powers through the diamond to corrupt me and convince me to set her free."

"Corrupt you? You seemed pretty eager to be king—I doubt *she* did that to you," replied Eira.

"While it is true I wanted to retake my family's place on the throne, my desire for it was magnified exponentially by the power of the jewel. The Blue Queen never intended to help me become king. She just wanted to be freed to take over herself. And I fell for all of it."

"How did you free her, anyway?" asked Eira. "You were locked up last time I saw you."

"My brother freed me."

"And where is he now?" asked Clea.

Dundan sighed, "The Blue Queen killed him the moment she was freed. My first tell that she was not who I had expected and perhaps I had made a grave mistake."

Everyone was listening intently to his story, trying to pick out any indication that he was lying.

"So," began Eira again, "how exactly do you think you can help us?"

"Eira!" interjected Theo. "You can't seriously be thinking of accepting his help?"

"We can hear him out and then decide."

Just then, Leon returned well rested. He walked through the flap of the tent and stopped dead in his tracks at the sight of Lord Dundan unguarded, standing before Eira, Killian, Theo, Clea and a couple of guards who were standing off to the side.

"What is he doing here?" he demanded, drawing his sword. Dundan backed away with his hands still shackled, raised in submission.

"See, told you he wouldn't use his fist," whispered Killian to Dundan.

Eira moved toward Leon with her hands up, motioning for him to put his sword away, "It's alright," she reassured, "our guards captured him and brought him here. He says he wants to help us."

"Help us! Are you kidding me? Eira, this man is responsible for everything that has happened to us up until this point. How can you honestly think of trusting him? We should be rid of him right now."

"I didn't say I was going to trust him! I said he came here offering his help and there's nothing wrong with hearing him out. Maybe he knows something we don't or maybe this is some elaborate scheme concocted by him and the Blue Queen to trap us. Either way, I've decided to at least let him say what he came here to."

"Eira," Leon replied with a heavy sigh and bringing his hand to his brow, "Why do you insist on seeing the good in everyone? It's going to get you in trouble one day—or worse."

"Well, that's why I keep you around," she smiled. "Everyone deserves to be given the chance to let the good in them out."

"Fine," he said through gritted teeth, "but I'm not letting him out of my sight."

"I wouldn't expect anything less."

They turned back to the group and let Dundan proceed in telling them what he had to say, "Look," he began, "the Blue Queen's power resides inside that diamond. When she was trapped inside, her powers bonded with the jewel and would remain inside the diamond forever, even if her human form is freed. She is tied to it for this reason, so if it is away from her for even a short period of time, it will start to affect her. Her powers will slowly diminish as long as the diamond is not with her until she has no power left at all."

"We already know that her power is tied to the Diamond of Azul. But we can't exactly get it away from her," sneered Leon.

"Well, what if I told you there is a way you could?" assured Lord Dundan. They all stared at him intrigued. "You may not have lived in that castle long enough to have discovered its secrets, but you're forgetting that my family lived in that castle for centuries before yours. And what you don't know is that they built escape tunnels leading out of the castle into the fields."

"That's how you got out, and how your brother got in," realized Eira.

"Yes, and that's also your way in," replied Dundan.

The group exchanged glances with each other until someone finally broke the silence, "I think I've heard enough for now," said Leon, moving toward Lord Dundan. "It's time you leave."

"Wait, Leon," began Eira. "We need to think about this. He just gave us a very crucial piece of information."

"Yeah—why, Eira? We don't know if we can trust him yet and I'm not going to let him play us. He'll stay here until we figure out what to do with him." Leon was not giving her room for negotiation and she knew it was best to let him do what he thought best to for the night. Leon moved toward Lord Dundan and pushed his back in a motion for him to start walking with him and the other guards followed close behind.

"If you think you're going to get into her head and convince her to trust you, you'd better think again," said Leon once they were outside of the tent. "We are not suddenly allies and we will certainly never be friends." He pushed Lord Dundan into a tent where they had ordered all available guards to circulate. He turned to leave when Lord Dundan finally spoke,

"I know you don't trust me and I would never expect you to, but believe me, your *wife* will see my side and I'm honestly not here to cause any trouble."

"What did you just say?"

"You think that the Blue Queen has no idea what the two of you have been up to? She has spies everywhere. Even the Valley of the Ethereal is no safe haven from her power and your best bet is to listen to someone who has been by her side for the last few weeks and knows the ins and outs of what she does. She wronged me and I want to destroy her just as bad as you do. Mutual hate is a much stronger foundation to build trust on. I'm sure you'll see it my way soon."

Leon didn't respond. He left Lord Dundan with the guards and headed back to his tent where Eira was waiting impatiently for him.

"You didn't kill him, did you?" she asked when he entered, only half joking. Leon gave her a look that implied he did not, and how could she possibly think that way? "What? You were ready to earlier."

"Yeah, well, I decided we should keep him around for now," he said, putting his sword on the table and taking his boots off so he could lay on the bed. Eira moved ever so slightly closer to him, shifting her weight in his direction.

"Can you please listen to me?" she started. "I know that we have no idea if he escaped from her or if the two of them fabricated this whole thing, but for now, he's here and we should at least give him the chance to prove himself."

"Prove himself? Eira, he's already proven to us the type of man he is. He forced you to marry him so he could take the throne, in case you forgot!"

"I didn't forget! And I also remember that *you* left when all of that happened. Why should I trust you any more than I trust him?"

"Seriously, Eira?" Leon stood from his horizontal position at that moment, "If you're going to hold that against me for the rest of my life, then maybe I'll just leave again."

"I'm not holding it against you, but people change. She killed his brother. You don't think that might cause a change of heart in him?"

"Depends. I don't know how close he was with his brother." Leon moved to put his boots back on and then walked over to the table where his sword was, but Eira caught it before he could reach for it. She held it close to her chest.

"Where are you going?" she asked.

"Out," he replied, trying to take the sword from her, but she backed up out of his reach. He moved closer to her, "Eira, give it to me. I'm not going to fight with you anymore."

"No! You don't get to just leave when things get too tough."

"See, there you go again, rubbing that in my face." He managed to grab the sword out of her clutches this time.

"I didn't mean it like that," she said, trying to get the sword back and blocking his way out of the tent. The two played a game of blocking each other with Eira trying to get the sword back until finally Leon had backed her against the side of the tent and held the sword high above his head and out of her reach.

"Give that to me," she pushed, reaching for the sword, "I'm not letting you leave like this." She jumped at him and wrapped her legs around his waist, still reaching for the sword. Leon lowered it to his side and placed his other arm around Eira's waist.

"Eira, I have to think about all of this. You need to let me leave. I'll be back, don't worry."

She jumped down off of him and finally let him take the sword, watching as he walked out of the tent.

By the time Leon returned, Eira was fast asleep and there were only a few hours left in the early morning before the sun would be making its appearance over the horizon. He quietly got into bed beside her and lightly ran a finger over her face to wake her.

"You have to go on another journey," he said.

"What?" she answered, not just in response to what he said but also because she did not fully hear him in her sleepy state.

"You need to go to Kesa."

"What? They don't like us," yawned Eira.

"I know, but if we're going up against the Blue Queen, we need all the help we can get. I think it's time to end the feud."

20

"Kesa!" spat Killian. "You want to go to that vile place? Have you lost your mind completely?"

"Look, we can't fight without their help," explained Leon. "The first time Ophelessa was defeated, it took the armies of all four countries, and there's no chance we can do it without them now."

"He's right," said Clea, "With our entire army under the Blue Queen's spell, the combined armies of Kevatia and Syysia aren't big enough. Talvia and Kesa are the biggest superpowers in this land—without Kesa, we don't stand a chance."

"We've been doing things without them for centuries. Been working out just fine," Killian added. He took a deep breath when no one joined his side, "But, I suppose if there's a queen who can unite all the countries again, it would be our Eira."

Eira smiled at him as if to say, *thank you.*

"What about us?" asked Clea. "What are we all supposed to do while you two are gone? I assume you're not inviting all of us."

"Oh, no," Leon shook his head, "I'm not going with her."

"Wait—you're not?" asked Eira.

"Why not?" asked Clea.

He paused a moment, thinking of the right way to approach what he was about to say next. "I'm sort of...banned from there."

"What?" asked Eira.

"Well, it was Killian's fault."

"Hey, don't throw me under the carriage." He turned to Eira, "And we're not exactly banned. There's just a very good possibility that we'd be arrested if either of us went there."

"Fine, maybe Clea and Theo should come with me, then."

"Well, what do you want us to do with Lord Dumbass then, while you're gone?" asked Killian.

"Just keep him here until we return and don't let him talk to anyone or go anywhere alone," said Eira. Then she leaned into Killian, "And don't let Leon kill him."

"I heard that."

"Uh, well duh," said Killian. "Okay, next question, how are you going to get out of here without Ophelessa's spies seeing you heading off to Kesa?"

"Well, we're going to take a play from Dundan's book and go through the tunnels," said Eira.

"What? You're going to trust him?" asked Clea.

"Not exactly. We had Lord Evian look into it, and he found an old map of the tunnels in his archives. There's a route that takes us far enough away from the castle, and we'll be able to stay in a small town on the Talvian border before we head to Kevatia. From there we can travel into Kevatia no problem, then hopefully we can take the train into Kesa without being noticed."

"They're never going to let you have an audience with the king. I don't know how you're going to convince him to send his troops to fight for us. They've refused any alliance with us in the past, and we've done the same."

"Well, we're going to figure it out when we get there," assured Eira.

"Well, they might let *you* in," said Killian nodding to Eira, "and Theo will probably pass too, but they'll catch Clea's Talvian accent right away and most likely refuse all of you."

"We'll work on that," smiled Eira. "Anyway, if we're going to do this, we need to go now. We don't have a lot of time to waste. Every minute spent trying to figure out how to destroy the Blue Queen is another minute she's ruling *my* throne and gathering her army."

They waited for nightfall to make their way to the tunnels from their camp. Eira, Clea, and Theo headed for the entrance to the tunnels when the sun had been down for hours, being extremely careful to not gain the attention of anyone or anything that may be watching. They knew the Blue Queen's spies were everywhere. They hurried, just the three of them and their horses, through the valley and to the hidden entrance.

"Quickly," called Theo after Eira when he made it to the entrance of the tunnel. He held the door open as Eira dismounted her horse and walked him through into the pitch black world below her kingdom. Theo ushered Clea through as well and then followed with his horse and shut the door behind them and lit the torch he had been carrying. Their surroundings now bathed in light, they could see a long stretch of empty tunnel before them.

"I guess we should get going," Eira said, taking the reins and walking ahead of the horse. The tunnel wasn't tall enough to ride through. Clea and Theo nodded in response and did the same with their horses.

It was a long journey through the tunnels, with none of them knowing if it had been an hour or several. Every so often there was a marker hidden high on the walls, which indicated they were heading in the right direction. There were many offshoots and without Lord Evian's map, they would surely be lost already. They were wary to take too many breaks as it was time they did not have to waste, but they also had to keep up their strength. They walked all night and before long, Eira could sense that they were getting to the end. She could see small bits of daylight peeking in through the tunnel and the smell of crisp morning air was piercing her nose.

They emerged from the tunnels as the sun was peeking over the horizon. By the time it was mid-morning, they had made it to the small town on the outskirts of Talvia. They were unsure of how far Ophelessa's curse had travelled and if the people of this town were under her spell just as the rest of Talvia was, so they tried not to bring any attention to themselves. Theo found a small inn and managed to get a room under a different name while Eira and Clea waited patiently outside with the horses making sure to cover their faces anytime someone walked past.

"Let's get a bit of rest and then head out. We should try not to stay here too long," said Theo as he placed their bags on the floor of the room. There were two beds. Clea and Eira shared and Theo took the other. They slept for a few hours and then headed out.

By nightfall, they were in Kevatia. They spent the night at an inn, one town over from where Leon's uncle Edmond lived.

"Oh, thank the gods you guys are alive," called Leon's uncle, as they made their way up the driveway late the next afternoon. "I had such nightmares after you all went into that pass. I was wondering what I would have to tell Leon's father—I let you go in there." He checked all of them over as if to see if they were still intact. "Why are you back?" he finally asked.

"We're passing through for the night, if that's alright?" said Eira. "We're off to Kesa in the morning?"

"Kesa? Why?"

"I have some business there," responded Eira.

"Hmm," Edmund pondered for a moment, "I'm not sure I like the sound of that, but it's your choice. Of course, you can stay here for the night. Come in. Maria is just starting dinner."

Edmund's wife was far less thrilled with the idea that they were going to Kesa for business, however, she was thrilled to have them for dinner.

"Your Majesty," she bowed to Eira as she served her a plate.

"Please tell her to stop calling me that," Eira whispered to Edmond as Maria backed away from the table.

"I have, multiple times. You may just have to get used to it."

Eira smiled at Maria as she stared Eira down, taking her first bit of food, "It's delicious, Maria, thank you," she smiled.

"Oh, wonderful!" Maria exclaimed. "It is my pleasure to cook for you." She finally felt comfortable enough to sit at her own table and eat the dinner she had made.

The dinner conversation was just that, small talk here and there amidst the chewing. After dinner, tea and cakes played out very similarly. Edmund asked them how their journey through the Quesnell Pass went and they gave him a brief summary of it. There was no need to worry him more about what had actually happened. When dessert was done, Theo, Clea, and Eira headed for bed. The train was supposed to pull into the station early the next morning, and while Edmund had offered to give them a ride there, it was still going to take an hour or so.

They awoke early the next morning with the first light of day and headed out for the train station hoping not to miss it passing through. Otherwise, it would be a long journey to Kesa; time they did not have.

"Enjoy your time in Kesa," called Edmund, as he left them at the train station.

They waved goodbye to him and thanked him again for his hospitality. Just like the last time Eira had been there, Maria was more than happy to give her and Clea something to wear that would suit Kesa more than the fur lined clothing she arrived in. Edmund did the same for Theo, and they headed to the train platform.

"Have you ever been to Kesa?" Eira asked Theo and Clea as they were waiting for the train.

They shook their heads in response.

"Well, I know they don't like us much, but I'm pretty excited," said Eira.

"You say that now, but I doubt you'll be feeling that way when the king wants nothing to do with you or your cause," replied Theo.

"We'll see about that. I can be pretty persuasive," smiled Eira.

The train pulled into the station right on schedule and they made it aboard and into their seats. It would be hours before they would arrive at the Kesa border and then another couple to the train station. Eira stared out the window, watching the scenery change for the majority of the trip. All she could think about was how to convince the king to become their allies again, after all this time. She wasn't even too sure as to why they were no longer allies.

When she first came to Talvia and was learning all about this world to prepare to be queen, she learned of the three other countries and their history with Talvia. At one time, all four countries were allies and lived in peace, but then something happened and Kesa and Talvia broke their alliance. She never fully got an answer as to why. The turning point in their history was hidden in some book somewhere and the real reason was lost over the centuries. All they had now were people's versions of it and who's to say if that is the truth or not. She tried to ask Theo and Clea if they knew about it.

"So, why are Kesa and Talvia no longer allies?" asked Eira.

"I don't know. They say we didn't fight for them in some war several centuries ago, and we say the same. They also claim that we didn't treat the soldiers they sent for us very well. In the end, it couldn't be resolved. Many had tried over the years, including marriage alliances, but ultimately they ended badly. One of their princesses poisoned our king and our princes refused to marry their princesses, calling them inferior. A lot of this happened when Lord Dundan's family was still on the throne," answered Clea.

"Well, I'm not his family and this king isn't his ancestors. Maybe we can finally put it behind us."

"I would like to think that way, too. Hopefully, the king can see it your way."

When they finally pulled into the Kesa station, Eira felt as though she was in some tropical paradise. The palm trees towered high above them and the humidity was present as soon as she stepped from the train onto the station platform. She had never been on a tropical vacation before, but she had always wanted to. The relaxed atmosphere was nice to be a part of with everything she was currently dealing with. For a moment, she could forget the real reason why they were here and just enjoy the warm breeze making its way across her face.

"Man, why don't we live here?" she joked. "This is pretty nice."

"Ah, the heat gets tiring after a while," responded Theo.

"So does the cold," she retorted.

"Fair enough." He looked around at their surroundings and then finally saw what he was looking for. He motioned for Eira and Clea to follow him and she could see the sign he was looking at that told them there was an inn not a far walk from the station.

It was a quick walk in comparison to the ones she had been on before. They passed many fruit stands and people simply enjoying the warmth. No one seemed to be in a hurry here and they were just living to enjoy their time. The small shops and markets were full of fresh flowers and shells made into necklaces and hair pieces. Others were selling fish, crab, and anything else you could catch from the water. Eira was in awe of it all and she wanted to stop and buy something from every vendor, but this wasn't exactly a vacation.

They settled into their rooms and were up bright and early the next morning to try to have a meeting with the king. They made their way down to the beach where there were many boats ready to take you across the water to the island where the Kesa castle was. They did not know what they would do when they got there, but there was no turning back now.

"No one is allowed an audience with the king today," stated one guard at the castle's gates.

"Please," pleaded Eira, "it is very important that I speak with him."

"What is this about?" asked the guard.

"Um, it's a business deal. An alliance between lands. The Queen of Kevatia sent us to make an arrangement with him."

"I didn't hear about any arrangement."

"It was very last minute. She sent us just early this morning and said it could not wait. It is for the good of both lands."

"You are not the advisor she usually sends. We only trust him."

"Well, he was sick today and this is extremely urgent."

The guard sized them up. "Alright, wait here. I'll go see if the king is willing to see you."

The guard left the three of them at the gates, wondering if he would actually come back or if they would soon be ambushed by more guards and forced out. They waited about twenty minutes when the guard finally made his way back to them and to the surprise of everyone involved, he opened the gates and led them inside.

His castle towered above the surrounding foliage, a mountain of white and yellow stone breaking against the greens, pinks, blues, yellows, and reds of the vines and flowers creeping all around the lavish palace built into the side of the cliffs overlooking the sea. They were led through the courtyard and past the magnificent fountain, spitting water from the mouths of aquatic animals with two mermaids at the very top, pouring water out of large shells.

They walked down the semi-covered hallways into the great hall of the castle. It was a grand room with glassless windows letting the warm breeze through. The king was sitting at the centre of the room, waiting for them, looking as if this was the biggest imposition on his day. He was an older man, possibly the same age as Leon's father or even older. His shoulder-length golden hair and informal attire made him look as if he was simply a retired man living out the rest of his life in this tropical paradise.

"Your Highness," bowed the guard, and Theo, Clea, and Eira followed suit. "This is the representative of Queen Isabella," he motioned to Eira.

"Yes, yes," he waved to his guard to signal him to back off, "what is this all about?"

Eira spoke, "I have come to talk to you about an alliance between our lands."

"We already have an alliance. There is nothing to discuss."

"I apologize, Your Highness but, we actually do not."

"What she means to say," interjected Clea with a bow, "is that our alliance has been torn for centuries now and it is time to reunite us."

The king was taken aback when Clea spoke, "You are Talvian!" he yelled in horror.

Gee, thanks, Clea.

"I'm sorry, Your Highness," interjected Eira. "We did not mean to deceive you, but we knew that if you were aware of the real reason as to why we are here, you would never talk to us. My name is Eira, Queen of Talvia."

"You are right that I would not talk to you, Queen of Talvia. Your people are not my concern. Get out now!"

"Please! King Elio, we don't mean you or your people any harm. Trust that we would not come here unless it was absolutely necessary. Just hear me out and then you can make your decision."

"No! You and your people lost any right you ever had to be heard by my people. This is the last time I will ask you nicely to leave."

"The Blue Queen is back. She has been released and is taking over Talvia. I have lost everything and we and the other countries alone are not going to be enough to defeat her again."

"The Blue Queen is back?" asked the king, slightly intrigued by what she had said. "That is a shame, but I will not send my troops to fight for you."

"Why not?" asked Theo. "You cannot keep punishing them for crimes of the past. Crimes of people who weren't even our ancestors. If your people came to us as a last resort; a plea for help, I am confident that this queen would not hesitate to lend you aid."

"Look, I commend your bravery coming here today, but I will still not waver," he paused a moment, "And don't think I haven't forgotten about what your little boyfriend did. He's still wanted here for stealing my prized painting of the founding of Kesa!"

So that's what they did—typical. "Hey," called Eira back, "allegedly—you have no proof it was him."

"Yeah, they were never convicted," added Theo, winking and pointing his finger at the king.

Eira sighed, *I should have just come alone.*

"Look, I'd suggest you three had better get out of here now while I am in a somewhat forgiving mood, and I can assure you, Your Majesty, it will not last long."

"No wait! Please, Your Highness," Eira tried again. "I don't know what started this war between us over four centuries ago, but when is enough, enough? At what point do we draw the line in the sand and say that everything that happened in the past is the past and we will no longer

292

punish each other for it? I have heard stories about what happened between our countries in the past and if I'm going to be honest, it all sounds like our ancestors were acting like spoiled children. My ancestors weren't even on the throne when this happened and even if they were, I am not them. And you are not your ancestors either. This generation and the generations before us didn't wrong your people, and neither did yours to mine. Living in the past doesn't solve the problems that already took place."

The king seemed to be quite interested in what Eira was saying. And she was hoping that by the intrigued expression on his face, she was finally winning him over. There was a long moment of silence before he finally spoke,

"You make some valid arguments, and I am impressed with your tenacity for such a young queen. I can see that you will serve your people well over the years. However, I cannot send my army to fight for you. Even if we say what's past is past, this is not our fight." He stood from his throne and walked a few steps closer to Eira, Theo, and Clea. "I have heard your plea just as you asked. Now please leave."

"Please, King Elio, do this for your people as well," Theo pleaded, bowing to him. "Do you not think that the Blue Queen will stop at ruling Talvia? The last time she was here she stopped at nothing to try to take over all four countries. Do you not think that is her plan again? You know as well as I do the tales from the past and what her reign was like. Talvia is only the beginning. She will not stop, and then you will not have any allies to help in your fight for your land."

King Elio took a deep breath. His anger could be seen as plainly as the nose on his face. "I said leave," he bellowed, and his guards did not hesitate to lead them out.

"Okay, what if I give you Leon and Killian to throw in jail for a night, and I will have the painting sent back to you, and then we call it even and you help us?" smiled Eira.

"Leave now, or I throw you all in jail! And I want that painting back!"

Elio's guards were leading them back through the halls of the castle when they heard someone calling out for them.

"Clea?" Then a man came running up to them and scooped Clea into a hug.

"Nevin? What are you doing here?" she asked when her feet were back on the floor.

Nevin motioned for the guards to wait a moment. "I came back last year, after the battle in Glasera. Everything that happened made me realize it might be time for me to make amends with my father. We had a heart to heart and worked everything out."

"I'm so happy for you," smiled Clea.

Nevin then turned to Eira and Theo, "What are you all doing here? It's pretty bold for you to just walk in here."

"We didn't have much of a choice," replied Eira. "The Blue Queen has been released and she's taken over Talvia. I need your father's army to help fight."

"I'm guessing he said no, and based on the fact that you're all still standing, he's in a good mood."

"He's not going to help us," sighed Eira.

"I'll talk to him. Maybe I can convince him."

"Thank you, Nevin, but I don't think he's going to waver, and we really need to get back to Talvia now. This journey was already an unfortunate detour from the problems at hand, and we can't waste any more time here," said Eira.

"Well, I wish you the best of luck then. I wish there was more I could do to help."

"You already helped us, last year in Glasera," smiled Eira.

"I'll come with you now. I'll help fight."

"I appreciate that, but no offence; one more person isn't going to make much of a difference."

"I still want to," Nevin smiled at Clea.

When they made it back to the train station to head home, they were feeling quite distraught—at least that's how Eira was feeling. She could not tell if Theo and Clea felt the same or not.

"You did your best," encouraged Clea. "It was a long shot and your ancestors probably would have never even tried. It's a commendable thing you did. We'll have enough to fight the army she's created."

"I don't want to fight, though. Those are our people fighting out there. She's turned everyone against me. If we have the bigger army, there's a better chance that we don't have to needlessly wound our own people. We can simply hold them off."

"Eira, I know but, it's looking more and more like we're going to have to fight them. The only people from Talvia we have left on our side are the few that didn't fall under the Blue Queen's spell. The majority of our army is coming from the armies of the other countries. I don't want to fight against my friends and neighbours either, but we have no choice," said Clea.

The train was pulling into the station and all Eira wanted to do at this point was to get back to Talvia and find a way to defeat the Blue Queen. She still had the King's Dagger, but it was useless without the diamond.

The journey back to the camp was long, and trudging back through the tunnels was not something Eira enjoyed very much. When she, Theo, and Clea finally made it back to the camp, it was as if no time had gone by since they left. Everyone was still holding down the fort and Ophelessa had not made a move on them yet. Lord Dundan was still in his tent surrounded by guards when Eira walked past. She could see him sitting at the table, his hands still cuffed. For a moment they caught each other's eye and Eira had this funny feeling inside that told her she may have to hear him out one more time.

Late that night, when everyone had succumbed to the blissfulness of sleep, Eira was wide awake. Her mind was tormenting her with thoughts of the impending battle, nothing different from every night for the past couple of months. She finally told herself there was only one thing that might put her mind to rest. She quietly and carefully got out of bed and slipped on her boots and coat. Pushing aside the door of the tent, she embraced the cold night air and walked toward the most intriguing tent in the camp. When the guards on duty saw her, they snapped upright and wondered what she was doing there.

"We cannot let you in, Your Majesty," said one of the guards, "I'm afraid we have orders from…"

"I know who the orders are from," interrupted Eira, "and since when do you listen to him over me?"

"He is the captain of the Royal Guard," said the other guard.

"He's not the king."

The guards stepped aside and let Eira enter the tent. It was pitch black inside, so Eira made her way over to the table where a small oil lap was sitting and lit it. She carried it with her over to the bed and when she was beside it, she swiftly kicked its occupant awake.

"Get up," she forced.

He did as was asked and followed her over to the table, sitting across from her. They stared at each other for a moment until he finally spoke,

"I take it that your adventures in Kesa were less than successful."

"How did you know about that?"

"People talk, this tent isn't exactly soundproof," yawned Lord Dundan.

"Fine, I'm guessing you know the reason I'm here?"

"Well, I assume you have finally decided to trust me, or at least just enough to let me help you. I told your husband you would come to my side soon enough." He leaned back in his chair, "He doesn't know you're here, does he?"

"That's none of your concern. You said you were here to help us, and you may be our only shot at defeating Ophelessa, so I came to bargain with you. You said you don't have a price, but everyone does. What's in it for you?"

"I want my family to no longer be outcasts in this land. I want to be pardoned for my crimes and be able to live out my life in peace. Once I realized Ophelessa was never my partner, I knew my life was going downhill drastically. The best chance I have at redemption is helping you defeat her and then hopefully I can just be left to live in peace."

"As long as you or any of your family members never try to take my throne again."

"My grandfather was the one in the family who was angry for his entire life about it. Most of my family has made peace with the fact that we lost the throne, but when he found out he could have been a king, he let it consume him for his entire life. He pulled me down with him and I realize now, it was a path that was never going to end in happiness."

"Where's your grandfather now?" asked Eira.

"He died last year, around the time you came back to take the throne. It seemed kismet that you had returned; a young queen not stable in her position as ruler. I could take the throne and make him proud. He bestowed the Diamond of Azul to me on his deathbed."

"That is an intriguing story. You must have had a lot of time to come up with it."

"It's the truth," insisted Lord Dundan. "I know I have no right to ask for your trust, but it is the truth. I swear on my life that I am not lying to you. Ophelessa will only grow stronger and if you don't get that diamond away from her and destroy it—it's game over."

"How do you suppose we get it away from her?"

"Not everyone in your castle has fallen under the queen's spell," he started.

"Here's the plan," said Eira. "We still have someone in the castle who is loyal to me."

"How do you know that?" asked Leon, as they were gathered the next morning in Lord Evian's tent.

"It doesn't matter how I know, but she's there waiting for us."

"What do you mean, she's waiting for us?" asked Clea.

"Okay fine...Dundan told me."

"Eira! Don't tell me you believe him?" asked Leon. "When did he tell you this?"

"I went to see him last night."

"Eira!"

"You don't get to tell me what to do. I can make my own decisions. Isn't that part of being a queen, to do what you think is best for your people? He is our only hope of ever destroying her." Eira turned back to the rest of the group, "Once Lord Dundan was imprisoned by the Blue Queen, Ceilidh was the only person who talked to him. She brought him his meals and he realized that she was not under the queen's spell. She knows that he snuck out of the dungeon and she's helping keep the idea in the Blue Queen's head that he is still in the dungeon. She brings food down there every day and pretends that he keeps pleading to have an audience with her. She's the one who has been keeping this war at bay."

"Why would Ceilidh trust Dundan?" asked Theo. "I thought she was better than that?" he sighed.

"I don't know why she trusted him, but if she does, then I do too," said Eira.

"So, what's the plan?" asked Leon with an expression that told everyone he was still not thrilled about the situation.

"We're going through the tunnels."

Eira led the group to where one of the tunnels let out. It was a small opening, hidden to the naked eye behind some overgrown winterberry bushes in the hills behind

Trillium Nivale to the north. When pulled aside, the bushes revealed the entrance to a cave which connected to the tunnels underneath the fields leading into the castle. Leon led the way and Eira and Theo followed as they made their way through the vast labyrinth. It was a long journey through the tunnels. Hours went by before Leon finally announced they were almost there. They arrived at a large outlet with various tunnels leading off in different directions. Leon went around and lit the torches on the walls that had not been lit for hundreds of years. He stood there for a moment looking all around and weighing his various options until he finally chose a path after carefully studying the map in his hand.

"We're almost there," he whispered. As if anyone would be able to hear them that many feet beneath the earth. "This tunnel should lead to a hidden door in the kitchen. It is our best bet at getting to the servants without anyone finding out."

When they reached the door, Eira could hear the sound of pots and pans clanging in the kitchen on the other side of the wall. They had to be careful about opening the door and revealing themselves. With extreme caution, Leon opened the door a crack and the smell of freshly baked bread wafted through the air only to be temptingly inhaled by their noses. Leon looked out through the crack and saw the baker there, but no one else. He closed the door and turned to Eira and Theo.

"Now comes the tricky part."

"What's that?" asked Eira.

"We wait."

What seemed like hours went by, but when you are hungry and being tormented by a kitchen of freshly baked goodies just out of reach, a few minutes can seem like eternity. Eventually, they received what they were waiting for and heard the voice they all recognized. Leon opened the hidden door once again and sure enough, there she was, sitting at the counter eating her dinner.

"Psst," whispered Leon, "Ceilidh," he called but, she didn't hear him. He was being unbearably quiet as to not reveal themselves to anyone but the intended.

"You have to be louder than that," whispered Theo.

"If I'm any louder, someone else might hear, and then we'll all be screwed."

"Well, you're going to have to risk it. She's our only hope," argued Theo.

While the boys were having their hushed bickering match, Eira found a small pebble on the floor of the tunnel and moved toward the crack in the wall. She aimed with precision and then let the pebble fly. It hit Ceilidh on the shoulder and then fell to the floor with a little knock and bounced back over toward the crack in the wall. Ceilidh looked in the direction the pebble came from and walked over to where it lay. She knelt down to pick it up and when she did, Eira called her name,

"Ceilidh," she whispered loud enough to be heard. Startled, Ceilidh jumped backward. Eira opened the door a bit more to reveal the three of them.

"Eira!" gasped Ceilidh, then covered her mouth quickly and looked to see if any ears were around to hear. "I mean, Your Majesty. You finally came."

"We need your help," began Eira, and she proceeded to tell Ceilidh all about what they had been through and their plan to defeat the Blue Queen.

Ceilidh agreed to help them out and over the next week, she delivered messages to Eira through the tunnels. Clea, Theo, Killian, Leon, and herself all took turns going into the tunnels to retrieve the information they needed. Finally, they had enough information to make their move on the castle.

"She is sending the necklace to the jewellers in town for cleaning and repair," started Eira. "That is our chance."

"What? You're going to steal it from the jewellers? I hardly think that'll work. How are you even going to get into town without her spies seeing you?" asked Theo.

"Wait," Clea, held up a hand. "She's letting the necklace out of her sight? I thought her power was tied to it and she couldn't be away from it?"

"Well, I guess she can for a short amount of time. Ceilidh said it is being sent with a guard to the jeweller's tomorrow morning and will be back by evening. The guard is not to leave the jeweller's all day until it is done."

"Okay, so again, how is this supposed to help us?" asked Theo.

"It's not being sent until morning, right?" smiled Eira. "So, we get to the jeweller first."

Eira dressed in the darkest clothes she could find and pulled a scarf over her head to shield herself from the prying eyes in town. Sneaking out across the fields was the easy part. Getting into town, on the other hand, took more skill. Leon led the way, hugging every wall of every building they passed, moving only in the shadows. Everything seemed darker and colder than Eira had remembered it. The wind blew in through her scarf and ran a chill down her spine, bringing a sense of increasing danger, more so than she already felt sneaking about in town.

When they reached the jeweller, it was closed, but the light was on upstairs in the jeweller's home above the shop. Leon knocked on the door while Eira stood beside him holding the scarf close to her face. Leon started calling loudly until the man came downstairs to address the person who was disturbing his night.

"Do you know what time it is, boy?" he said unlocking the door. "What is it?"

"Please," begged Leon, "you have to help us. My wife is quite sick and I saw your light on. We were travelling through when she struck ill and I'm afraid everything we have is not helping. It's far too cold for her to stay in the carriage."

"Yes, of course," said the man. "Come in." He moved to the side to let Leon and Eira in. They made their way over to a small chair in the corner of the jewellery shop, and the man turned on a small lamp resting on the table beside it. Eira removed the scarf from her face and the man stepped back, "Your Majesty!" he gasped, falling to the floor. "You cannot be here. It is not safe." He stood up and made for the door, "Leave now, please, before anyone sees you."

"No, please," pleaded Eira, standing to meet him, "we need your help."

"What could I possibly do for you? The Blue Queen has taken over this land. I'm afraid I do not serve you anymore. No one does, not after she has threatened everyone who lives here."

"That is why we need your help," said Leon. "We need to stop her."

"I would do anything for you but, how can you be so sure I will not be persecuted for helping you and acting against the Blue Queen?"

"We can't," replied Eira. "But we need you to have faith that you are our only hope."

The man sighed and looked at the two of them standing there, begging for his cooperation. "Alright," he whispered, "what can I do for you?"

"She will be sending a guard tomorrow with a necklace that she needs cleaned and repaired. We need you to study every detail of that necklace and then once the guard has left, make an exact copy of it, so good that even she will not be able to tell the difference."

"I cannot make a necklace of such extravagance in a day. I've seen it around her neck when she comes through town. It is an intricate piece."

"I'm afraid you have to," said Eira, "and I will make sure you will be adequately paid for your services."

"A request like this will take me all night. You will not get it until the next morning."

"That is alright. Just please get it done. Leon will meet you on the borders of town, in the hills the next morning, to get the necklace."

The deal was done and the door of the jewellery shop shut behind them as the lights went out from within and the jeweller went back to his small apartment to rest for the task at hand tomorrow. Eira pulled the scarf over her head once again.

"Do you think this is going to work?" asked Leon.

"I hope so," Eira replied.

A guard delivered the necklace to the shop the next morning as planned and the jeweller was able to fix it while studying its craftsmanship and every detail. Every setting of every jewel he noted down on a piece of paper to use later when creating the replica. The guard remained waiting, watching the jeweller's every movement all day as instructed—he was not to let the necklace out of his sight.

"What are you writing down?" the guard asked the jeweller, suspicious of his actions.

"I am just noting the fixes I have made to the settings. I have to keep them for my records for payments."

The guard seemed satisfied with his answer and sat back in his chair, crossed his arms again and continued watching the work the jeweller was doing.

When the necklace was done, the jeweller handed it over to the guard. He held it up to the light, studying the piece. He looked satisfied with the work done and paid the jeweller, placing the necklace back into its box and tucking it safely into his pocket. When the guard left, the jeweller began work on the replica and by sunrise the next morning it was delivered to Leon as planned. Now all that had to be done was make the switch.

****

Eira knew the risk Ceilidh was taking, but her loyalty was something she would not trade for anything. Ceilidh was happy to take on the challenge and knew exactly how to get it done. The necklace replica was slipped to her through the secret door in the kitchen, and she waited to make her move. When Ophelessa was sleeping would be her best chance.

She walked calmly down the hall to the door of the queen's chambers. When she rounded the corner, she saw one of Ophelessa's guards outside—a rather large and brooding one at that.

"What are you doing here so late?" demanded the guard as Ceilidh walked slowly over to the door. She had no excuse for being at the queen's chambers so late at night, and the guard knew that as well.

"Nothing," she said softly and smiled, turning to head down the hallway as if that was the direction she had intended to go all along. What the guard didn't know, however, was that Ceilidh knew every inch of the castle, and there is more than one way to get into a room. Ceilidh snuck into the queen's chambers through a hidden passageway in one of the corridors.

There it was, the newly repaired and shining necklace sitting safely in its box. She quickly switched them out, glancing at Ophelessa to make sure she was still asleep. She watched as her chest rose and fell with every breath of sleep. As quickly as she entered, she vanished once more into the hidden passageway, with the diamond tucked safely in the pocket of her apron.

The necklace was wrapped in a neat little package and laid on the doorstep inside the tunnel that led into the kitchen, where it was picked up by Eira and Leon.

Just as they were about to head out of the tunnels, they heard the echoed voices of Ophelessa's guards advancing on them.

"What do we do now?" asked Eira as she looked at Leon. They were trapped, with nowhere to go that wasn't being guarded by Ophelessa's men.

"That is enough now," Ophelessa waved a hand at Ceilidh. "Bring me my jewellery box, will you?" she asked as Ceilidh put down the brush she was using to work the queen's long hair into an elaborate up-do. Ceilidh smiled at Ophelessa's reflection in the mirror and walked over to the dresser on the other side of the room returning promptly with the blue wooden necklace box, placing it on the counter. She bowed to Ophelessa and disappeared out of the room. Ophelessa moved to the counter and opened the box ever so carefully to admire its contents. She rubbed a finger over the jewels and sighed, "Simply marvellous," she beamed with satisfaction.

She glided into the great hall with all the ease and grace she thought she deserved to present herself with. She was truly the Queen of Talvia now and she had the key to her rule displayed around her neck. It was glowing with every ray of light that caught the diamond and reflected a deep teal-black colour. She smiled, sitting down on the throne and addressed the people brought before her,

"Did you really think you could trick me?" she asked, as Eira and Leon were thrown in front of her. "Not the smartest idea, sweetheart. Especially in your delicate condition."

"What?" Eira replied.

"The baby. What? You didn't know?"

"Eira?" asked Leon.

"Yes, the royal heir. How wonderful. It's going to make this so much better when I defeat you, and take away everything you love."

"You're lying. You're just trying to get into our heads. How could you possibly know that?" demanded Eira.

"I know everything. And not just because I am who I am." She rose from the throne and slowly walked over to them. She snapped her fingers and a guard dragged a badly beaten Ceilidh in by the wrist. "You should have thought twice before you risked the life of your dear friend."

"Don't hurt her," begged Eira.

"Oh, no, I'm not going to...anymore. I think she learned her lesson. She won't be helping you anymore.

She's on my side now—everyone is. Including a *dear* friend of yours."

"What are you talking about?" Eira warily asked.

A voice came from behind, "Hello, darling."

21

Eira turned. She could not speak. She simply watched as Killian made his way past her and stood beside Ophelessa.

"What have you done to him?" Eira finally demanded.

"Oh, well I figured it would benefit me having someone you trust dearly on my side, and how convenient for me when he came walking into my castle all on his own with a message from you. So, if you think about it—you're the one who did this to him." Ophelessa took a breath and looked at Leon who also wasn't saying anything. He just found out his wife was pregnant and his best friend had betrayed them—he was understandably a little out of it.

"You see, it was just too easy. I took him over and then sent him right back to you completely unaware that anything had happened. Then, when I needed information, I went into his mind and took it. And now," she looked at Killian, "he's mine to control as I wish." Her vindictive smile grew, "Anyway, I'm done talking to you now. It's your husband who I think might be of some use to me." With a snap of her fingers, Eira fell to the floor.

"Eira!" Leon called, running to her side. "What did you do?" he turned back to Ophelessa.

"Relax, handsome, she's just asleep."

Leon stood to face her, "What do you want?"

"You know what I want. I want this kingdom, and I want you to stop fighting me for it. It'll be so much easier on you if you just give up. I'll let your friends and family go, and you'll never return to bother me."

"Somehow, I find that hard to believe. You won't give up until you rule everything."

She snapped her fingers again and Eira awoke, sitting up with a gasp, "What happened?"

"We're leaving." Leon took her arm and helped her off the floor.

"And, oh," Ophelessa called after them, "take this damned thing with you," she tossed them the replica necklace. "I have no use for it. Maybe you will."

They didn't speak again until they were halfway back to their camp, when Leon halted his horse and turned to face Eira, "Are you really pregnant?"

"I…I don't know," Eira stammered. "She's probably just trying to get to us, to force our hand into giving up."

"Eira, she's known everything else. Why would she lie about this?"

"She knows because Killian told her!" Eira cried. "He doesn't know this; he couldn't." The tears kept falling at monsoon pace.

"Hey, I know, I'm upset about Killian too, but she's not going to hurt him. She used him to get to you. We'll defeat her and get him back—I promise."

"How can you say that?" sniffled Eira.

"I don't know, okay. Let's just head back to the camp."

When they arrived back at camp, Eira ignored her friends trying to ask her what had happened. She headed straight for her tent and stayed there, crying into her pillow, until Leon arrived a few minutes later with a doctor.

"Good afternoon, Your Majesty," the doctor smiled.

"What's going on?" she asked Leon.

"We're finding out for sure."

The doctor moved over to where Eira was sitting on the bed and placed his bag on the spot next to her. He pulled out some vials and a needle, "Now, Your Majesty, your arm please. This might sting a bit, but we only need a small amount." He tied a band around her arm and drew some blood. Leon waited patiently, leaning against the table with his arms crossed. "Won't be long now," assured the doctor as he took a few drops of blood from the vial and mixed them with a few drops of something Eira didn't know. The doctor swirled the new mixture together and looked closely at the results. "Congratulations," he smiled, "you are indeed expecting."

"Thank you," said Leon, and showed the doctor out. Eira stood from the bed, not saying anything. She looked at Leon who was standing so placidly. He seemed to have no emotion or thought on the matter, but then he hurried to her and pulled her into a kiss. She smiled up at him and he smiled back. "We have to stop her, more than ever now, and...you can't be a part of it anymore."

"What?" said Eira, pushing back from him.

"I'm not putting my wife and child in danger. You can't be anywhere near this fight anymore."

"If you think I'm just going to sit back and watch everything happen around me, you have another thing coming. I'm the queen and I'm not giving up on my people."

"Eira, you cannot be serious. I'm not letting you put both of your lives in danger."

"And what happens if you die in all of this? You're just going to abandon me and your child? We're in this together. This is what we signed up for."

"I'm not letting you fight. I'll have the guards surround this tent indefinitely until the war is over if I have to."

"You have no right to do that," she spoke sternly.

"Really? We're married now, and that means technically I'm the king."

"No, technically, you're my husband. You're not the king yet."

Later, when they were all in Lord Evian's tent,

"So, are you guys finally going to tell us what happened? Where's Killian?" asked Theo.

"She got him," sighed Eira. "He's been feeding her information. We were caught."

"What?" gasped Theo. "Oh, he's never going to live this down." Eira glared at him. "What? He would appreciate the making light of the situation," he replied and Eira smirked slightly at the truth in that.

Leon took off his jacket and was about to sit when he noticed something. He reached into the pocket and pulled something out, "Hey, I didn't put this in here," he said as he tossed the necklace on the table.

"What? Is that the necklace?" asked Theo.

"No, it's the replica. A guard must have put it in your pocket when we were leaving," said Eira.

Suddenly, a new voice entered the conversation. It was a voice that was familiar to Eira, although she did not have the pleasure of ingraining it into her memory as she would have liked. The last time she heard it was a few months ago and only for a brief few days. She turned towards the voice and saw someone she thought she would not see again for a long time. "Man, you've been queen for less than a year and you already lost the throne?"

Eira looked to the entrance of the tent. She smiled, ignoring his opening remark, "Oren," she ran to hug her brother, "what are you doing here?"

"I heard you might need some help—and it sure looks like it. I was in Kevatia when I heard they were gathering troops to come to your aid. So, how can I help?"

"We're still working on that. Our latest plan didn't exactly go well." Eira was about to elaborate when she reached across the table to grab the necklace replica—

"Eira!" was all she heard, then everything went black.

****

Ophelessa was sitting in the great hall with Killian by her side. The first of many people who had come to see her that morning was sheepishly walking into her presence. They were all the same—begging for more food or help with their land. It was all trivial to her. She simply smiled and said she would give them everything they needed, trying to buy their affection. She waved every person off and then called the next in line to bow to her. Ophelessa loved the way the people came and groveled at her feet. This was the moment she had been waiting for years, the moment she felt her power seep into every crack and crevice of the land, into every person's heart to where they would not be able to come back from it if they tried. There was no way to stop her now. She was determined to prove to the people that they were better off with her as queen, and she was going to get every last person on her side by any means necessary. Since the necklace came back from the jeweller, all shined and gleaming, a newfound poise heightened her already overflowing confidence. There was nothing that could stop her now. She looked out over the vast fields below the castle, over to where the camp of a certain former queen lay in the shadows of a true ruler, unwavering and unable to come any closer. She loved having her enemy right on her doorstep. That pretentious sense that as long as they were there, she always knew where they stood and could keep a watchful eye. It is better to have your enemy in your sight and know where they will attack from, than not see them coming at all.

****

"What happened?" Eira sat up, reaching for her head. No one was answering her. When her vision became clear again, she looked around. There was no camp, no people. She was alone in the field. She looked out to the distance and could see Trillium Nivale. "Wait a minute," she looked around again and felt the earth beneath her bottom, "where's all the snow?"

22

Five years ago.

Eira stood and stared at her surroundings for a moment. She couldn't figure out what had happened. One minute she was in a tent with all her friends and the next she was lying in a field. She headed back in the direction she thought was camp, but she couldn't find it. After walking for some time, she was finally in town. *Great. At least this is familiar.* She headed for the only place that would be open this late.

As she walked through the streets, the people passing her along the way didn't seem to notice her, or notice who she was. She was just another citizen to them. When she finally made it to the pub, she didn't quite know what she was going to do. Was she just going to walk inside and ask the first person she saw where all the snow went?

She was staring at the doors to the pub, trying to decide her next move when they opened. Eira looked up and saw a familiar face. She rushed forward and tucked her arms under his and around his back, "Thank goodness! I've been looking all over for you. What happened?" She released the hug and looked up at Leon, not noticing that he looked slightly different.

"Eira?" he replied, pushing her forward to get a better look at the person who had just embraced him. "What are you doing here?" He then grabbed her by the hand and dragged her off into the alley so no one would see them.

"What are you talking about? Why wouldn't I be here—and what the hell happened to all the snow?"

He just kept staring at her until the silence was broken by another voice calling out, "Dude, where did you go?" Eira knew that voice—knew it too well. She pushed Leon aside and emerged from the alley.

"Killian?" she said, marching toward him.

"Do I know you?"

Leon was soon behind her. "What, of course you know me," added Eira.

He looked to Leon, "Oh good, there you are." He quickly changed the subject, "Oh man, that was great,"

Killian clapped Leon on the shoulder. "Did you see the look on that guy's face when you took all his money?"

"Okay, what is going on here?" asked Eira.

"Um, this is Eira," said Leon to Killian.

"This is Eira? The princess? What is she doing here?"

"That's what I'm trying to figure out." Leon turned back to Eira, "You're not supposed to be here. The last time I saw you was a month ago at training."

Eira went silent and stared at the ground, trying to make sense of everything that was happening. When she glanced up at Leon again, she caught a glimpse of his forearm, "Wait," she said grabbing his sleeve and pushing it farther up his arm, "where's your tattoo?"

"I don't have one," he said, yanking his arm from her.

"Oh, this is bad, this is not good." She was pacing in front of them and then stopped, "How old are you?"

"Um, okay—weird question," replied Killian.

"No, no, no, hang on. I want to see where this is going," said Leon. "Uh, twenty-two."

"What? Okay, no big deal, I'm just five years in the past!" She started talking to herself, pacing around the boys. "Okay so two options here. Option one: I can wait five years and not touch that stupid necklace again, except it won't be me, it'll be the other me that hasn't come here yet, so I'd have to warn her and that's just weird. In the meantime, I'm still stuck here." She let out a groan, "Ugh, time travel is so confusing! And option two: I need to figure out a way back except I have no idea how to do that! Okay, calm down, you have gotten out of worse." She took a deep breath and walked over to Leon and Killian, "Okay this going to sound absolutely insane, but a couple of hours ago I was in a tent with you figuring out how to defeat the Blue Queen, and I touched this necklace and passed out and ended up here."

Leon and Killian simply stared at her until Leon finally said, "Okay—what? Look I've had a lot to drink tonight, but even this is a little weird for me."

"I know it's weird, but you have to believe me. Right now the future you is fighting to get our kingdom back from the Blue Queen and I'm stuck here. I have no idea how to get back, but there's one person at the castle who may be able to help us."

"Wait—what am I doing?" Killian piped in.

"Um, I should probably not get into that."

"Alright, look, *Princess*," began Leon.

And we're back to calling me, Princess, Eira rolled her eyes.

"You're not supposed to be here, and we need to figure out a way to get you out of here before someone sees you. I don't buy this time travel thing—I don't know what's wrong with you, but Feya is going to kill me if she finds out you're here with me instead of with her where you're supposed to be."

"Are you serious? You have a freaking dragon in this world, but time travel is hard to believe?"

Suddenly, another voice joined the group, this time from a female. A woman about Eira's age stumbled out of the bar over to Leon and threw her arm around him, "Hey, you're leaving? We were just getting started. You said I could see the castle."

He smiled at her, "Sorry, it'll have to be another night."

Eira scrunched her nose at the sight of them and the woman was not too pleased with Eira's presence. "Who's this?" asked the overly affectionate with Leon woman.

"No one," replied Leon. "Don't worry about it."

"I'm his wife," smiled Eira.

"What?" gasped Leon and Killian.

"She's joking—she's *not* my wife," assured Leon.

"Yes I am," Eira said holding up her ring.

The woman pushed Leon away, "You're married?" and slapped him across the face. "Pig!"

He turned to Eira and glared down at her. "What?" she asked innocently.

"We're not married."

"Well, you and I aren't, but the future you and I are. That was a weird sentence."

He rubbed his brow and gave a sigh, "We're seriously married?"

"Well, technically yes. But man, did you drag your feet with proposing. I mean, it took you almost letting me marry someone else, and then me almost dying to finally do it."

A snort came from behind Leon, "That's so you," mocked Killian.

Leon glowered at Killian. "What?" he turned back to Eira.

"Oh, don't worry—I obviously didn't die," she assured him.

"Well, I probably didn't propose because we're technically already engaged being betrothed and all," he shook his head. "But anyway, that still doesn't help this situation that we're in right now. And how do I know you're the real Eira? You could be some imposter just trying to get into the castle. You *do* look slightly older than her."

"Well, yeah, I'm five years older than what you know me as. What? I'm like, seventeen to you." He stood there with his arms crossed until she spoke again, "Fine, ask me something only I would know."

"I have no idea what only you would know. I barely know you. I've known you for less than a year."

"Well, then you're just going to have to trust me."

"Dude, I like her. You should totally take her home," smiled Killian.

"Fine, we need to get you out of here before we attract too much attention. Let's go," he motioned for her to follow him.

"Hi, buddy," smiled Eira, scratching Harwin's nose when Leon led her over to him.

"That's weird. He doesn't usually like strangers."

"I'm not a stranger," she smiled.

"Well, if he hasn't met you yet—yes you are."

"Well, maybe somehow he just knows."

"Whatever," he motioned for Eira to get on the stallion and then he hoisted himself up, sitting behind her. He smirked slightly and was about to say something when Eira cut him off.

"Don't say it."

"Say what? I wasn't going to say anything," replied Leon.

"Yes you were—and then I was probably going to call you a prick."

****

"Eira!" shouted Leon. "What happened?" The others looked around just as stunned as he was. "Where did she go?"

"Don't look at us," replied Theo. "We know about as much as you."

"She's not the only one that touched that necklace. Why did it only do that to her?" He knew the others didn't actually know what happened either. "What did she do to it?" he asked.

"Who?" Theo asked.

"The Blue Queen. She must have done something, and I'm going to find out what." Leon stormed off, necklace in hand toward the door.

"What are you doing? You can't just march into the castle and ask what happened. You need to think this through," urged Theo.

"No, that is exactly what I'm going to do and I don't care what happens to me. She's the only one who knows what happened to Eira." He headed out of the tent and toward Harwin.

"Leon!" called Theo after him. He was running toward him with Oren trailing behind.

"Look, we know when it comes to Eira we can't stop you, but we can at least go with you," smiled Theo.

"You guys don't have to. We shouldn't risk all of us ending up in jail—or worse."

"Ah, I've been in worse places with you," nudged Theo.

"Alright fine. Let's go then."

The three of them headed off toward the castle. When they arrived, it was dark. It was as if the entire castle had fallen under some sort of sleeping spell.

"This isn't weird at all," pondered Theo as they rode up to the gates, no guards to greet them, or rather prevent them from entering. They left their horses outside and walked in. The halls were empty and quiet.

"Is everyone sleeping?" asked Oren.

"I don't think so," replied Leon warily, placing a hand on his sword. "I doubt Ophelessa lets her guards sleep." They headed for the great hall and sure enough, there she was, as if they had arrived with an invitation.

"I'm assuming you're here to find out where your little queen has gone," Ophelessa called out across the room.

"What did you do to her?" yelled Leon.

"I sent her away. A little insurance that you would never be able to stop me. The minute she touched that necklace, poof—gone. And there's no way back."

"What are you talking about? I touched that necklace too."

"Well, I don't need you out of the way, handsome." She walked toward him, casually circling him as he glared at her, hand still on the hilt of his sword. "No, you I could actually use. Still want to be king, sweetheart?"

"I swear, Ophelessa, if you don't tell me where Eira is, I will remove your head from the rest of you right here."

She sighed, "Oh darling, don't be so dramatic. She's fine, she's just in a place where she has no power over me, or anything really. I sent her back—five years, roughly. I didn't quite specify it when I enchanted that necklace."

"What?" piped up Theo.

"Your beloved little queen is hanging out in the dry desert Talvia used to be, and there's no way back. No one has ever successfully enchanted anything to travel through time—well, until me, that is." She waved her hand goodbye to them and gave a cackle that echoed through the hall.

"No!" Leon lunged after her, but his sword was stopped by a familiar force and he stared Killian in the face. "Bring her back!" he yelled through the struggles of fighting Killian. They had fought many times as kids and men, but it was like the spell Ophelessa had over him had made him stronger. He couldn't win. Finally, he broke free and Ophelessa ordered Killian to stop.

"What do you want me to do with them, Your Majesty?" Killian asked.

"I don't care—throw them outside. I don't need them cluttering up my dungeon. There's nothing they can do to me now."

"You don't know Eira, Ophalessa! She'll find a way back—she will!" Leon's calls echoed down the hall as they were dragged off.

****

"Okay, well here we are, at the castle," Leon announced as he helped Eira off of Harwin.

"Great, let's go get Gideon and find me a way back home."

"It's the middle of the night. Everyone is sleeping."

"Well, we need to wake him up then. This isn't exactly something that can wait until morning."

"What difference does it make?" Leon argued back as they walked the halls of the castle.

"I don't know, but I feel like it needs to happen now."

"And I feel like I need another drink." Leon grabbed Eira's hand and pulled her in the opposite direction.

When they got to where they were going, Leon rummaged around a moment for a few glasses and something to drink. He pulled out an old bottle that was half full with the snow-berry-infused liqueur she had enjoyed herself a number of times since being in Talvia and proceeded to pour the drinks. He handed one to Eira and then to Killian. They all took a sip when Eira remembered she couldn't and spat the drink back into her glass.

"Not a fan?" asked Killian.

"No, I just remembered I can't...I'm pregnant." Leon nearly spat his drink across the room. "It's new," she smiled.

"Aww, congrats man," said Killian, clapping Leon across the back. "Nice work."

When Leon was done choking on his drink, he stood and looked at Eira, "Okay, I'm sorry. All of this has got to be some weird joke, or dream, or something. I'm going to bed and when I wake up, *you* will not be here and everything will be back to normal. Okay? Good." He placed his drink down and walked out of the room.

Eira leaned over to Killian, "It's not going to be back to normal."

"Well, you know that, and I know that, but I can't wait to see the look on his face tomorrow."

Leon awoke to grumbling beside him the next morning. He rolled over to find a shirtless Killian sleeping peacefully beside him.

"Dude! What are you doing?" he jostled Killian awake.

"What?" Killian sat up and looked around. "Oh, yeah. I gave Eira my room." Leon was still staring at him, needing more information. "Well, what? I wasn't going to sleep in the same bed as your pregnant wife."

"What?"

Suddenly, the door swung open and Eira walked in, "Hangover?" asked Eira when she was at the foot of the bed.

"You're still here?"

"That's the face!" smiled Killian.

"Yeah, and unfortunately this isn't the first time I've seen you two like this," she motioned to the two of them in bed. "Anyway, I know this is still weird for you, but I seriously can't waste any more time. I need to talk to Gideon and see if there is a way I can get home. One day you'll understand what is at stake."

Leon took a deep breath and got out of bed. Dragging Killian out of bed too, he pulled him into the bathroom. "How are you not freaking out about any of this?"

"Well, she's not my wife," replied Killian.

"You're not helping!"

"Look, I think we need to believe her. Take her to Gideon—he'll know if she's crazy or telling the truth. And if she is telling the truth, we need to help her."

"I know, but it's just all a little much," added Leon.

"Come on, it'll be a fun story to tell your kid later."

Leon's face fell unimpressed. "Okay, you seriously have to stop. And you could have slept on the couch."

"I tried, it wasn't comfortable. You know I need proper support."

They headed back into the bedroom, "Alright, give me a minute to get dressed and we'll go to Gideon, but no one else can know you're here. We don't need the whole castle knowing this," insisted Leon.

"That's probably a good idea," replied Eira.

Leon headed to the closet, and a few moments later he emerged. He took a deep breath, "Okay," he motioned his hand to indicate Eira should head toward the door. She opened it slightly to make sure no one was in the hall, then they slipped out and headed for the library. They walked stealthily down the halls, checking around every corner before they continued. While there was a good chance that no one, especially the staff, would recognize Eira, they still didn't want to take any chances with anyone asking who she was. They managed to make it all the way to the great hall, but then they heard a voice billowing down the hall.

"It's your dad!" whispered Eira as she grabbed Leon and pulled him around the corner to hide. Killian followed close behind. "Quick, this way." She led them back down the hall in the opposite direction when she stopped at a tapestry and pulled the corner over to reveal a hidden door. She pushed it open and motioned for them all to get inside.

"Okay, I am starting to believe you may be who you say you are," whispered Leon as he flipped the switch on the wall to illuminate the passageway. Eira just smiled in response and they headed to the Library.

Gideon was nowhere to be seen when they emerged from the passageway into the library. They called out for him, but there was no reply until finally he wandered through the door holding a plate with a sandwich on it. They all turned to stare at him as he looked up, taking a bite of his meal.

"You're not supposed to be here yet," he stated through a mouthful of ham and cheese. He swallowed, "Well, not for another one thousand three hundred ninety-two days. Give or take."

"Wait, you know who she is?" asked Leon.

"Of course, I would recognize Adela's daughter in a heartbeat."

"See," Eira nudged Leon.

"So, the question is, my dear, why are you here?" asked Gideon.

"Well, that's the weird part..." Eira proceeded to tell Gideon what had happened. He stood there listening to every word of it, as if nothing she was saying was out of the ordinary. When she was finished, he wandered over to a bookcase and started looking for something.

"What are you looking for?" asked Killian.

"A book—what else? Ah, here it is." He headed back over to the three of them and placed the book on the table and flipped through it until he found the page he was looking for. "Well, this is a predicament you have gotten yourself into. I have only ever heard of one enchantment that can turn back time. Only a really powerful sorcerer has the ability to cast that spell. Without someone like that, I'm afraid you're stuck here."

"Well, what if we did have someone like that?" asked Eira.

"I suppose if you did, you could, in theory, enchant an object to become a time turner, but, Eira, there is no one in this world as powerful as the Blue Queen."

"There is one person, but I don't exactly know where to find him. The last time we did, he found us," said Eira.

"Who?" asked Leon.

"The caretaker of the owls. His name's Al, but he lives in the Land of the Owls. Only the owls can take us there, and they don't seem to listen to me very well."

"He's still alive?" asked Gideon.

"Yeah, but it took a lot of convincing to get him to help us last time, and even if we can find him, I don't know if he still has the power to help me."

"Well, that would be your best shot at getting back home," started Gideon. "But even if you can find Al, you need the enchantment first and that's a bit harder to find. It would be in the Library of the Seasons. It's the largest library in the world and holds millions of works from all around. Finding the scroll itself would be like finding a needle in a haystack, but it's your only chance at going home. It's also not a place you can just wander into—you usually have to be invited by the steward of the library himself. It's also heavily guarded considering it holds documents of this nature, and you cannot take anything out. You'll have to copy the enchantment and make sure it's right because one wrong word, and who knows what will happen."

"Okay, well, I guess that's where I'm going," Eira shrugged.

"We're going with you," smiled Leon. "You shouldn't do this alone."

She smiled back at him, "Where is it?" she asked Gideon.

"On the border of Talvia, where the snow would start to fade into Spring—if it were still here."

Huh, convenient. "Well then, I guess we had better get going." Eira walked over to the corner of the library where the hidden door was.

"Where are you going?" asked Leon.

"To the door—it'll get us there faster. We don't have time to head all the way to the border on horseback."

"Yeah, but we should probably hit the armoury first. You don't have anything to defend yourself and you heard Gideon, it's heavily guarded. How do you suppose we actually get into that place?"

"I don't know. I was going to figure it out when we got there."

"Well, lucky for you, you have two of the stealthiest men coming along with you. We've snuck in and out of many places," Leon put an arm around Killian and smiled.

"Yeah, you and I both know Killian is about as subtle as a tornado." Eira grinned, "That might work to our advantage, though. While he may not be the best at sneaking into places—he has *distraction* written all over him."

The Library of the Seasons was a massive building hidden in the forest that bordered Talvia and Kevatia. Its spires towered five stories high, and the domed roofs just poked over the treetops from the surrounding forest. The vines on the Kevatia side were overgrown, crawling up every stone on the Spring side of the building. They could see the guards surrounding it. Gideon had not exaggerated the security surrounding this place.

"So, now what?" asked Killian as they crouched in the forest, watching the guards at their posts.

"I don't know," replied Eira, studying every entrance they could see to the library. The front doors seemed like the obvious choice, but they were also the most heavily guarded. There was a skylight in the atrium at the centre of the building, but she wasn't so sure that would be the best choice. Eira could see that there was a massive tree at the heart of the library soaring up into the atrium and out of the skylight. That could work if they could get into the roof somehow.

"Well," suggested Killian, "why don't we just walk up and ask to go in? Most people probably don't try that."

"And say what?" started Eira. "That I'm the Queen of Talvia and I need to get in there for the sake of everyone's future. I'm sure that'll go well."

"Well, we can ask for an audience with the steward. Maybe he'll let us in—it's worth a try."

"Well, whatever we do, we had better figure it out quickly. I still have to go train with the past you this evening," added Leon.

"What? You couldn't have mentioned that earlier?" asked Eira.

"I might have forgotten until right now," shrugged Leon.

Eira let out an exasperated groan, "Alright, fine, let's just walk right in," agreed Eira.

The three of them walked up to the entrance of the library. The doors towered over them—three stories high.

"Do you have an appointment?" asked one of the guards.

"Yes," replied Eira.

The guard looked them up and down, "Follow me."

The three shared the same look of, *that was easy.* The doors opened to reveal a massive entryway with stained glass domed skylights depicting various scenes of spring, summer, autumn, and winter. At the centre of the room, was a large domed skylight with a night sky scene with the moon at the centre and various constellations around it.

"Sign in there. You have three hours," informed the guard.

Killian shrugged and signed them in, "See, I told you we should just walk right in."

"Yeah, that was way too easy," said Leon.

"Well, maybe they only like to spread the rumour that this isn't a place anyone can just walk into, to keep it less busy. It looks like we're the only ones in here. I mean, it is still extremely heavily guarded," Killian added.

"Okay, well, where do we start then?" asked Leon.

"I have no idea," sighed Eira. "Gideon said it would probably be a scroll, so where are the scrolls kept?"

"Fifth floor," replied Killian, looking at a directory on the wall. "There are seventeen scroll rooms, though."

"Seventeen!" gasped Eira and her voice echoed through the library. A guard gave her a stern look and she quieted. "This is going to take longer than three hours."

"Well, we should get started then," motioned Leon to the stairs.

When they finally reached the fifth floor, after what felt like two thousand steps, they could see all the various rooms filled to the brim with shelves upon shelves of scrolls. Each room had years written over their arched entrances to indicate which centuries' information was held within.

"I guess we should start from the beginning. Gideon said it would be an ancient spell," said Eira. "You guys probably know more about Talvia's history than I do, though."

"Oh yeah," Killian rolled his eyes, "I was totally paying attention to the part of history class where they would have gone over this."

"Let's start here," suggested Leon. "I doubt it'd be right at the beginning, but not too far in."

They walked through the archway and looked at the shelves. Each shelf also indicated what types of scrolls were held there: mathematics, science, history, fiction, non-fiction, philosophy—you name it. "Well, at least it's organized," said Eira. "What do you suppose ancient spells are under?"

"Guys," called Killian from another part of the room. "I don't think it's going to be on one of these shelves." They followed where Killian's voice was coming from and found him staring at the entrance to another part of the room labelled: *Forbidden,* over the archway. "I'll bet you a hundred gold pieces it's in there."

Great. "How are we supposed to get in there?" asked Eira. It was strange it was not guarded, but they could all sense there was something in the air near the doorway that led them to believe it was enchanted and no one would be able to enter.

"You three do not have an appointment," came a voice behind them. They turned to find an older man standing behind them—the steward. His long robes puddled around his feet, and his greying hair was unkempt. "What are you doing here?"

"Please," began Eira. "We need to find a certain spell, to enchant something to be able to turn time—it's a matter of life and death."

"Now why would anyone need something like that?" Eira was slightly shocked that the man did not instantly call the guards to drag them out of there. He seemed intrigued, but how far was that going to get them? Eira was unsure of how much to tell him, however if he was the steward of the library, he would know of the Blue Queen and her history—he should want to help.

"Look, this is going to sound insane, but I'm not from here. I was sent back here from the future, and I need that spell to go back. My name is Eira and four years from now I defeat the dragon and bring back the snow. Then a year later, the Blue Queen is released and wreaks havoc on this land. She's the one who sent me back, so I wouldn't be able to stop her."

"That is an interesting story," pondered the steward. "A quite elaborate one at that. I'm not sure if anyone would be able to fabricate something so outlandish, therefore—it must be true," he smiled. "But I'm afraid the scroll won't help you much. I'm guessing none of you are a powerful sorcerer?" They all shook their heads. "Without someone to perform the spell, it will be utterly useless to you."

"We know, and I do know of someone who can help us," replied Eira.

"And who is that?"

"The man who trapped Ophelessa inside the Diamond of Azul in the first place. I've met him, and he battled her not long ago, but unfortunately, she defeated him. However, five years in the past, he's still here."

"You do know what you are talking about," said the steward. "Any information on anything you have just told me resides only within these library walls, and I certainly have never seen you before. So, either someone who has been here and has researched this very topic told you, or...you truly are the Queen of Talvia," he bowed. "I will help you, Your Majesty."

He unlocked the room and the three waited until he emerged with a small scroll, barely bigger than Eira's index finger. They copied the spell exactly and thanked the steward for his help.

"Hey," stated Leon when they were back in the forest, "do you think we'll remember all of this when you go back? Like, will we talk about the time you showed up and freaked the hell out of me by telling me you were my pregnant wife?"

"I don't know, but I'm guessing neither of you will remember this. Why would Ophelessa send me back if there was a chance I could screw up her future from the past? It would be too easy for me to just wait five years and never let this happen in the first place. I don't think anything I do here is going to have an effect on the future. If I were her, I would have made sure of that."

"So what did you mean when you said you didn't want to tell me what I was up to in the future?" asked Killian.

Eira looked at the ground and her voice turned solemn, "Oh, um. Well..." She didn't know if she should tell him, but she felt like she owed it to her friend, "You sort of fall under her spell. You brought a message to her from me and...she cursed you." Eira was trying not to cry. It had been a while now since she was able to talk to her friend. "But don't worry, we're going to get you back as soon as I'm out of here. I know you would never intentionally betray me—or any of us."

Killian didn't say anything, then finally, "Damn, we really do need to get you back to the future."

Eira smirked, *ha—back to the future*. "Yeah," she sighed. "But, hey," she held up the piece of paper, "we're one step closer now." She reached for her jacket pocket and unzipped it to put the scroll inside, but felt something else in her pocket at her fingertips and pulled out the small silver whistle. It was so light in her hand; barely there at all.

"What's that?" asked Leon, peering into her palm.

She looked at the guys and smiled.

23

Eira desperately wanted to go find Al, but she was forced to wait until the next morning. By the time they had arrived back at the castle, Leon was already an hour late for his training with the past Eira, and he wasn't about to let her go without him.

When Leon returned, he found Eira sprawled out on the chaise in the sitting area in his bedroom waiting for him, reading a book. "Ah," he called out. "Sorry, I'm still getting used to this. I just saw you—but now you're here too." He sighed, "Look, I'm just going to shower and then we can do the owl thing."

"Okay," she smiled.

He headed for the bathroom and a few minutes went by before the door cracked open, "Hey," he called. She turned to where she could see him poking out of the bathroom. "Can you come here a minute?"

"Uh, sure," she smiled. She walked over to the bathroom and stopped at the doorway where Leon was leaning with an arm overhead. She looked up at him, his eyes watching her intensely. Why did he keep doing that? Seriously, did he do it on purpose when she was around? See, this—this is how she got pregnant.

"Look, this is weird," he began, "but I recognize that you've probably seen me like this before. Anyway, you seemed to have got me good in training today—you were pretty pissed I was late—and I have a scrape on my back that I can't reach. Do you mind?"

"Sure," Eira smiled. He opened the door to reveal he was only wearing his boxers. She took a breath and composed herself. He walked over to the counter and handed her the bottle of ointment and some gauze. She wiped some of the ointment over his cut and like magic—well, it *was* magic—the scrape was gone.

He turned to face her when she was done, "You don't remember me being late? I mean, I wouldn't have been if it weren't for all of this." Eira shook her head. "Huh, I guess whatever happens here really doesn't affect the future." He looked down a moment and then back, eyes fixated on her, "You know, it's weird. I just saw you an hour ago, but you're right. It's not you—you're different. I'm starting to see why I fell in love with you." He was leaning against the bathroom counter with his arms crossed. She didn't respond. "What?" he looked suddenly uncomfortable.

"Oh, nothing," she smiled, placing the bottle of ointment down beside him. "It's just I have a lot of hormones in me right now, and..." she motioned to his bare chest, "you're not exactly helping the situation." She took a step back, "So, I'm just going to..." she pointed toward the door to indicate she was about to leave. But before she could, he reached out a hand and pulled her between his legs.

He smiled, "Oh, yeah? And what would the future me do to help you with that?" He spun her around and lifted her onto the counter, her legs now around his waist and his arms on either side of her, supporting himself against the counter.

This isn't technically cheating, right? Although, if you have to use the word, 'technically'? He kissed her. *Yeah, no.* She pushed him back and jumped down from the counter. "Nope, this is just weird," and she walked out of the bathroom with Leon chuckling, now sitting on the counter where she was moments ago.

"Alright, I guess we should head out then. The sooner we get you back the better," announced Leon as he emerged freshly showered from the bathroom.

She nodded, "Yes, I am so ready to be back where I belong and this can just be some weird, slightly out-of-place, chapter in my life."

Killian had already declined going with them—he wasn't a bird fan. Eira and Leon walked out onto his balcony. "You know what you're doing?" he asked as Eira held the whistle in her hands.

"Not really. But how difficult is it to blow a whistle?" She put the whistle up to her lips and blew. No sound came from it, but she figured it was like a dog whistle and only the owls could hear it. They waited a few minutes, but no owls came. "Great—what now?"

Leon shrugged, "Blow it again?" She did, but still no sound came from it.

They waited again until finally Eira heard the cry she was hoping for.

As if the owls knew exactly why she had called them, they soared through the night sky into the mountains where the great birds lived. They landed in the same room they took Eira and her friends before. Eira and Leon slid down the owl's back onto the cold stone floor, and looked at their surroundings. "Yeah, Killian would have hated this place," said Leon, as he stepped around some owl droppings.

"Al," called Eira, her voice echoing into the highest parts of the mountains. "Al," she called again.

"Who is there?" came a voice, finally. "How did you call my owls?" Al emerged from another room and saw Eira and Leon waiting by the large tree at the centre of the room.

"With this," she held out the whistle to him when Al was finally close enough to them.

"How did you get my whistle?" he asked as he reached a hand into his pocket to ensure his whistle was still there.

"You gave it to me. I know this is going to sound crazy, but we have met before. My name is Eira. I'm the Queen of Talvia and I really need your help."

Al's expression remained the same through Eira's tale. She explained everything to him and he didn't seem the slightest bit surprised by any of her story. He took the scroll from Eira and looked over the spell. "Do you think you can do it?" asked Eira.

He sighed, "This is not a spell anyone in history has ever been able to successfully master—well, I guess one did. If anything goes wrong, I have no idea what will happen to you or where you will end up."

"Please, I'm willing to take that risk. You have to do it," pleaded Eira.

"I will do my best."

Eira and Leon waited as Al worked for hours until finally he had it. "Okay," he said, placing the whistle he had given Eira on the table in front of them. "You touch this, and you should be back, exactly where you were before—so long as you are sure you explained to me every detail of where you were and what was happening when you touched the necklace."

"I did," Eira nodded. "I guess this is it," she turned to Leon.

"Look, as you may know," began Leon, "I wasn't exactly looking forward to having to marry you one day—but now...I think I'm really looking forward to the future."

She smiled, "Thanks. And I'm going to apologize in advance for how many times I hit you when I first ended up back here."

"What?"

"Okay, bye," she smiled and was about to touch the whistle when she was pulled back by Leon and held in his arms. She smiled up at him.

"Bye," he said as their eyes locked and finally let her go.

Then she touched the whistle.

****

She was on the ground again. This time her butt was freezing from the snow all around. Eira gasped awake and inhaled the sharp, cold air around her. *Thank gods*, she smiled. She still didn't know for sure that she was back, but she was hopeful. Eira stood and brushed the snow from her behind and could see the camp in the distance. She was right on the border of it and when she got closer, Lord Evian's guards noticed her and rushed over.

"Eira!" called Leon, as he rushed to embrace her when she walked into their tent. He held her back to look her over, "Are you okay? What happened?"

"I'm fine," she smiled, "just glad to be back."

"Ophelessa said she sent you back—did she really?"

"What? You knew where I was?"

"Yes, as soon as you disappeared, I headed straight for the castle and demanded she tell me what she did. How did you get back?"

"Well, you helped me, and...Killian," Eira lowered her voice. She then proceeded to tell Leon everything.

"Wow," said Leon when she was done. He grinned, "So, did anything happen between us?" he raised his brows.

"What?" she stared at him.

"Come on—really?" His eyes narrowed, "Nothing?"

"No. Okay, you did kiss me, but that was all."

His stupid grin made Eira frown. "Yeah I did."

"What? If the roles were reversed, you would have tried something with me?" asked Eira.

He nodded, "Oh, yeah. I would have had so much fun trying to convince you that we're married. Although, you did hate me back then—a lot." He sighed and smiled, "Ah...fun memories."

"Whatever, this is all just so weird and I'd rather just forget it ever happened."

After dinner that evening, and after Eira had filled in the rest of the group about what had happened to her, they were finally back to figuring out what their next move should be. While she was gone, they were busy trying to figure out how to get her back from their end and put the trying to defeat Ophelessa on hold for a while, so they were still no closer to defeating her than they were when Eira left.

Eira found her brother standing outside in the frigid night air, after they had been discussing a new plan for hours. "So," she started, "how long are you here for this time?"

"Not sure. Maybe I'll even stick around afterward. Clearly you need help ruling."

"I do not," she shoved him and smiled. She had known her brother for all of a week, over a year ago, and for a few days here and there afterward. She never really got to know the only family she had, and his presence here tonight made her hope that there was some truth behind what he was saying, that he would stay this time.

"This is going to be a tough one, Eira," he said, looking out toward the little yellow slits of the castle windows illuminated in the distance. "Much more difficult than the dragon."

"Yeah, I'm starting to see that." She sighed and then changed the subject, "So, how's Bianca?"

He shrugged, "We're not together anymore."

"Oh, sorry. Clea never mentioned anything."

"Don't be. People go in and out of relationships, Eira. It's not that big of a deal."

"Well, okay," she replied. She could tell he didn't exactly believe what he had just said, but it was clear that he didn't want to talk about it. "I guess I'll head to bed then—goodnight."

She walked back over to her tent, leaving him standing there in the darkness. The tent was lit with the glow of an oil lamp on the bedside table. Eira fastened the canvas flap to the tent pole to ensure no cold air could make its way inside to disrupt her night. Leon's arms were ready and waiting for her to nestle herself into when she crawled onto the bed.

"Do you think he's staying this time?" asked Leon

"I hope so. I hope he realizes with everything that has happened that he can't just leave anymore. I need him here."

"I know you do, but you've been fine without him for years and you have family here," added Leon.

"Yeah, but I never knew what I was missing."

Leon held her tighter and kissed her forehead, "Look," he began, "I have no idea what is going to happen in the next few days and I just want you to know—"

"Don't," she said, sitting up on the bed and turning to face him. "Don't do this—everything is going to be fine. We'll find a way to beat her. I mean, I found a way back from the past—how hard can this be?"

He smiled warmly and pulled her back into him, "How are you feeling?" He placed a hand on her belly.

"Good," she smiled. "I was a bit nauseous earlier, but dinner seemed to help."

"That's good." He paused a moment, staring off into the distance, "You know, I still don't like you being fully involved in all of this now."

"I know, but what are we supposed to do? You know I can't just sit back and not fight. We're in this together—we agreed on that." Eira rubbed the small braided silver band on his finger—the match to hers made by the Wintren-elves.

"I know."

****

"Are you alright, Your Majesty?" Ceilidh asked Ophelessa when she brought her lunch. "You looked a little tired today. Should I turn down the bed for you? Perhaps a little rest would do you some good."

"No!" snapped Ophelessa. She did not know what was coming over her and she did not want anyone to know she was feeling her powers fade. Ceilidh was taken aback by Ophelessa's response and moved closer to the door to leave her in peace. "No, I mean," she said in a calmer tone, then held her hand out to the girl. "Come here, child. I promise I won't bite." A shy smile spread across Ceilidh's face as she moved slowly to where the queen splayed herself across the chaise. When she got closer, her hands were taken from where they rested against the front of her dress and she breathed in as they were hidden inside Ophelessa's. Ophelessa pulled her down so she was sitting beside her on the chaise and patted Ceilidh's hands as they rested in her lap. "Now, I don't want you to think I am as mean and ruthless as they say. Of course, I do take pride in my ability to instil terror in my enemies, but anyone worthy of being a great ruler should," she looked at the bruising on Ceilidh's face, only now beginning to lighten. She held a hand to her chin to examine the markings better, "I think you know what I am capable of, and I think you have certainly learned your lesson—you've been nothing but loyal since our little misgivings."

"I'm—I'm sorry, Your Majesty," said Ceilidh. "I was just startled is all. I didn't mean to offend you."

"You didn't, my dear child," she said now moving her hand to Ceilidh's cheek. "Now run along and tell everyone how kind I have been to you. I do hope we can be friends someday," she smiled and forced Ceilidh on her feet again, moving her legs back to resting across the chaise and taking her glass from the coffee table. "Soon you will forget that dear little saviour queen of yours. I am much more gracious, I assure you."

Ceilidh curtsied and vanished through the door, closing it tightly behind her.

Forcing her way down the winding steps into the dungeon and making her way to the farthest cell, Ophelessa could see the man within, hunched over his knees sitting on the damp floor. Two guards were trailing behind her and when they reached the cell door, one of them took the keys from the wall and unlocked it. She sauntered into the cell.

"They tell me you are the wisest man in this castle and you know all the legends of old and events of the past."

Gideon looked up to see his visitor. "I suppose you could say that," he answered.

"Tell me what you know of me," she ordered, "and what you know of this diamond."

"I cannot tell you anything you don't already know."

"Well, maybe you can." She reached down and pulled at Gideon's tattered clothes, forcing him onto his feet. "Why are my powers weakening when I have not removed the diamond from my body?"

"Are you sure about that?" he asked her in a plain tone, not at all fazed by her forcefulness.

"I removed it once to have it cleaned. It was gone for less than a day. That would hardly have an effect. Besides, it is back around my neck now. It should be doing its job."

"I don't know what to tell you, Your Majesty. You're right. It should be doing its job then," he said with an air of satisfaction in his voice.

The Blue Queen let go of his collar and shoved him away from her. He slunk down back to his spot on the floor and picked up the book he was reading. She moved to the cell door and just before she left Gideon in the darkness, he turned his head toward her one more time, "Perhaps it is because the power you draw from it is being spent too frivolously," he said plainly. "All your power comes from within that little piece and once it's gone, you cannot get it back. Perhaps you need to spend it more wisely."

She stormed out of the cell and into the great hall where Killian was currently residing over the throne, sitting in it with his body shifted to one side and resting his head on his fist, looking utterly bored with a royal life.

"What's wrong with you?" asked Killian as he watched Ophelessa stomp over to the throne beside him and slump down into it.

"Nothing," she shot back at him.

"Okay." He seemed uninterested in whatever she had to say.

"That stupid little queen," she muttered. "That stupid little friend of yours is making me use my powers too much. Sending her back must have taken more of a toll on me than I thought."

"Yeah, but she's gone now, so your powers can recover. Just don't use them all the time." There was a moment of silence while Ophelessa thought over what Killian had said and refrained from punching him for the obvious comment. "So," he started again, "why do they call you the Blue Queen? You're not blue."

Ophelessa shot Killian a glare, then leaned into him, "Have you ever seen blue ice? The kind on the underside of icebergs—a powerful force just waiting to be released and obliterate anything in its wake."

Just then, a guard marched into the hall, "She's back, Your Majesty."

"Who is?" Ophelessa sneered at him.

"The queen—sorry, the old queen," he bowed. She shot upright. "We're not sure how, but we just received word that she has arrived back at her camp."

"That is impossible," she turned and grabbed Killian by the collar and pulled him closer to her, "How did that little wretch beat my time-turning spell?" She threw him back and screamed, the echoes in the great hall deafening all around them.

"Relax," said Killian, "even though she managed to find a way back doesn't mean she can defeat you. You're still far more powerful than anything she can throw at you. Now maybe you should go get some rest. You look...haggard."

She glowered at him, the rage building in her veins. "I do not need rest! I am a queen!" she forced.

****

The sun was nowhere to be found the next morning. Grey light cascaded across the sky as Eira sat at the breakfast table in Lord Evian's tent. "Okay," she finally said after she had finished her breakfast. "I've thought a long time about this, and I think it's time we fight. We give her all we've got and just end this. I have no idea what will happen, but we're out of options and out of time."

"Are you sure you want to do that?" asked Leon. "We're probably all going to die."

"Then we'll die together. I can't sit here in this camp anymore, useless, while she sits up there in the castle and terrorizes my people. We still have the dagger and maybe we can fight our way to that necklace and destroy it once and for all."

"We're behind you all the way, Eira, but—" Theo was cut off by the sound of horns bellowing outside their tent. They all turned to listen more carefully.

"What's that?" asked Eira.

"I don't know," replied Leon, getting to his feet and walking to the entrance of the tent. He pulled back the flat and peered outside, then turned back to the group, "You're going to want to see this."

An army dressed in colours of emerald green like the fresh grass of summer, were making their way through the camp. Their flags displayed the crest of a great golden tree from the roots to the canopy on an emerald shield. On either side of the tree, was a tiger reaching its mighty paws up the trunk.

"Who are they?" asked Eira as they all stood outside the tent watching as the commander of the army dismounted his horse and strode over to them.

"That is the Kesan army," smiled Theo. "I can't believe you actually did it."

"I don't think I'm the one who did it," smiled Eira, nodding toward a familiar face. Nevin dismounted his horse and was soon walking over to them as well.

"So," greeted the commander, "I hear there is a battle to be won here."

The Kesan army was larger than Talvia's, Syysia's, and Kevatia's combined. They greatly outnumbered Ophelessa's army just on their own.

Commander Harris was a tall, thin man. Not someone who looked like he had seen many battles, or that would do well in one, but perhaps his physique made him more agile on the battlefield. His golden hair was well kept, and he stood with a poise that challenged any royal or nobility in his company.

He soon laid out a plan of attack for the field below the castle while Eira and the rest of her friends made a plan for taking back the castle itself. Commander Harris would make a show of the battle in the fields below while Eira and the rest headed for the castle.

"And how are we getting into the castle?" asked Theo. "The tunnels again?"

"Oh, no," said Eira, eyes drenched with spite, "we're marching right through the front doors."

****

Ophelessa was on the balcony as she watched the advancement of Eira's troops on her territory.

"Your Majesty," called Killian, bursting through the balcony doors, "they are moving on us. What should we do?"

"Call the troops to fight. If Eira wants a war, this is the war she is going to get. The first one was merely practice, but she has arrived just in time for the final show. And I'm not sure she will like the ending."

****

"Where are you guys going?" asked a voice when Eira and Leon were walking through the camp to their horses. Eira turned to see Lord Dundan, standing at the entrance of his tent, guards at either side of him and hands and feet still shackled. "I can't believe you got the Kesan army to fight for you." Leon simply ignored him, but Eira paused a moment. "Please, let me help you fight. I want to take down Ophelessa just as much as you do."

Eira walked over to him, "Did you know about Killian?" she asked.

"Who?" he replied.

"Our friend. The one she's controlling. The one who betrayed us because of a spell she put over him."

"No," he answered, eyes fixated on hers. "I swear to you—I didn't know."

"Eira, what are you doing?" asked Leon, walking up beside her and grabbing her arm, pulling her away from Dundan.

"He wants to help."

"So. He can stay right here until all of this is over and then he can be tried for everything he has done."

"I think we should let him fight."

"Eira," Leon sighed sternly.

"Please, just listen to me."

He looked into her eyes and finally moved to the guards beside Dundan and took the keys from them, "You had better not make me regret this, or I will hunt you down and make sure that you pay," said Leon as he unlocked Dundan's restraints.

"I believe you," he replied.

"This is it, soldiers," called Arlen on the back of his horse, looking to the oncoming battle. The air grew still and all that could be heard was the heavy breathing of the horses as they huffed in the frigid air and exhaled warm steam. Clouds of snow rose and tumbled around their hooves as they pounded the ground. These horses were bred for battle and they wanted nothing more than to charge.

Her footsteps echoed through the corridors with a pounding force. Her soldiers were lined in the hall ready to defend the castle, while more marched into battle on the fields below.

Inside the stone walls of the castle, another battle was brewing. Eira, Leon, Theo, Clea, and Oren made their way through Trillium Nivale toward the castle. They rode the stone bridge and when they neared the courtyard it was lined with guards.

It took them no time at all to break through the castle doors—their rage fuelling them and pushing them forward.

Eira had instructed more soldiers to enter the castle through the hidden passageways and they came pouring in, one by one, through the hidden door in the kitchen, taking out as many of Ophelessa's guards as they could.

Eira marched straight through the castle. She still didn't exactly know what she was going to do when she faced Ophelessa, but she was hoping that with every step closer to her she got, she became a step closer to finding the courage it would take to finally defeat her. Leon, Oren, and Clea made their way through the castle, taking out any guards they passed on the way, while Theo headed to the dungeon to free those imprisoned by Ophelessa.

When he got to the basement, he swiftly took out the one guard who was down there and unlocked the cells.

"Quickly, we have to get back upstairs and help Eira. She has the dagger and is going to destroy that diamond," said Theo.

"Wait," said Gideon. "She has the King's Dagger?"

"Yes," replied Theo, trying to hurry Gideon upstairs.

"That is not good," he replied. "If she uses that dagger to destroy the diamond the force might be so great that she will not survive."

The grand choreography of the battle beginning in the fields below could be heard as they made their way down the corridors of the castle. Eira saw the sacrifices that were being made for her on the reddened battlefield outside of the castle windows and with every ounce of strength she had within, she pushed herself forward to where she hoped Ophelessa would be waiting.

"Where is she?" demanded Ophelessa, tapping her fingers on the armrest of her stolen throne. Killian was beside her while her guards were standing at the doorway preventing anyone from making their way in—anyone but the very person she was waiting for.

"We seized these two just outside the great hall, Your Majesty," said two guards as they entered, dragging Clea and Oren with them. "The whole castle has been run through. There are few guards left standing."

"So this is it?" laughed Ophelessa at the sight of them. "Your brave queen sends you to do her dirty work? She can't even come and face me herself? Where is that rat, anyway? You know, it's rude to show up to a party late."

Clea and Oren didn't respond. They struggled in the arms of Ophelessa's guards as she rose from Eira's throne and strode slowly toward them. "And how is your wonderful queen going to save you now?" she asked when her face was so close to Clea's that she could see into the depths of her ice-cold eyes. "Take them away," Ophelessa ordered the guards. "I have no further use of them."

"But I do," announced Eira, making her way into the great hall with Leon behind her.

"Well, well. So you finally decide to show up. I guess everyone's here for the party, then. We may as well begin." Ophelessa glided across the stone floor toward her, "And I can't wait to see the look on your face when you see the surprise guest I invited." She snapped her fingers and out walked a guard, dragging Nell along beside him.

"Eira!" screamed Nell. She squirmed in the guard's clutches, "Let me go, you dis-proportioned brute! You know, skipping leg day is never a good idea." Killian headed over to where Eira stood. "Eira, no! There's something wrong with him, he's not himself."

He tried to disarm her, but she dodged out of the way. One benefit of training with Killian from time to time was that she knew all his moves. It wasn't difficult for her to outsmart him, although he seemed to be going easy on her somehow. It was as if he was holding back.

"Oh, Eira, what are you going to do now? You can't destroy me. Any hope of that died with Alareison on the battlefield. Did you really think that he could entrap me again?" Eira's expression remained placid as she looked Ophelessa up and down and glanced past her at Killian. "You see, I have everything you hold dear. I have two of your best friends—one of whom I think will make an excellent king," she stroked a finger up and down Killian's chest, "and the other one. Well, I'm not exactly sure what I'll do with her yet, but I'm sure I'll think of something really fun." Her eyes darkened as she dug into Eira's soul. "Or maybe...I'll just have him kill her." She nodded her head in the direction of Nell, and Killian began slowly making his way to her, unsheathing his sword when he was only a few steps from where she stood.

"No!" screamed Eira, "Don't, I'll give in. You can have the throne—don't hurt her."

"Oh, I figured you would, darling, but it's just not enough for me to take your throne—what will bring me the greatest joy is knowing that I sent you on your way utterly destroyed from losing all that you love." She nodded to Killian, and he advanced on Nell.

"No!" screamed Eira again, cutting between Killian and Nell. Leon joined in and fought to free Nell from the guard while Eira was in a standoff with Killian.

"Killian, stop!" screamed Nell through tears. "This isn't you. You have to wake up." He just ignored her and kept advancing toward Eira until Nell ran between the two. "Please," she pleaded with him, "please, stop." Killian paused a moment as if the familiarity of Nell's voice was getting to him, but he shook it off and moved forward, pushing Nell out of the way, but she pushed back. "Please," she said one last time, pushing against his chest and looking into his eyes. "This isn't you. I know the real you, the one who would stop at nothing to protect Eira—and me." Killian was backing them into the centre of the room where Ophelessa stood, watching with pleasure. "This isn't you—this isn't the man I fell in love with. Please—I love you, don't do this." He paused at the sound of the words coming from her mouth. He took his eyes off of Eira and looked at Nell and smiled. He walked straight up to Nell and pushed her to the side, turning to Ophelessa and tearing the necklace from her before she could react.

Her screams echoed through the hall. "What have you done?" she yelled at Killian. "I ordered you to kill them."

"You can't tell me to do anything," he smirked. "You never could." He tossed Eira the necklace and she caught it out of the air before Ophelessa could move.

"You're forgetting I still have my powers. I'll destroy all of you with the snap of my fingers."

"Not if I destroy you first." Eira pulled the dagger from her belt and placed the necklace on the floor, ready to plunge the diamond blade of the dagger into it.

"No!" yelled Ophelessa as she ran toward Eira. She threw a hand up and the marble column behind Eira began to crumble. Eira turned back and rolled out of the way with the necklace just in time to witness the marble crashing to the floor in front of her.

Marble scattered across the floor. The guards holding Clea and Oren were startled just long enough for Clea and Oren to free themselves. More guards rushed in, and Leon and Killian took them out as they came in. Stone was crumbling all around them as Ophelessa followed Eira around the hall, bringing down every column in her path. Everywhere Eira turned, more of the castle seemed to explode in her path, creating a mess of dust and blurring her vision. After a few times of forcing the stone to the floor, Ophelessa could feel her powers fading. She bent over her knees as if to catch her breath.

"Give it up," called Ophelessa when she regained her strength, "you cannot beat me now." She was calling and looking for Eira who was hiding behind some fallen chunks of stone, slowly making her way around and behind Ophelessa. Ophelessa threw her hand up one last time and sent stone flying toward Eira. She managed to just avoid it but slipped and fell to the floor.

Eira was moaning in the rubble when Ophelessa found her and stood at her side, staring down at her. She placed a foot on Eira's hand which was still clutching the necklace and ripped it from her grasp.

She sighed, "Now, that's better," she said, holding out the necklace in front of her. But it was ripped from her fingers just as she had pried it from Eira's. "What are you doing?" she screamed at Lord Dundan as he held the necklace in front of her.

"Fixing my mistake." He motioned for Eira to give him the dagger and when it was firmly in his grasp, he threw himself to the floor and plunged the dagger right into the centre of the cold stone floor beneath the necklace.

Ophelessa's laugh radiated throughout the hall, "You think you can destroy it that easily?" she cackled, holding the necklace out with her index finger as it swung back and forth.

Eira climbed atop one of the fallen pieces of stone and leapt behind Ophelessa with her sword. She turned quickly and caught Eira's sword in the air and forced it from her hands. Ophelessa was slowly backing Eira into a corner as Clea, Oren, and Leon were taking out the last of the guards. She raised her hand and lifted Eira off the ground by the neck. She was struggling against the wall as she gasped for breath, not giving in to Ophelessa.

"Eira," called Oren. He lunged for Ophelessa and knocked her off balance just long enough for her to release her hold on Eira. She dropped Eira instantly and she slumped to the floor, gasping for breath. Ophelessa turned her attention now to Oren as she still grasped the necklace firmly in her hand. Eira managed to find her breath and make her way back to her feet. She looked all around the room. Ophelessa's guards were no more—lying in the rubble. Ophelessa was the last one standing from her side. The rest in the room were, and always will be, loyal to the only true Queen of Talvia.

She took a deep breath and fastened the necklace once again around her neck. "Well, that was easy," said Ophelessa brushing off her dress and picking crumbs of rubble off her sleeve.

"Eira. Eira," said Leon, as he ran and knelt beside her. She slowly sat up, holding her arm. "Are you okay?" asked Leon. As he did, he heard Ophelessa's voice coming over the dust from the crumbling castle around them.

"My people," she announced to the battlefield below. The soldiers turned their attention to the castle above them. "Your queen has fallen. I am the Queen of Talvia now and you will all obey me now and forever. This will be a new era for Talvia and its people. I am sure you will all find, in time, that following me will be best for everyone."

The crowd below remained silent as the snow began to fall around them. Eira's troops did not know whether to keep fighting or not.

"What should we do, Captain?" asked Nevin, looking to where he knew his friends were fighting.

"I'm not sure," answered Arlen.

"It can't be over—can it?" They stared up at the Blue Queen standing over them and looked at the faces of the other men fighting for Talvia and did not know if there was still a Talvia worth fighting for.

25

"Where is it? Where is it?" said Gideon as he rummaged through drawers and boxes on his desk in the library. Then he remembered something. He climbed the spiral staircase and moved the ladder against the bookshelves along its track until he got to the right place. Climbing up four rungs, he outstretched his hand and removed a book from the shelf. Opening the book, it revealed a hollowed-out centre only about the size of his pinky finger, just big enough to fit the small glass vial that was resting inside. "There you are you little devil," he said as he pried the vial out. Quickly, he tucked it into his pocket and placed the book back on the shelf.

"And what do you think you're doing?" called a man's voice just as Gideon was coming off the last steps of the ladder. He turned to see another of Ophelessa's guards standing in the doorway, blocking his exit. The guard moved to where Gideon was standing and as he turned, he crashed into a somewhat hidden bookshelf, causing the books to tumble out one by one, hitting the guard until the entire contents of the bookshelf and the bookshelf itself fell atop him.

"I've been meaning to move that," said Gideon, looking at the unconscious guard. He stepped over all the books, "Excuse me, I'll just..." He hurried out the library door and down the hallway to meet Theo.

"What took you so long?" asked Theo.

"Ran into another guard," Gideon said, taking in a deep breath. "Don't worry though, I took care of him. A real bloodbath; you don't want to go down that hallway," he pointed.

Theo looked at Gideon, unarmed and looking like he didn't have a scratch on him. "What did you do? Take him out with a book?" Theo asked.

"Several, actually."

The halls of the castle had never seemed so long as Theo and Gideon ran toward the great hall. The crowd below on the battlefield was silent as Ophelessa placed her hands on the railing and looked down at her kingdom. Then she was thrust backward by the force of something on her back.

Eira managed to undo the clasp of the necklace as Ophelessa was swinging around in an effort to remove the burden now hanging off her. She tore the necklace from its owner and jumped to the ground, falling behind Ophelessa. Eira scrambled to her feet quickly, dodging every attack Ophelessa threw at her. Ophelessa stood up and Eira backed slowly off of the balcony, watching Ophelessa as she took heavy breaths and locked eyes with Eira.

For some reason, Ophelessa remained motionless on the balcony, making no attempt at Eira's or anyone else's life. Eira turned her back finally and ran over to where the dagger lay, nestled in between a couple of pieces of fallen marble. When she did this, Ophelessa finally let out a blast of anger directed toward Eira, but she grabbed hold of the dagger just in time and jumped out of the way. Wasting no time, she held the dagger high above the jewel and—

"Eira, no!" called a voice and just before the dagger would have hit the diamond she turned to see Theo running straight at her and before she knew it, she was sliding across the floor in Theo's arms, the diamond still intact and the dagger now in Theo's hand. He dropped it to the ground and it rocked from side to side before remaining still, next to the necklace. She looked at him, wide-eyed and in shock from what had happened.

"If you destroy that diamond, the force created by it will likely kill you," said Theo helping Eira to her feet.

"Oh darn, and just when things were about to get interesting," said Ophelessa. "You may as well hand over that necklace, sweetheart. No one is going to destroy it. No one is going to risk that kind of catastrophe."

"It has to be destroyed," Eira said to Theo.

"If you destroy it, you'll die. There is no way you can survive that kind of power."

"We can't lose you, Eira. Talvia needs you as queen," added Clea. "If we take the diamond away from Ophelessa, won't her powers slowly fade anyway?"

"And what are we supposed to do with her in the meantime?" asked Gideon. "It's not good enough—the diamond needs to be destroyed." He reached down and took the dagger in his hand.

Ophelessa finally had enough of their conversation and decided to step in. "Well, I'll make this easy for all of you," started Ophelessa as she moved closer to Eira and the necklace. "If I kill you, none of this will matter anyway."

She moved toward Eira, but before she could, Gideon looked purposefully at Theo and Eira was being pulled out of the way while he pierced the diamond with the dagger.

"No!" screamed Eira as Theo took her by the waist and carried her off to safety behind some larger pieces of the fallen castle.

Ophelessa was held in her tracks by the mighty force of the diamond cracking. "No!" she screeched. Cracks that resembled lightning ran through the dark diamond and all the power that was contained within began to escape and was finally released in a large column of blinding light and dust that tore through the ceiling of the castle, and could be seen all through the land. Just like the diamond splitting with cracks of light, the Blue Queen was split by the blue lightning that emerged from the diamond before shattering into millions of pieces. When the diamond finally exploded, Ophelessa was engulfed by the light and vanished along with it. The force of her exploding powers tore through the hall like a hurricane—a pounding shock wave that destroyed everything in its path.

Gideon was finally freed from his hold on the dagger when the diamond burst into nothing more than fine shimmering coal powder. When the dust settled and the tower of light had disappeared into the sky, all was still around them. Eira ran out from behind the shelter the stones had given them and slid over to Gideon's body laying on the cold hard ground.

"No. No," said Eira as the tears started to flow down her cheeks. "You can't die on me. You just can't. I can't be Queen without you." She touched his face and brushed his hair back with her trembling fingers.

The seconds that went by until he finally stirred felt like an eternity—and then he moved. He coughed and his eyes opened to the sight of Eira over him, wiping the tears from her eyes. "I hope those aren't for me?" he uttered as he tried to sit up on his forearms.

"Of course not," she answered with a smile as she wiped the tears dripping off the end of her nose. "I'm just crying because...because..." She looked up around the room and noticed Lord Dundan trembling in the corner. "I'm still quite upset that I almost married that guy," she gave a small laugh with the upward curl of her mouth and nodded toward the man curled up like a baby in the corner. Gideon smiled when he saw him and laughed as well.

"What? She almost—what?" said Oren.

Theo shrugged his shoulders as if to say, *Well that's what you miss when you're not around.*

"Okay, yeah, I'm definitely sticking around this time. Too much happens when I'm gone."

Eira stood as Leon and Theo helped Gideon to his feet. "How did you survive that?" she asked when he was standing upright.

"I always have a trick or two up my sleeve," he smiled and then pulled on the chain around his neck. "My good luck charm," he said when he revealed a small glass vial inside of a silver holder stopped with a small cork that was attached to the chain. Inside there appeared to be blue sparkling dust. "Fairy dust—it's powerful stuff. Not easy to come by, however. This particular vial was given to me by the High Lady of the fairies herself many years ago, when I was just a boy. One of its many powers is that it provides protection to any who wears it." He brushed off his shoulders and ruffled his hair, letting some of the blue sparkles fall to the floor.

Eira smiled, "Fairy dust—who knew?"

"Yeah, I'm not helping clean this up," announced Killian walking past them and brushing off some dust on his jacket. He was then tackled by Eira, but managed to stay upright and embraced her hug. "Okay, I missed you too," he smiled. "You know," he started when Eira was back on her feet, "for years this little piece of paper has been in my dresser and I never knew where it came from or what it meant." He handed a small piece of paper to Eira that read: *Don't betray her.* "But something was telling me to take precautions when I delivered that message here. So I got Evian to put a protection spell on me. It didn't completely do the trick, but it did enough that she didn't have complete control over me. I figured it might help us to have someone on the inside," he winked.

Eira smiled and she looked at Nell standing in the distance. She headed over to where Leon was standing as Nell made her way to Killian. "So, you love me?" he smirked as she got closer.

"No," she stated. "I just said that to try to get you back from whatever spell was over you—and clearly it worked, so..."

"No, you love me—you said it." She rolled her eyes at him. "And it's about damn time," he added.

"Okay, fine. I said it; I love you. Are you happy now? You can stop trying to do all those stupid little things you've doing for the past few months to get me to fall in love with you."

"Why would I do that?" Killian asked. He moved closer to her, "I'm never going to stop trying to make you fall in love with me over and over again, because I do it every single day."

Nell smirked, "You fall in love with yourself every day?"

He gave his head a slight shake, "Shut up, Penelope," and he closed the gap between them, kissing her.

Theo leaned over to Eira, "Her name is Penelope?"

"And yes," began Killian, pulling away from Nell only slightly, "I do—because I'm awesome."

"Well, now that that's all sorted," smiled Eira, "I'm going to go throw-up."

"What?" asked Nell. There was a shared confused expression amongst the group.

"Oh—guess what guys?" smiled Leon.

Killian's eyes widened. "Yes!" he shouted and ran to Leon, picking him up and bouncing him in his arms. "Is this why you two got married already?"

"Gods help this child," sighed Eira as she made her way back from puking behind some rubble. Killian put an arm around Eira and kissed her forehead. "So," she looked at Leon, "there are no more evil queens or lords who want my throne, right?"

"Not that I'm aware of."

Eira smiled and sighed in relief, "Good. Because I'm kind of over this shit."

"So," started Theo, "what in the world are we going to do for fun around here now?"

26

Three months since the day she had set out for the Spring Country to find Leon, Eira and Leon were walking with Polar and Olaf in the winter gardens of the castle. The dogs were bounding through the snow, completely carefree and in an utter state of bliss—chasing snowballs thrown for them. When they reached the largest evergreen tree the garden contained, Eira and Leon walked under its snow-frosted branches. Eira always loved the smell of fresh evergreen mixed with the cold sharpness of the snow.

"I think it is finally time I ask you something," said Leon, turning to Eira.

"Really?" she asked, turning to face him.

"I think I owe you a real proposal. Not a rushed one in the middle of a war," he smiled, kneeling on one knee in front of her and opening a ring box. "I managed to finally track down the ring I wanted to give you in the first place. It was your mother's." Inside was a far more beautiful ring than the one that now belonged to a pair of happy ravens. It was a thin white gold and diamond-covered band interlaced with gold vines and leaves spiralling up the sides. At the top lay three oval-cut ice blue diamonds, side by side with small diamonds separating them. Eira couldn't speak at the sight of it and it took her a moment to refocus on what Leon was saying.

"Eira, from the moment I met you, I knew my life was never going to be the same. And while neither of us probably would have agreed to marry each other when we first met, I know now that you're the only one I would ever want to share my life with. Through dragons, evil queens, lords that want your throne, and even you injuring me—a lot, I have grown to love you more than I ever thought possible, and I would gladly go through all of it again, a thousand times again, if it meant having you in my life, for the rest of it. Will you marry me?" asked Leon. "Again?" She looked into his eyes and smiled, not answering just yet. "Um, it's kind of cold and wet down here, so if you could—"

"Yes!" she answered; the most important word in the world at that moment. He slid the ring onto her finger and stood, brushing the snow off his knee. Then he wrapped his arms around her in a warm embrace.

The glass chapel shone in the noonday sun as the guests inside watched the snow slowly drifting from the

377

heavens to the world below. It was a grand chapel nestled in the woods of Talvia where the trees towered around it, sheltering it from the harshness of winter. And as the sun peeked through the trees and made its way inside the chapel creating a warm glow against the white world outside, the doors opened and Eira emerged.

Her eyes were only on Leon's, but the eyes of all others were fixed on her grace and elegance as she walked down the aisle. The long sheer white and gold train of the gown she had been dreaming of her whole life, trailed behind her while the rest of the gown graduated into white lace and made its way up her body touching all her curves and finally cascading out across and off just below her shoulders and down again to meet her wrists where at the end of them, her hands clutched a bouquet of gold roses and evergreen boughs. Her hair was done up with a golden headpiece and a long cathedral-length veil with golden appliqué around its edges came out from underneath her hair. By the time she made it to the altar, the entirety of the guests were in tears and she was struggling herself to hold them back.

Killian was failing to compose himself beside Leon.

"Dude," whispered Theo, "pull it together."

"I'm trying," he whispered back.

All Eira could think about at that moment was the man standing before her, waiting at the altar, smiling. There is something about a man's smile that when he has your heart, your whole heart, he can break you with a simple curl of his lips. That smile was meant for Eira and Eira alone, and it took her through time itself, on the journey of her life.

When she was before the altar, she handed her bouquet over to Nell and took Leon's hands just like she had done months before at Lord Evian's palace.

It was the happiest moment of Leon's life; the day he married the Queen of Talvia.

The months went on and the most dramatic change in Eira's life was the fact she could no longer see her feet or wear the beautiful gowns that adorned her closet, for her midsection had grown to the size of a beach ball until one faithful winter morn when the cause of her fashion predicaments came into the world, and Leon had a new happiest moment in his life.

"So," began Leon, sitting beside Eira who was holding their sleeping new daughter, "we still need a name."

"Yeah." Eira looked across the room to where there hung a portrait of her mother and as she looked into the eyes she never knew growing up, she glanced back at her waking child, bright-eyed and beaming with the same eyes she would now watch grow up. "I think I have the perfect one in mind," she said with a smile.

"Yeah, what's that?"

"How about, Adela?"

Leon looked at Eira and then back to the baby who was once again drifting into sleep and replied, "She looks like an Adela."

Eira had never thought of herself as the motherly type, but when she gazed into her daughter's bright blue eyes for the first time, an overwhelming sense of love fell upon her. As the first couple of days turned into weeks and then into months, she took on the role with all the grace and ease expected of her. After everything she had been through in the last couple of years, she finally felt as though she could feel her family around her, especially her mother, whose eyes she looked into every day reflected in the eyes of her daughter.

The kingdom was preparing for another grand event to celebrate the new princess's first few months in the world. Snow fell on the ground outside as the party began and the great hall was decorated from floor to ceiling with shades of rose and gold for the baby princess. Everyone had come out for the presentation of the baby. It was a happy day with no dragons, witches, or angry lords to ruin it and there was no chance of this baby growing up with any less than two parents and lots of aunts and uncles that loved her as much as humanly possible.

"I'm so glad she looks like Eira," teased Oren as he looked at his niece in Leon's arms. "That could have been an unfortunate life," he added, kissing his sister on the cheek.

"I should be offended, but I'm really glad about that too," answered Leon. "I'm also really glad we're out of the newborn stage and I have Eira back."

"Hey!" interjected Eira.

"What? You once yelled at me in the middle of the night for having stupid, useless nipples."

Eira just grumbled and rolled her eyes at him, "Well, you do."

"Seriously though, sis," said Oren before Eira could leave, "Mom and Dad would be proud. I know I never knew them and you really have no memory of them, but something is telling me that this, all of this, is everything they ever wanted for you."

"Dude, quick," said Killian, rushing over to Leon, "give me the baby."

Eira watched as Leon began to hand her over. "Wait, you're not going to ask why?" Leon shrugged. "Why?" Eir asked Killian.

"I pissed off Nell, and for some reason she can't seem to stay mad at me when I'm holding that kid." He took the baby from Leon's arms.

"I'd be careful of that if I were you," said Eira, as she watched her daughter smile and grab at Killian's face, "or you won't need to be borrowing *our* baby for much longer."

He looked at Eira and shook his head, "Uh uh, I'm careful—unlike you two." Nell appeared beside them. "Hey, babe, what's up?" grinned Killian.

"Don't. You can't take their kid every time I'm mad at you."

"But look how cute we are." He held Adela up by his face and smiled as she removed her fist from her mouth just long enough to give a drooly baby grin to her aunt. He wasn't wrong. It would be difficult to resist him in his formal wear while holding a baby in a ball gown.

She sighed and rolled her eyes. A couple of familiar faces soon joined the group.

"Clea! Nevin!" called Eira, embracing them both in a hug. "I'm so glad you guys made it."

"Of course," smiled Clea, "we wouldn't miss this."

"Yes, and my father sends his congratulations as well," smiled Nevin. He then looked at Leon, "And his thanks for the return of his painting."

"I don't know what you're talking about," replied Leon, taking a sip of his drink.

"Anyway, how are you two?" Eira looked at Clea, "Settling into life in Kesa well?" Eira asked.

"It's taking some getting used to. But honestly, I'm enjoying the warmth. I never grew up in a snow-covered Talvia," answered Clea.

"Fair enough. I think I'm actually the only one here who has ever experienced snow before," Eira joked. "And I think you're going to make a great queen one day," she squeezed Clea's hand. "You know, if Nevin ever gets around to it."

"Yeah, well, that's still a long time in the future," said Nevin, joining Eira and Clea. "My father has no intention of abdicating, or dying, anytime soon. He reminds me of that every day."

"Well, I'm still glad we were able to put everything behind us and move forward," smiled Eira. "Mostly because I'm really looking forward to a beach vacation."

The evening went on and when the baby was sound asleep in her crib, Eira was enjoying the fresh air on the balcony wrapped in a plush blanket.

"So," came a voice behind her as Leon made his way onto the balcony and sat behind her, just like he always did, "that was a nice party."

"Yeah, it was," smiled Eira, snuggling into him.

"So, you ready for another one?" The death glare she gave him was unmatched. "Okay, I'm just kidding," he kissed the top of her head.

"Yeah, we're not having another one until Killian and Nell have one. I'm not doing this mom thing alone."

"Well, we have to make it through their wedding first."

"Yeah, that's going to be fun," Eira replied, it dripping with sarcasm. "They've been engaged for a month and she's already turning into kind of a bridezilla."

"A what?"

"Nothing. It's just something you call a bride who is a bit crazy and over the top about everything."

"Ah, she's not that bad."

"You're not her maid of honour. You guys just have to show up on the day."

"Yeah," smiled Leon.

"Anyway, I'm sure she'll calm down. She's just excited right now—I get it."

"It is pretty exciting getting to marry the love of your life." He grabbed her and pulled her on top of him, so they were now face to face.

Eira rolled her eyes at him, "Really?"

"What? I can't want my undeniably sexy wife and the gorgeous mother of my child?"

Eira sighed, "No, you can. I just haven't felt very sexy since Ella was born."

"Eira, I can promise you that since Ella was born, you have only become sexier, and the amount I have to control myself around you every single day is unfathomable. You make being a mom the sexiest thing in the world."

"Well, I guess if you put it that way." Eira placed her hands on either side of his face and brought her lips to his, then ran her fingers through his dark chestnut hair. Leon's hand grasped the back of her head and with the other arm wrapped tightly around her waist, he rolled them over so they were laying side by side, his arms wrapping tightly around her, never letting go.

About the Author

Alexandra Louise lives in Alberta, Canada with her husband and daughters. She spends most of her time writing and taking care of her littles because she enjoys being bossed around by tiny dictators, retreating to her own fictional worlds, and getting paid for neither. Her books are full of relatable characters, fun adventures, low spice/ fade to black for everyone to enjoy, swoony moments, and of course happily ever afters.